What the Monk Didn't See

Emma Batten

First published in the UK by Emma Batten.
This second (amended) edition published in 2021

ISBN 978 1 9995820 1 2

Printed and bound in the UK

A catalogue record of this book can be found in the British Library

Edited by Maud Matley

Further editing and proofreading by Rosemary Bartholomew

Cover painting by Kean Farrelly

www.emmabattenauthor.com

To Kean, who shares my love of St Nicholas Church, with huge thanks for taking on the challenge of painting the 1287 storm cover picture.

About the Book

I am taking you back to the 13th century, when violent storms battered the south coast of England causing damage to towns and villages and, in some cases, changing the features of our coastline forever.

New Romney, once a thriving port, was suffering badly. The Rother estuary had silted up, as tides pushed sand and shingle into the river mouth and the king ordered that a manmade watercourse be made to flush out the harbour. But this was all to no avail as, in 1287, there came a great storm causing irreversible changes to New Romney and the surrounding areas.

My story of the travelling monk was inspired by reports from Matthew Paris, a monk who reported on the 13th century storms and wrote in detail about the destruction of Old Winchelsea.

All characters in the novel are entirely fictional, and only the surname Craythorne was taken from a manor house which existed to the north of the town. Within the town, St Nicholas Church still stands and, incredibly, it bears the marks of the great storm. St Martin's Church is long gone, but its name lives on in an open space near to the town centre. Part of the medieval priory can still be seen opposite St Martin's Field.

Acknowledgements

Many thanks to Maud Matley for her encouragement and enthusiasm as she edited the manuscript, tirelessly pointing out any phrases which were too modern and correcting my grammar. Also, for inviting me on the Historic Churches Tour, where I learned about the possible anchorhold at St Nicholas, which became such an integral part of the story.

With thanks also to Rosemary Bartholomew for her thorough editing and proof reading, and to Joan Campbell from the Romney Marsh Historic Churches Trust for reading the novel and pointing out some changes needed for historical accuracy.

With thanks to local shops and cafes for enabling me to sell my work locally, and on-going support in promoting my novels.

A huge amount of research has gone into this novel, and I have tried my best to give an accurate representation of New Romney in the 13th century. I couldn't have done it without the following resources:

Jill Eddison's *Romney Marsh Survival on a Frontier*
Gillian Draper and Frank Meddens' *The Sea and The Marsh: The Medieval Cinque Port of New Romney*
www.theromneymarsh.net

Also by Emma Batten

Stand-alone books in order of era:

What The Monk Didn't See (1287)

A Place Called Hope (1580s)

But First Maintain the Wall (1758)

The Saxon Series:

The Pendant Cross (680AD)

The Sacred Stone (694AD)

The Dungeness Series (1873—WW2):

Still Shining Bright*

Secrets of the Shingle

Stranger on the Point

The Artist's Gift

* prequel, this could be read first or after the others.
To be followed by a second prequel in winter 2021/22

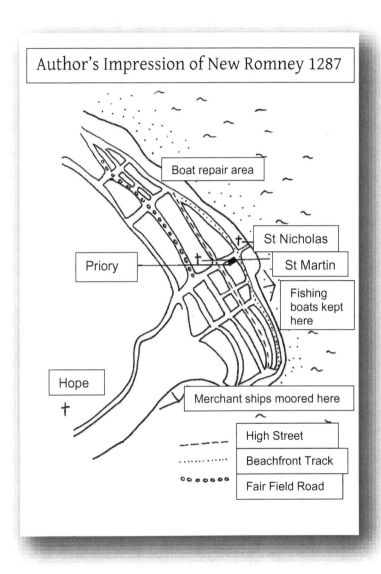

Author's Impression of New Romney 1287

Boat repair area

St Nicholas

Priory

St Martin

Fishing boats kept here

Hope

Merchant ships moored here

High Street

Beachfront Track

Fair Field Road

Part One
The Storm – 1287

Chapter One
The Monk

From his small room nestled under the eaves of the priory, the monk could hear signs that the wind was whipping itself up into a frenzy. The south coast, including the prestigious Cinque Port of Romney, was going to take a battering overnight. Roof tiles were being lifted, then slapping down upon one another. Most would keep their hold on the priory roof, but what of the reed-thatched cottages and wooden shacks on the seafront?

The sky had darkened prematurely, and he could no longer rely on the weak light already restricted by the small, salt-encrusted window. He didn't care to write by the flickering, yellow light of a tallow candle. Reluctantly, the monk put down his quill and closed his leather-bound notebook.

He was the predecessor of the modern-day news reporter and, months beforehand, had set off from his home monastery at Arundel in order to record events along the south coast of England. It was a solitary life, as he passed through towns and villages. He was an onlooker, an observer in people's lives but not a part of them. At birth he had been given the name of Nicholas – that of the patron saint of the sea – and this is why God had ordained he should follow the coast and record the stories of the people living at the sea's mercy.

His writing cut short, the monk took his rough woollen cloak and wrapped it around his shoulders. He closed the narrow, wooden door behind him and set off along the corridor, then down the steep, stone steps to the iron-studded front door leading onto the street. For a moment, he stood in the shelter of the doorway. Opposite was the church of St Martin's and as he looked at the graveyard he was filled with a feeling of foreboding. *The gravedigger will have plenty of employment by the time the night is over, and the storm spent. He would be wise to start his digging now, although he may find himself toppling into the grave. I would put nothing past the power of this wind.*

While he hesitated in the doorway, the rain began. It was by no means torrential, but what there was came down fast – sharp and spiteful as it battered the monk's face. Shoulders hunched, he pulled his hood low on his forehead and, with his head bowed, turned towards the beachfront. He was heading for the stocky church tower of St Nicholas and although every step would be a battle against the wind, he was determined to reach his goal. *From this tower in its glorious position overlooking the coast, I will have a fine view and can watch the storm unfold. There is no better place to be. The rain may soak me to the skin, but I shall see the Lord's fury at its best. I was placed on God's Earth to witness great events and will gain nothing from cowering in the shelter of the priory.*

With his cloak wrapped firmly around him, the monk staggered to the road junction. Here, the High Street stretched left and right. Now he was caught out by the sheer force of the south-westerly gale as it pushed on his throat, making him gag. It pulled at his long robes, almost causing him to become a human sail. The combination of early dusk and high winds had forced the market traders to pack up in a hurry. They had been slack with tidying up that day, and the street was strewn with debris.

As he paused for a moment, the monk's ankle was assaulted by the dead body of a chicken as it flew along on the wind. *What a life – bred as human food, only to be rejected at the marketplace. What a waste, it would have given a hearty meal to some poor family.* A cabbage rolled by. It was not in the nature of the townsfolk to let good food go uneaten. The market truly had been abandoned in haste as the storm took hold.

With a glance at his goal, the monk crossed the High Street to a short road leading towards the church and harbour. Now there was nowhere to shelter. To his left, St Nicholas Church stood as an example of fine Norman architecture at the edge of a natural harbour. The churchyard walls held iron rings. These, in turn, held fishing boats, lashed securely by ropes. A sandy beach stretched to his right, shelving gently into the turbulent sea. At the top of the beach, beyond the reach of a spring tide, were more boats and the tools of the fishermen's trade.

"How long until high tide?" a fisherman shouted.

"An hour or more," was the reply from his companion.

"God's bones! It will take the lot."

"Not if we can help it."

The tide was not ready to turn. Fishermen desperately tried to pull their boats further up the shingle bank or secure them with more rope to the wall of the churchyard. For a moment, the monk took in the scene of frantic activity. The sea was licking at the debris marking its usual limits, then taking its chance to leap further. It clawed at ropes, nets and baskets as the townsfolk fought to snatch them back and drag them up to the beachfront track.

The smell of the sea was rich in his nose and mouth. It could be tasted on the monk's lips, pungent with seaweed and laden with salt. The seascape before him was a palette of dark blues, greys and purples, all highlighted by sporadic light beams that came and went as the clouds raced past the face of the moon. But the greatest assault to his senses was the tremendous noise – a commotion like none he had ever experienced. As the sea forged landwards, it took shingle from the top of the beach. The air was filled with discord as pebbles were pulled back with the tide, then returned to be spat out further up the bank than ever before. They rattled down at a great pace, causing both a terrible racket and danger to the men on the beach.

Whilst the sea threatened the fishermen, all men of the town gathered, whatever their trade, to help save the livelihoods of those who braved the elements to feed them. The monk, set apart by his vocation, did not consider helping. He saw himself as a scribe, a messenger, and his duty to the town was different. By watching it all, he could record this great storm so it could be remembered beyond the fishermen's lifetimes. He was doing a service to the people of Romney in a less obvious way. By recording their history, their struggle would not go forgotten. So, he turned towards the best viewpoint that he knew of – the tower of the Norman church.

"It's going to be a rough night." A fisherman passed by with an armful of rope.

"We are in God's hands," the monk replied piously. "I wish you His protection."

12

"Let's hope He sees fit to spare us." The reply was whipped away on the wind. The fisherman turned his back on the monk.

No one noticed the loner as he opened a wooden door, set at the base of the church tower. In near darkness, the monk felt his way around cool stone walls until he reached a stone spiral staircase and began his ascent to the tower roof. As he climbed, he paused on platforms of wooden planks. Narrow, round-topped windows let in shafts of welcome grey-blue light, for any light, however meagre, was better than none. Up he clambered, past the bells hanging steady, barely knowing of the tempest outside the stout Norman walls. Finally, the monk reached a trapdoor and used all his strength to push it open. He then settled himself to crouch on the roof, against the low stone parapet. At once, he was so enraptured by the storm that he longed to put his quill to vellum, but this was not possible, so he was forced to say the words aloud, committing them to memory:

"The moon, swollen to twice its usual size and glowing, sent shafts of light across the raging sea." He imagined the curling lines upon his vellum; they would look fine. "The sea raged, throwing itself beyond its usual limits, seizing boats and pulling them from their moorings, taking them for its own." Looking down, he saw the sea was by no means ready to ebb and was now throwing its spoils back upon the beach track. As the waters forged on, he prepared more lines in his mind: *No man was safe in his seafront home as the sea savaged them, battering them with their own boats and spitting shingle out onto the streets.*

That evening, the monk had a perfect view of the harbour and beyond. He believed that he could see everything that happened in the town. He believed that nothing of significance would happen that he could not

13

see and record for the town's history in his fine curling script.

He was wrong. Unseen by the monk, huddled in her father's pig shelter, a young woman was suffering her own terrors while the storm raged.

Chapter Two
Agnes

Earlier that day, while the fishermen were muttering that there was a storm coming and their wives went about their daily chores, a young woman walked to the street market. It was a day like any other and she was unaware that the night of the storm would change her life forever. Not just her life – it would change the fortunes of Romney forever.

"Here you are, Agnes." The stallholder wrapped a piece of cheese in paper and placed it in Agnes' shopping basket alongside the butter. "I'll be packing up now. There's not many more folk who will come out in this wind."

"Thank you." Agnes tucked the basket under her arm. "See you tomorrow."

"Take care. They say there's a storm brewing."

"I'll keep safe." Agnes smiled, her dark eyes lighting up. "I've got my pa and two strong brothers to look out for me."

"Aye, you have. Give my best wishes to your ma – she's a good woman."

"I will, and I hope you get home before the rain starts."

Agnes turned and hurried back along the High Street. The local people who traded daily from the market were all packing up early. The wind was already catching at the stalls, and they didn't want their goods scattered along the street. It was only mid-afternoon, but already the town had an air of being deserted. With no customers, the shops would probably close early too.

Agnes walked swiftly, holding onto the skirt of her tunic to stop it being lifted by the breeze. Her curtain of long, dark hair was being whipped up by the wind, pulling it out from the restraints of her hood. At fourteen years old, she was on the brink of becoming a woman, with a petite frame of gentle curves. Her eyes were absolutely beautiful – large pools of darkest brown, framed with almost-black lashes; now they were lowered to the ground as the wind swept into her face.

Turning from the High Street towards the beachfront, Agnes could see the sea was darkening and becoming wild. To the west, the sun was covered by purple clouds, causing dusk to come early. As in the market, the fishermen who traded on the beach were already packing away. Small fishing boats, which usually sat midway up the shingle bank, beyond the sandy beach, had been pulled higher up, to the top of the bank. Above, gulls soared and swooped, cackling and mocking the people below. They would do well if freshly-caught fish were abandoned before the storm took hold.

The shutters of her wooden beachfront home had already been closed. Agnes pressed down on the door latch and entered the one-room cottage. It was dark inside, with the only light beaming from a solitary tallow candle and the open fire. The girl's eyes smarted as thick smoke from the fire hit them. She breathed in an aroma of woodsmoke, mingling with the savoury steam coming from the pottage of leeks and grains simmering in the pan.

"There's a terrible wind gathering," Agnes told her mother, as she removed her cape and put the butter and cheese on the heavy oak table.

"Aye, Robert came in not long ago," Mary replied. "He said the sea's getting rough."

"He didn't stay then?" Agnes asked.

"Nay, he was needed to help pull the boat further up the beach. Pa was worried – he had a feeling that the tide would be high this evening."

"I saw them all out there, on the beach. The boats will be safe enough. They've pulled them up as high as the ridge. I've never seen them so far up." Agnes placed her basket on the floor. "I'll cut the bread, shall I? They'll be in for supper soon enough. No one would choose to stay out in this weather. The market's all shutting up."

"No point in staying open. Not in weather like this," Mary stated.

Agnes' home was set midway between the church of St Nicholas and the mouth of the River Rother. Between these two points stretched a shallow, sandy beach from which small boats went out fishing and fishermen sold their catch. Her home, facing the beach, was vulnerable to the open sea and fierce winds. Yet Agnes loved the changes in the mood of the sea: its varying colours and the smell of salt in the air. All this made her feel invigorated.

At the mouth of the Rother the water was deeper, the seabed having been scoured away by a strong current. Here, visiting ships moored stern to bow along the riverbank. This gave a tenuous sense of security within the estuary, slightly removed from the main body of the English Channel. The larger ships came from other parts of England and abroad. From countries so different and exotic that Agnes could not begin to imagine what they looked like. Sometimes the sailors had dark skin or different-shaped features, firing the interest of the local people who longed to know what they said as they called to one another and traded their goods. Spices and dried fruit came from these ships and added new flavour and variety to the diets of the townsfolk. They never knew what would be coming in on the next ship or from which country it had come.

On flat, marshy lands beside the river mouth there was also the busy salt-making industry. Here salt was collected from shallow pans of seawater. It added much-prized flavour to their food and was sold to the people of inland settlements.

Beyond the town there were miles of flat countryside, interspersed with reed-lined drainage ditches, stretching towards the hills between Hythe and Appledore. To the west, towards Lydd and the sea cliffs at Rye, the land was less mature. It was still frontier country – winding creeks that filled with seawater, earth banks built to keep the sea at bay and irregular-shaped fields which were at the mercy of the incoming tides.

Supper was ready and simmered in the three-legged pan with its blackened base, which stood over the fire. It wasn't long before the front door was flung open again and Agnes' father came in with her two older brothers.

"By the blood of Christ!" Agnes' father, John, swore as he removed his cloak. "I fear for our safety tonight. That wind is ready to tear our homes apart and now it rains."

"Rain? It was dry not long ago," Agnes' mother began to ladle pottage into wooden bowls.

"The rain will set in now, Ma," Robert replied, seating himself on the bench.

They ate without speaking, but not in silence, as they listened to the storm around them. Wind pushed at the end of the low wooden cottage and whistled as it forced its way through gaps in the shuttered windows. Intermittent crashes could be heard outside, and unease showed on the faces of the whole family.

"I'll just take the scraps out," Agnes edged towards to door, curious to see the storm.

"Be careful, sweeting," her mother cautioned.

Before feeding the pig, Agnes peeped around the side of the cottage and looked out towards the church and the beach. Now, as high tide approached, the sky had taken on a sinister look, with clouds racing across the face of the huge moon hanging low. The wind had whipped itself into a frenzy and was thick with salt and icy splinters of rain. It tore at the beachfront cottages and the boats that lay tilting in their new positions higher up on the shingle bank. Already the tide was licking around the hulls of the boats and foaming at the ridge of the shingle bank, trickling down the other side and onto the beach track.

Agnes looked on in fascinated horror until a wave launched itself beyond the usual limits, slapping down upon the track and spitting its salt-spray towards her. She threw the scraps in the direction of the sow and raced back to her home.

"I've never seen the sea so high," Agnes reported, wiping the spray from her face.

"You've got yourself in a right mess," Mary replied. "The pig could have waited."

"I wanted to see...."

Agnes' father stood, the force of his sudden movement upsetting the bench. "I can't settle here, not hearing the sea roaring like that."

"It's out to cause trouble, that's for certain," Mary replied.

"I'm going to check on the boat," John was opening the door as he spoke. The wind took its chance and rushed inside, scattering the fire. His sons were right behind him, pulling on cloaks as they left the home.

"May God protect you." Mary's words came as the door slammed shut.

Mother and daughter spent a few minutes tidying the remains of the meal, and then Mary could wait no longer. "Stay here, Agnes, and tend to this. I need to check on the old folks." Her mother was picking up a shawl. "Don't go out, you'll get swept away, a little wench like yourself."

Agnes did her chores, then sat listening to the wind pushing at her timber-framed home. The reed-thatched roof was already lifting at one corner and wind forced its way through the gaps in the shutters, causing the candle to flicker. In her hands, she cradled a cup of ale. Her ears were alert to the sounds of the storm, and she feared for the safety of the fishermen.

The pains started as high tide hit Romney Bay. Not the usual high tide: this one surged beyond its usual limits and then further. As wooden boats ripped from their moorings, spasms ripped through Agnes' fourteen-year-old body. As the sea leapt upon the beach track and salt water surged between the cottages, a spate of watery liquid rushed from her body. The pottage must have been rotten, Agnes thought, but never had a bellyache caused such pain. And, how shameful to have messed herself. What use would she be to her parents and brothers when they returned to find her sitting in her own filth? Still the pains continued in the depths of her stomach – rhythmic spasms that left her fit for nothing.

When the roof was torn from her home, scattering years of dust and broken strands of reed-thatch over Agnes, she was forced to stand and staggered to the back door. With her arms wrapped around her belly, she lurched towards the low pigsty and pushed open the wooden gate. Desperate to be out helping her family, she wanted to be of some use. But the pains, coming in regular spasms, rendered her useless. All she could do was crouch against the warmth of the sow.

Time passed – how long, she had no idea – and still the pains engulfed her as she huddled, listening to the sounds of shingle spraying over the town, and fearing that the tide may yet encroach on the place where she sheltered.

As the tide finally ebbed and the wind eased, a baby boy broke free from Agnes' body. *I had no idea. How could I have not known?* These were the first thoughts coming clearly amidst the confusion and aftermath of intense pain. It was these words that were repeated over and over in her mind. Soon, the words of disbelief became intertwined with memories of stolen, guilty moments spent with a man who was another woman's husband and fifteen years her senior.

Instinctively, the new mother took a handful of clean hay, and wiped first the baby, then herself clean. He was so tiny: legs and arms thin and fragile, his stomach softly rounded. In the half-light she couldn't see his delicate features, but wiped the soft, dark hair, feeling her way with her fingertips. They were still attached by the throbbing cord, but Agnes knew what to do, having seen the births of her niece and nephew. She tore a thick length of material from the hem of her tunic and knotted it tight around the lifeline between herself and her son. Then, having taken her eating knife from her belt, Agnes cut the cord in one swift move. Minutes later the afterbirth slipped from her body.

All this time, the sow slept on, gently snoring. She had provided invaluable warmth and a backrest for Agnes. The regular breathing and solid form gave Agnes a sense of peace and stability at a moment when her childhood had been firmly left behind and the future was at its most terrifying.

The baby began to mewl and so Agnes brought him to her breast and gently guided him to her milk. All her life she had watched relatives and neighbours feed their babies. It was obvious what her son needed. At that moment, the moon shone through the doorway. Although she was stunned and afraid, Agnes saw his tiny snub nose and delicate features, and fell in love with the child. She fed her baby and cradled him within the folds of her shawl, then they slept, oblivious to the chaos around them.

When they woke, Agnes ached from sitting on the hard earth floor. Her limbs were stiff with cold, making it awkward to stand. But she had no choice and manoeuvred herself until she stood, holding her baby securely. She realised the storm had eased – the wind was no longer howling, and the tide would have retreated some time before. Knowing the town was in chaos and soon her family would be looking for her, Agnes realised she would need her wits about her if she were to protect her son.

For the first time, Agnes peeped out of the pig's shelter and looked upon all that had been familiar. Her wooden home had only the western end wall standing and part of the back wall. The cottages either side had been destroyed, with their walls folded in upon themselves and topped with the remains of reed-thatch roofs. The land surrounding her was not only strewn with debris from homes and broken-up boats but had been engulfed with sand and shingle. She was forced to climb up and out of the pigsty. A piece of cloth was caught on some wood; Agnes tore at it and used it to swaddle her baby before setting out.

With her son held close, the new mother pulled at her shawl, so it covered her head and the whole of her tiny bundle. She trudged steadily along the shingle-strewn beach track. The sea had now slunk back in shame, its fury spent. In the moonlight, the townsfolk were busy – frantically salvaging all they could. No boat was left whole after the storm. No seafront home, smokehouse, or net shed was left undamaged. Agnes could see how men and women would work through the hours before dawn, collecting wood, rope, netting and cloth. They pulled them away from the beach determined that, on the next high tide, the sea would take nothing more from them. These things – meagre as they were – would be used to rebuild their homes and restore their livelihoods.

Agnes made eye contact with no one, and they were too busy with their own concerns to notice her. She had survived through the terrors of the night and now, in order for her plan to succeed, she must remain unseen and not be recognised. She approached the parish church, heart pounding, but fully resolved to do her duty by her son.

St Nicholas Church was now sunken. Its doors had been smashed open by the force of the tide and swathes of shingle had entered, piling up against Norman pillars and walls. Agnes had no need to enter the church; it was not part of the hastily-constructed plan for her son. Instead, she hurriedly scooped at the pebbles just within the doorway, making a secure nest for her baby. Then, having placed a gentle kiss on his forehead, she left him.

Agnes loved her son above herself. By leaving him in the church doorway, she had done her best for him. He was sure to be taken in by someone more capable of caring for him. What could she do for a newborn baby? She was young, homeless and, most importantly, unmarried. To keep the child could only bring shame upon her parents. *How could my father support my child? We have no home, and the boat is destroyed. I could not ask it of him or my mother. I could not burden them with my troubles.* The thoughts ran through her mind, confirming that Agnes had done the right thing by the innocent newborn.

When she turned away from the baby, Agnes knew she could not stand by to watch him grow up. She could not be an onlooker to his first smile, first steps and first words. Unbeknown to her, at that moment her parents had returned to their home and were desperately searching for their daughter in the wreckage. But Agnes was on the beach and walking out of her son's life.

From his vantage point on the tower roof, the monk, who had watched the storm unfold, gazed out to sea. He marvelled at how it now swayed gently to and fro, with all its previous rage gone. He hadn't seen Agnes leave the precious bundle or walk away. She strode out along the sands which had been left clear as the tide retreated and set off in the direction of Dymchurch. So, when the baby was discovered, there was no one to tell how during the chaos of the storm, the gift of a child had come.

Chapter Three
Matilda

Matilda sat on the edge of her son's bed, stroking his blond curls. How could he sleep? How could he rest whilst the storm buffeted the town? It was his youth which allowed him this respite, she knew that. At two years old, what did he know of danger? There was chaos and devastation ahead – that was clear enough. Matilda knew the storm was going to cause destruction as it hit Romney and would leave misery in its wake.

Just hours ago, on her return from the High Street, the wind had been gathering momentum as skies darkened. While Matilda had hurried home, she'd met the old soothsayer, Gundred. She had attempted to avoid the wizened old crone, as Oliver tugged on one arm, and her basket weighed heavy on the other. But it was not to be: Gundred had Matilda firmly in her sights and a need to share her premonitions:

"There's dark deeds happening tonight. I've never had such a bad feeling. Pray, Matilda. Pray for your family and the town."

"Pray for the town?" Matilda repeated, alarmed, for she tended to be drawn into the soothsayer's cautionary tales.

"Aye, the town. Cinque Port, sunk port. That's what I hear over and over: Cinque Port, sank port, sunk port. It rings in my ears and fills me with terror." Gundred stood on the street before Matilda, barely reaching the younger woman's shoulders, her back was that bent.

As always, she was draped in a thick shawl. Scraggy brown-grey hair escaped in tendrils from beneath her hood, her nose was aquiline, and her eyes were like small dark currants.

"That makes no sense to me," Matilda stated with a bravado she didn't feel. "But I'll pray, nonetheless. There's a storm brewing and damage will be done tonight."

"Cinque Port, sunk port," repeated Gundred. "I can't say I understand it either. It's a curse, those words that come to me. I tell you Matty – it's a curse the things I see and hear." Now the old hag stretched out her arm and clawed at Matilda's woollen cloak. "You didn't listen. You didn't take heed. I know you're feeling the sorrow already and have been feeling it for these last few years. I pity you, Matilda. You've made a mistake and are suffering for it. I feel it in my bones. I feel your regret."

Matilda lowered her grey eyes. She didn't want her secrets laid bare for Gundred to see. She had a fine stone-built home, plenty of food and a healthy son. And if her husband wasn't all she had hoped for, he was neither a drunkard nor violent.

"All is well with me," Matilda replied curtly, shaking off the gnarled hand and with it the spell Gundred held over her. "But there goes Oliver – he's slipped free of my hand!" She took a step away. "I'll pray for the townsfolk. Of course I will. I'll pray for their wooden homes and fishing boats because I can see the devil himself rules the sea tonight."

"He's the very picture of your husband, your Oliver is," was Gundred's last comment, thrown at Matilda as she scurried after her lively young son.

It was true. There was no mistaking who Oliver's father was. And there was no good in being the son and image of Hugh Alcock. That's what people thought, and

Matilda knew it. But they were wrong. Her son would be his own man with his own values. He was a fine, sweet boy and she loved him dearly.

With her basket cumbersome on her arm, Matilda soon had Oliver's hand firmly in her own and was making him retrace his steps, back to St Martin's Church. Ignoring his wails of frustration, she marched him straight down the aisle and to the image of the Virgin Mary. Here the young mother made peace with her son by handing him a biscuit from her basket. He willingly sat down to enjoy it.

Now Matilda stood before the shrine and made the sign of the cross upon her body before dropping to her knees and feverishly beginning to pray:

"May God forgive my sins. Forgive me my doubts. Forgive my treacherous eyes that see things they should not see. Save me from my unfaithful thoughts that dwell on things they shouldn't. Mary, Mother of Jesus, guide me. Help me to be an obedient and loyal wife."

As Oliver began to stir and she became aware of her son and his needs, Matilda desperately rushed the words of her final prayer: "Lord, help the people of Romney and keep them safe from the storm. Amen." Backing away, she feared a disservice had been done to the townsfolk. She had not prayed with enough devotion for them.

Matilda closed the heavy wooden door and paused in the church porch to take in the changed scene. She noticed that in just those last five minutes, the wind had gathered strength and the purple-grey of the sky had darkened. Now, rain came down in small, sharp droplets, driven sideways by the force of the wind.

Directly opposite, the iron-studded door of the priory opened. Matilda saw the monk appear and momentarily cower in the doorway. He gathered his robes around him and, with his body hunched against the power of the storm, he moved away in the direction of the High Street.

Unbeknown to the monk, Matilda had studied him over the ten days he had lodged at the priory. She secretly envied his simple life. She selfishly wished for his life, seeing it as unhindered, beholden to no one but God. He, the monk, could go where he wished and spend hours in quiet contemplation, or preach to enraptured audiences about the places he had visited and the things he had learned. Whereas she, Matilda, was a mother, wife and daughter who could only snatch at a few minutes of prayer. She had to fulfil all those roles before she could serve the Lord. And then her precious time was spent apologising for her sins.

Matilda and Oliver reached their home – a low stone-built cottage under a tiled roof. It boasted three rooms: a central living area, as well as two bedrooms, one at each end. The frontage onto the road was substantial, with strong window frames, carved shutters and a sturdy front door for all to see. No wonder it was the envy of her friends and family, most of whom lived in one-room cottages. At the back, the pig lived in more splendour than some of those poor families on the beachfront and her cousin kept the vegetable plot in good order.

The road, known affectionately as Fair Field Road, was the one travelling entertainers took as they journeyed into Romney and set up camp on the field opposite St Martin's Church. They would entertain the townsfolk before moving onto the next town or village. From the front of her home, looking past the cottages opposite, she could see the seafront boat-builders' sheds, barrel-makers' stores and the smokeries. The men were there, securing anything that might be vulnerable to the gale which was rapidly building up momentum.

Matilda couldn't see Hugh. The men were all of a likeness in the premature dusk, with the rain blurring their features. He'd be there somewhere, though, ensuring that his tools were safe, and his sheds were secure. She didn't expect him home any time soon, as Hugh's working hours were changeable.

Soon Matilda and Oliver were settled in the comfort of their home. The fire had come to life and the pan of pork stew warmed through over the open flames. Mother and son had eaten at the wooden table and then Matilda had sat, with Oliver on her lap, and told him the stories her own mother had shared with her children. As for her husband, she would reheat his supper when he came in.

It was only when Oliver was sleeping on his straw-filled mattress, that there was time to reflect on the soothsayer's messages, and those beady eyes peeping into Matilda's soul to read her secrets. Three years ago, when Matilda had captured the heart of the prosperous and handsome boat-builder, her friends had been envious and her family proud of her. What was it about Matilda with her chestnut hair, grey eyes and trim figure that had tempted Hugh to marry? She was pretty enough, they agreed, but perhaps a little serious? Matilda was decent, devoted and God-fearing, of that there was no doubt. But how had she attracted the confident, handsome man who strutted along the beachfront overseeing his fishing boats and boat repair business? It was only the old hag, Gundred, who told Matilda the truth of it:

"There's no love for you shining from those blue eyes of his. He's not got any to share. He's kept it all for himself." Gundred had begged Matilda to listen. "I see you turning to sin, Matty, I see great sins before you."

"Why ever would that happen?" Matilda had shrugged away the threats.

"A black heart such as his can turn one as pure as yours," Gundred had cried out.

But Matilda was young and enamoured by the promise of a stone cottage, a job for her brother at her husband's boat repair yard and plentiful fish for her father to smoke in his shed. She built a small altar in her marital bedroom and was determined to deal with any sin swiftly. She had protected herself from Gundred's warnings and set out on the path of marriage and motherhood.

It was still early evening, but it felt like the dead of night as Matilda walked through her living area to the comfort of her altar. The shutters rattled and roof tiles creaked. She paused and opened the front door to glimpse at the street scene. The moon hung large and low in the sky, an ever-changing pattern of clouds racing across its surface. Rain was still being driven diagonally by the wind, pushing relentlessly from a south-westerly direction.

In her bedroom, Matilda moved aside a wooden trunk then, on her knees, she carefully prised a loose stone from the floor and reached into a hollowed-out area of earth. She withdrew an object wrapped in cloth and carefully removed the thin cotton covering to reveal a wax figure, which was about the length of her own slender hand.

"You should not covet another woman's husband," she whispered and stuck a nail in the soft stomach of the doll. "He committed to his wife and what God ordained, no woman shall put asunder."

Matilda held the figure by its slender waist, moving aside the thick strands of black wool that fell down her back. The face was featureless, but Matilda saw those large, dark brown eyes, full red lips and the soft unblemished skin of the child-woman who had tantalised and lured her husband with her youth and innocence. She pictured the temptress, hips swaying, long black hair reaching her pert bottom, often running barefoot across the beach or selling fish on the seafront.

She was not the only one. Matilda was sure of that. Women lowered their eyes as they passed her in the street or scuttled away from the boatyard as she approached, Oliver in tow. And where was her husband when he claimed to be working these long hours? She saw his eyes follow a pretty face and she knew as well as anyone how attractive Hugh was to a woman. Hadn't she admired him for years? As a girl, she had watched him working, shirt sleeves rolled up, his body golden brown from the sun and muscles toned from hard physical work. His blond hair was sun-bleached and blue eyes dazzling. But it wasn't just his looks that made Hugh Alcock attractive – it was his air of confidence and the wealth he was accumulating in his various trades.

Matilda knew Gundred had truly seen into her future, although she would always deny it. She could almost feel her heart blackening as the soot from the fire blackened the stone on the back wall. A gradual build-up of black soot, and a slow but steady growth of black sin upon her heart. The darkness grew whenever she pictured the slim young figure, with her curtain of dark hair falling to the waist and the round pools of her eyes which gazed at Matilda with false innocence. The sin of hatred towards Agnes from the beach track was tarnishing Matilda's heart.

As she replaced the wax figure in its wrapping and into the hollow under the floor, Matilda whispered to herself, "I'll not suffer this for much longer."

The bitter woman took a few steps towards her low altar, which was adorned with candles and a metal cross. A thick rug was laid before it and she knelt to pray for guidance. After a while she rose, feeling more at peace with herself. She sat in the dim light of the candles, in front of the dying embers of the fire, sipping a mug of wine and listening to the storm howling around her, yet leaving her untouched in her stone-built home.

Hugh did not come home and when the candles burned low, Matilda prepared for bed. She checked on Oliver, who slept on unaware of the storm. Then, in her own room, she pulled aside the curtains surrounding her bed and settled down to sleep.

When Matilda woke a little later, something was different. She lay still for a moment, listening. Hugh was not there beside her. Perhaps he sat by the fire? Then she realised what had changed – all was quiet. There was peace outside. How odd that she had managed to sleep through the sounds of the storm, yet now it was calm; it seemed almost eerie.

She swung her legs out of the bed and stood, the long nightgown falling to her ankles. Then, having taken a shawl and wrapping it close, Matilda walked to the front door. She felt compelled to look out on the new silent night-time world, at the aftermath of the storm. As Hugh had not returned, the door remained unbolted. Matilda lifted the latch and pulled the door open, into the living room.

The breeze was now gentle, and the tide must have ebbed as Matilda could no longer hear the roar of the approaching sea, nor the crashing of shingle smashing upon the top of the beach. The moon hung higher in the sky with its usual soft grey colour. Trails of cloud still crossed its surface, but they had lost their urgency; now they languished in the night sky. The rain had ceased and so it was a serene night-time world that Matilda gazed out upon.

Looking up and down the Fair Field Road, Matilda noticed the storm had not passed without causing damage. The cottages opposite had suffered the loss of their roofs and clumps of reed-thatch lay strewn about the place, caught up on low walls, trees, bushes and even on the corner of her own stone house. The occupants must have gone to shelter in St Martin's, she assumed, and vowed to go there in the morning to offer whatever help she could give. Pebbles from the beach were scattered here and there. Later, in the light of the sun, Matilda knew she would see every surface covered with a fine layer of invasive sand, so easily carried along on the wind.

At the front of her home, which was set back from the beach, Matilda saw nothing of the huge damage caused by the storm. She didn't know that the beach-track homes lay like piles of kindling wood and a thick layer of shingle and debris had spilled beyond the beach into the church of St Nicholas and onward to the High Street.

From his viewpoint on top of St Nicolas church tower, the travelling monk who had watched the storm unfold and marvelled at its fury, could not see Matilda standing at her front door. He looked down upon the devastated beachfront with its ruined homes and livelihoods lost. He realised his departure from the tower would be tricky, as it seemed the church itself had been flooded with both seawater and spoils from the beach.

Neither Matilda from her doorway nor the monk from his tower could see along to the further end of the town, where the River Rother met the sea. They were unaware that the river mouth had been blocked. This was to cause disastrous effects on the stricken town. The fishermen and those who lived at the seafront were dealing with the immediate effects of the storm, unaware of further tragedy.

Matilda turned her attention beyond the scattered cottages and to where her husband's boat-building trade took place on top of the shingle ridge before the beach. It was hard to tell in the darkness if the wooden workshops had suffered damage, and now Matilda could see dark figures of men moving amongst the smokeries and sheds. What time was it, she wondered? It must be the early hours of the morning. What damage had been done that kept the men from their beds? Or was Hugh keeping another woman's bed warm?

With her shawl wrapped close, and nightgown brushing over bare feet, Matilda stepped out of her home. Moving slowly, her feet pressed against loose shingle and slipped through the lengths of reed thatch. She passed between cottages standing empty of life, and now the sea was before her, glistening in the moonlight, swaying to and fro as it retreated. The ground she stood on was soaked, and not just from the rain. Matilda realised the tide had gone beyond its usual boundaries and this explained the boats... one in the back wall of a cottage, others listing on their sides amongst the sheds, rather than on the beach-bank.

It was now that Matilda realised while she and Oliver had stayed safe within their stone house, the town of Romney had been destroyed by the storm. For the first time she feared for the safety of her husband and family. Her throat tightened and heart began to pound. She felt driven to find Hugh.

"What are you doing here, Matilda?" Hugh appeared from between the remains of the cottages. He hauled a bundle of netting. "This is no place for my wife. Get back to the cottage. It's one of the few left standing."

34

"I came to see..."

"You see it now. God has vented his rage on Romney tonight. Now get back to my son and let me get on with salvaging all I can. I tell you, folk will be poorer for this, and we'll be suffering with them."

"The shed... your shed?" Matilda could see now that the huge barn in which Hugh carried out his trade was tilting badly in the direction of Dymchurch.

"I've a couple of men helping me there. Get home, Matilda. I've no more time for you."

Hugh now dumped his load within the doorway of the broken shed and called out impatiently, no doubt expecting someone to be at his beck and call. Matilda stood for a moment, in the shadows of a ruined cottage. She watched Hugh move to the far side of his workplace before she moved on.

Hugh Alcock was not a popular man. Women admired his lean body, golden curls and clear blue eyes, but most of all they were impressed by his air of importance. Many had been spurned in their quest to become his wife, while others had both the pleasure and shame of being his lover. Men admired his ability to trade well and make money but suffered a growing resentment as they realised Hugh's gains were their losses. As for his wife, she both adored and detested him.

The shed in which Hugh carried out his trade was by far the largest on the beachfront. He did not want to see it fall and was sure that if a few of the local men would come to his aid, it could be propped up and made secure. There was a good post, just to the side of the building. It had probably come from another shed and could now be of some use to him. He called out for help, but in the meantime Hugh pulled at the post, dragging it under the listing wall and making a move to pull it upright.

In the eerie silence following the storm, everyone along the beachfront stopped their work to turn towards a new terrifying sound: the creaking and groaning of wood as it split and tore. Then the tumultuous crash as tall plank walls fell bringing with them the vast beams and bundles of thatch, which had been the roof.

At first, in the darkness, few of the men labouring on the beach realised that their leader lay crushed under the might of his own shed.

Chapter Four
Will

The human chain stayed strong while yet another wave slapped down hard, causing the men to gasp and pause for a moment. But the sea was relentless and even while they gathered their breath, the next assault was mounting. This time it came in the form of the ragged end of a broken plank, catching Will on his shoulder. With one hand held fast to the next man, and the other to the sail they were salvaging, he was helpless to defend himself. Then the plank was gone, tossed up and onto the beach track. *Perchance it will be of some use to someone. There will be many homes and boats lost tonight.* As the clouds passed by the huge moon, its light shone out and they saw they were winning. The sail they were trying to save was still in their hands and the men were hauling it up the steep slope.

Exhausted from hours of battling against the sea, Will slumped on top of the shingle ridge, not caring that saltwater still sprayed upon them. The others took the precious prize and dragged it to safety beyond the frothy clutches of the tide.

That night fishermen worked with merchants and farm labourers – alongside any fit man who was able to help save a portion of their livelihood. Will was a cobbler with a home and business on the High Street, but if the fishermen were to lose their boats and homes then he, along with the rest of the townsfolk, would suffer for it.

Lifting his head, Will surveyed the scene beyond the patch of beach. His gaze fell on the top of the church tower, and he thought he saw a figure revealed by a fleeting shaft of moonlight. "Who's that on the tower?" he asked a man who came to rest beside him.

The fisherman looked up with disinterest. "Who would be up there on a night like this, watching us working as slaves?" The moon was again covered by clouds and the tower was indistinct. "There's no-one. You've drunk too much seawater."

Will shrugged his shoulders. What did it matter? He scanned the beach and got up. There was nothing to be done to save the boats that had been lashed to the churchyard wall, only to be lifted and smashed upon the stone until they gave up the will to remain whole. All he and the others could do was pick up the remains and drag them free from the sea. Standing stiffly, Will felt the discomfort of his sodden breeches clinging to his muscular thighs. The material was heavy with saltwater. Will had lost count of the times he had plunged into the sea to claim a piece of wood, cloth or net from its clutches.

As the two of them trudged towards the next dark mass being carried towards them on the raging waves, a call came:

"The tide has turned."

"Thank God," muttered Will, as he grasped at a tangled net.

As the tide turned just before midnight, the wind eased, and rain stopped. Will had spent hours helping the fishermen, and now he needed to check on his own home and business. But first he paused on the shingle-strewn track to look at the piles of wood and swathes of reeds that had been the beachfront cottages. The homes lay like heaps of kindling wood. Some smouldered – dry thatch and wood had fallen onto the hot embers of abandoned fires.

How will these families manage when they have lost both their home and boat? They had so little to start with but owned the vessels and skill to feed the people of Romney and their own families. What purpose will they have now?

One had been the home of Agnes. Now just the western wall stood tall. *Where is she – my Agnes with the beautiful dark eyes and long black hair? Please God, she fled her home before it fell.* She would be sheltering somewhere or helping her mother, Will told himself. He could see straight through remains of the cottage, and smiled briefly to note that, amidst the chaos, the pig remained secure in her shelter. If, God willing, his home was standing, this would force the wedding. They'd been betrothed since she was eleven and her father would be pleased to have her off his hands. Will smiled again as he pictured taking his bride to his bed under the eaves.

"Have you seen her?" It was Agnes' brother, Robert.

"Nay, I've just come from the beach," Will replied.

"She'll be at the church, no doubt," Robert informed him. "That's where I sent my wife and the children. St Martin's, that's where they're gathering. The homeless."

"You've lost your home too." Will shook his head in sympathy.

"Christ's teeth, there's not one standing along the beach track."

"I'm going to check on mine." Will turned from the smouldering ruin which had been the home of his beloved. "Good luck to you, Robert."

He walked stiffly to the High Street. The September wind was not cold. It began to dry his shirt sleeves and breeches until salt-laden cloth scoured his skin. His boots were sodden, and he longed to change them for clean ones. How lucky he was to have two pairs, Will reflected. Luckier than most.

The High Street was littered with debris from the hastily-abandoned market as well as shards of roof tiles and swathes of reed-thatch. The path leading from St Nicholas to the High Street was thick with sand and shingle, while at the road junction it spilled out in either direction. Throughout the night Will had been astonished by the force of the sea but imagined it had taken its fury out on the beachfront. Now he saw that it had used its strength to fling its load through any available crevice between the beach and main road. Ribbons of wet sand and shingle glistened in the moonlight.

In contrast to the beach, the town was nearly deserted. Will stepped over stones, tiles and ridges of sand-mud before reaching his shop. His business was that of shoemaker and repairer, working the leather tanned by his cousin and using the wooden blocks shaped by his brother. He walked under the furled canopy where he would work and serve customers on a fine day and, after kicking a wooden pole aside, pushed his shop door open. It was dark inside, but he could feel the gritty sand beneath his saturated boots. Sand could get through any crevice when carried by the wind; it wasn't unusual to have a fine layer of it within his shop and rooms above. Beyond the shop, the kitchen was also in darkness, with just a shaft of moonlight coming through the small back window.

Will felt his way to the roughly-hewn steps and climbed up into the room above. Again, the room was in darkness, and he gave a sigh of relief: the roof was intact. He felt over his bedcovers. There were some patches of dirt, as if the tiles above had shifted but it was dry, thankfully.

He sat on a bench to fumble with shoelaces in the dark. At last the boots were removed, and thick woollen socks peeled off soggy feet. He replaced the socks with clean ones but reluctantly pulled the same boots back on. There was no point in getting another pair wet and the night's work was not done. His shirt sleeves had dried in the breeze, but the thick jerkin remained sodden against his back, so Will replaced this and hung the wet one over the bench.

The shop backed onto St Martin's churchyard, which was Will's next stop. The young man picked his route through the yard, threaded his way past the vegetable plots and the chickens who remained secure within their run. He pressed on the gate latch and stepped into the eerie churchyard. He then took a winding route amongst the graves to the porch, which faced the priory.

The door to the church was open, and Will peeped in. Within the ancient building, family groups huddled together under blankets borrowed from the more fortunate. They had come as they were when their homes began to fall: children in only their nightclothes and many of the people barefooted. Families were incomplete, as the menfolk were still out salvaging what they could from the sea. In the morning they would begin to take stock of their homes and gather their belongings. Will didn't spot any of his own family, but saw Agnes' mother, a grandchild in her arms. He walked down the narrow nave, stepping over bundles of blanket.

"William, have you seen her?" Mary looked up, her face weary in the light of the candles.

"Agnes? No, I thought... I expected to see her here, with you."

"I told her to stay safe at home. Safe!" The anguish could be heard in Mary's voice. "Have you seen it?"

41

"I have." Will knelt down beside Mary. "Every home has gone on the beachfront. But you don't think...? She'd have got out, wouldn't she?"

"I'm sure of it. Her father had a good look everywhere. Agnes has gone off somewhere, perhaps to look at the river. She was keen to see the storm, but I had said not to go out. Would you go and look for her, Will? I have to stay with the grandchildren."

"Aye, I'll go over to the river mouth and send Agnes here if I find her. The wind has dropped, so she'll be safe enough to walk home. I won't come with her because there is more helped needed on the beach. I only came back to see if there was still a roof on my home."

"And is there?" Mary asked.

"It seems fine. Good enough." Will stood up. "I'll be seeing you."

"Godspeed, William."

He stood aside to let another bewildered family enter the church. They came from the area by the repair sheds, he noticed. So, the cottages there had not survived the storm either. On leaving the church, Will walked briskly to the road and then straight on at the High Street crossroads, kicking shingle from his path as he went. The church tower of St Nicholas loomed ahead of him, and he looked up, recalling the figure he had seen earlier. There was no one there. He frowned – there *was* a figure – a shrouded figure standing at the parapet, looking over the sea. He was tired. Imagining things. Who would stand up there and not be amongst the townsfolk doing all they could to help? A cloud began to obscure the light from the moon and the figure, imaginary or not, could no longer be seen.

Will paused again briefly at the wreckage of Agnes' home. He could offer her parents shelter for a month or two. His upstairs room was a fair size and could have a partition put across it, probably in the form of a blanket. *I would rather bring my bride home alone. Just the two of us. Selfish thoughts. Her parents need somewhere to live and so they must come along with their daughter. How can I leave them to bed down God-knows-where when I have a good roof over my head? At least I think I do – it will be clearer by day. But what of her other brother?* Will sighed. *He must bed down in the living area.*

"Any news?" the shout came from Agnes' brother, Robert. "Have you seen Agnes?"

"Nay, there's no sign of her, but your parents have checked the ruins and she's not there. It's likely that she moved to safety, but God knows where," William replied. "She's probably gone to help someone, and we'll see her soon enough."

"Aye, Ma told her to stay safe in the cottage, but I thank the Lord that she saw fit to leave."

"I've just seen Mary in St Martin's. She's with your wife and little ones."

"I took them there myself," Robert told him. "Then came back to do what I could here on the beach."

"At least you know they're safe." Will paused to look at the beachfront in its new form.

"How fares your business?"

"Not bad. Not bad at all. When I see the state of things here, I can't complain about a few loose tiles and a bit of dust on my bed. The Lord vented his fury on the fishermen last night – he truly did. The shop is full of sand, but it still stands, and the rooms above seem to have survived. As the sun rises, we'll see the true extent of the damage done."

"Aye, we will."

"Mary asked me to go over to the river mouth, as Agnes wanted to watch the storm and it's a favourite place of hers." Will started to move away. "I'll be seeing you, Robert, and hopefully with news of your sister."

"I hope so. We've suffered enough tonight."

As they went their separate ways, the first rays of dawn were coming over the horizon, fingers of soft yellow and pink gave a curious light to the sky and sea. The stones of the Norman church were bathed in a soft hue and the shingle would soon glisten as the morning sun tentatively shone on the stricken town. It was in this half-light that Will trudged along the track towards the river mouth.

The area where the Rother meandered into the sea through a broad estuary was at the south-westerly corner of the town. It was a short walk, but for Will, who had been up since the previous dawn, it seemed like a struggle to be kicking aside stones and stepping over wreckage from boats and cottages.

On reaching the far edge of the town, it was too dark for him to see across the mudflats and reedbeds to the other side of the estuary. The wide expanse of mud shimmered grey, and rivulets glistened as they wound their way through silt and sand. It was both magical and eerie to see the estuary in the first moments of a new dawn.

Over the last century, the river had begun to silt up, and it was no longer possible for ships to moor end to end along the riverbanks all the way to Hope and Old Romney. Romney still had its haven, though, and good access to the sea, so became the main trading point. But where was the river that ambled along the channel forged through the mudflats? In this half-light of the new dawn, Will strained his eyes to spot a darker, deeper movement of water. *I am tired. What does it matter if I can see the river or not? It will still be there when the sun rises above the horizon, and for all the tomorrows.*

He sat on some stones, his head in his hands, fighting sleep. *It won't hurt to stop for a moment. Just for a while. Until... until there is enough light to show the tower of Lydd Church on its distant island. That will be enough, and I can go back to see the damage done to Romney in the light of day. I can close my eyes... just for five minutes... just for ten minutes. Then I must go back to help the townsfolk. But where is Agnes? Not here.* Will's body gave into exhaustion and slumped.

When Will woke, the sun had peeped above the horizon and the sky was shot with shades of orange and yellow. The water now took on those colours and dazzled him. What had woken him? Was it that the damp stones made an uncomfortable bed? Or was it the light shining upon his eyelids? Will sensed a movement behind him and turned slowly, his body stiff with cold. A young woman stood, her eyes weary and pale skin drawn from lack of sleep. She clasped a thick woollen cape around her slim frame. The hood came low, covering her brown hair and reaching her thick eyebrows.

"Cecily! What brings you here?" Will stood and turned towards the woman, who was both sister of the local vicar and wife of the town's doctor.

"I just came to be on my own. Away from the chaos." She spoke quietly and without emotion.

"Has anything happened? Your home? Your family?"

"No, the house stands solid behind the priory. My husband is on the beach or in St Martin's." She hung her head. "He is wherever he is needed, and I came here."

"I came here too," Will acknowledged her guilt. "I've worked all night, though, and you have too. I'm sure of it."

"Aye, I prepared the church for the homeless."

"We are tired. We worked all night." Will looked across the estuary. "I was looking for Agnes. Have you seen her?"

"I've seen no one."

"You're cold. Go home and get to bed, Cecily. You'll be able to help better after getting some sleep. You'll feel better for it."

"I have no child. I'll never feel better."

Will had been about to turn and walk back to the town, but now he paused. This was women's business, or at least something to be discussed between man and wife. Not for his ears. Was this why she had come away from the town? To be alone with her wretched thoughts? To be alone by the river?

He turned back, remembering his vow to see the church tower of Lydd before his return. There it was across the estuary... across the river... The river. But where was it? Will was about to ask Cecily where the river had gone, but it sounded foolish, and her thoughts were on her childless state. It was true, she had been married for several years and there was no child, or children, yet. What could he say to her?

"When God is ready, you'll be blessed, Cecily." He sounded like a priest. The words were too pious. Will faltered, gazing once more across the estuary. "I'm sorry, I don't know what to say. How to respond."

"I've been married five years, and last night I came here, having given up hope. But something strange happened..."

Five years. She has been five years married. A long time – there is no denying it. Some couples would have had as many children in those five years.

"Something happened? Was it the river? It doesn't flow. How can it not flow?"

"The river? No, I sat beside the mudflats, thinking of walking on and on. Thinking to spare my husband and

46

allow him to take a new wife. A fertile wife." Cecily looked up at Will, brown eyes puzzled. "Something came to me... a fairy... a fairy from the marshes. A little wisp of a thing and she told me... she told me a child would come to me. I would hold a baby in my arms."

How do I respond to this? Is it best that she lives with hope? It must be. "So, you came back, Cecily. That's good. Come along with me now and we'll pray for you and your child as we walk."

"Thank you, Will."

They turned away from the estuary but didn't follow the beach track. Instead, they took a parallel road which soon widened into the High Street. Will's mind, befuddled by lack of sleep, struggled to put the events of the night into any order. *Agnes – she will be found. She will be with her family by now. Cecily – she will regret confiding in me. What a good woman she is. I can only pray she will be blessed with a child.*

But the third thing playing upon his mind was the mystery of the Rother. *Why did it not flow to the sea? That was its purpose, what else would it do?* He shook himself. *Everything will become clearer after some sleep.*

Like Will, the monk had watched the sun rise over the horizon and gradually light up the land. He was curious to see what changes the storm had brought. From his viewpoint on the church tower, he saw the wet shingle shimmer under the dawn's rays. He saw the tide had deposited debris further than he could have envisaged; in both directions the beachfront was destroyed.

The monk looked towards the river mouth and harbour where the merchants docked, and he saw the remains of yesterday's Rother. As the sun shone on these muddy puddles, they shimmered, and so he believed the river flowed as always. The monk didn't

47

see – he couldn't see from that distance – that the Rother had gone and would never flow past Romney again.

He turned from the scene. It had been an exhausting night. Time to descend the spiral staircase to the base of the tower.

Part Two
The Aftermath

Chapter Five
George and Beatrice

The storm was spent and the sea, having ravaged the town, had retreated. In its wake, a thick layer of shingle and debris covered the beachfront track and spilt onto the High Street. Piles of wood, ropes and sails were stacked throughout the town, beyond the new high tide mark. One man's helm had been jumbled with his neighbour's mast as they were gathered in haste before the sea took them for its own. Later, when the people of Romney had slept, the salvaged goods would be shared fairly.

Homes and livelihoods were destroyed. Yet, amidst all the terror, the only recorded death was that of Hugh Alcock, boat builder and repairer. As the first light of dawn appeared, the sea had retreated fully. Now it swayed gently to and fro, lapping on the sand, oblivious to the panic and destruction it had caused.

A man passed by the church, looking for anything to recover. He was weary from first trying to protect his boat and smokehouse, and later collecting the remains. His feet sank through the shingle as he neared the church entrance in the base of the tower. St Nicholas was on the seafront and was the only building strong enough to withstand the repetitive onslaught of the sea. It had resisted the sea to a point, George noted. He had approached the building from the east and seen the end wall had fallen.

Now he reached the tower and found himself standing at a height which took him halfway up the curved Norman doorway. How would this ever be cleared, he wondered? The wooden doors had been smashed open by the force of the sea. It had no respect for the sanctity of this building and had flowed relentlessly into the building, depositing its seabed as it retreated. Was there anything here to reclaim? He took a few more steps and saw a small bundle on the ridge within the doorway.

To his shock, George saw that a baby nestled there. A tiny scrap of a thing wrapped in a piece of rough cloth. Tentatively, he scooped the child into his arms and gave a sigh of relief to see it was alive. Something wasn't right though – it was too quiet. This baby should be objecting loudly about its mistreatment and demanding its mother's milk. Carefully, George picked up the fragile child and held it in the crook of his arm, hoping to share the warmth from his body.

"What do you have there, George?" The vicar approached from the direction of the High Street.

"A baby boy, Vicar, and newborn I'd say," replied the bewildered man.

"Why do you bring him here to the church, after such a night? Is he ill?" The vicar looked at the bundle with mild curiosity.

"I didn't bring him," stated George, "I found him, just here in the doorway."

Half a dozen others had now gathered, and questions were flying at the vicar:

"Whose baby is he?"

"What does this mean?"

"What are we to do with him?"

"Will he live?"

The vicar felt unable to answer, to explain the arrival of this child. He opened his mouth a few times, but no words were formed. He stood, gazing upwards at the clear blue sky, silently seeking guidance from his Lord. There came a crunching sound of feet upon the shingle within the base of the tower. As if in answer to his prayers, the travelling monk appeared on the rise of stones within the doorway. Who better to answer their questions than this wise man who was known to have travelled extensively and experienced more than their humble vicar?

"You came from within the church," the vicar said in surprise, and all faces turned to the dishevelled monk who stood, on the shingle, several feet higher than themselves. It was almost as if he had descended from heaven.

"I watched the storm from the tower," informed the monk, who was a man of few words. "I saw it all."

"And did you see?" The vicar asked. "Did you see anyone put the baby here? Just here in the doorway?"

"A baby? I did not. I saw no one put a baby there." And so that became the truth.

"But you were there?" The vicar's words came out in a rush. "You said you saw it all, from the tower. You watched all night from the tower?"

"I saw it all from the tower," the monk repeated.

"Then how, in the midst of this storm, did a baby arrive?" The vicar looked up at the wise monk. "Tell me how."

"He is a gift from God," stated the monk, and no one considered to doubt his wisdom. "Romney has indeed been blessed."

With that, the monk turned his back on them and slid awkwardly out of the tower. He nodded his head towards the group of men, placed his forefinger briefly on the baby's head, and made the sign of the cross. Then he turned and walked away. It was not in his nature or profession to stand around gossiping. He returned to the priory, his temporary home before he moved on to the next town or village.

"Whoever he is, he still needs feeding." George felt responsible for the baby. "I'll take him to my sister to wet-nurse until you decide what to do with him."

"Thank you, George. Thank you. That seems to be for the best." And, nodding to himself, relieved of the burden, the vicar scrambled up and into the doorway of the church.

With the newborn gently cradled, George picked his way along the road, pushing aside the debris with his boots. As they reached the High Street, the baby boy stirred and began to cry in desperation. George's expression had been serious, with deep lines etched in his tanned face, but now as the newborn opened his blue eyes and his tiny mouth, George grinned down at him.

"There, there, we'll get you some milk in no time," he said. The tension flowed from his body. He had believed the little scrap would not survive. It wasn't natural to lie there so quietly.

Having turned left at the priory, George passed the doctor's house and a few minutes later he rapped on the door of his sister's cottage. He entered without waiting for a response and smiled down at Beatrice, who was sitting with her drowsy six-month old daughter at her breast. Beatrice moved her baby and pulled her tunic back in place. *She looks tired too. Who doesn't after the storm?*

"Who do you have there?" Beatrice asked as she placed her baby in a basket. "Take it back to its mother. It needs feeding."

"He has no mother." George passed the tiny bundle, whose crumpled face was now red with anger.

"By God, another death in the night? Who?" Beatrice shifted her tunic to partly expose another swollen breast and gently guided the newborn to it.

"I don't know," George slumped on a bench. "Not a death. Not that I know of. Just a baby." He put his head in his hands. "I found him, at the base of the church tower. At St Nicholas."

"He's newborn." Beatrice stroked the fine dark hair on the baby's head. "But who would put him in the church porch? I can't think who would do that."

"Neither can I," George paused for a moment, unsure of how to voice his words. "There was a monk... you know the man... staying at the priory. He was there. Came out of the tower."

"The church tower? What was he doing there?"

"Stayed up to watch the storm, he said. Could have come down and given us a hand."

"But he couldn't. Could he, George? Not a monk." Beatrice adjusted the baby slightly. "He suckles well."

"We needed all the help we could get. I'm not proud."

"What's the monk got to do with this little one?"

"Well, everyone's crowding around, asking about the baby. Asking the vicar where he comes from. Then down comes the monk, from the tower, and the vicar thinks that he might have seen someone put the baby there. But he hadn't seen a thing. Said that he had looked out at the storm and along the beach all night and no one had put a baby there."

"What did the vicar have to say about that?" Beatrice asked.

"Not much, not much at all because then the monk said that the baby was a gift from God. A gift to make amends after the storm."

Beatrice gazed at the baby in awe. He opened his dark blue eyes and looked up at her. She had no words to express her wonder. He stopped feeding and she busied herself with wiping his mouth, then said to George, "Can you pass me a cloth... over there, he needs making clean and comfortable."

Beatrice cleaned the baby and swaddled him in a blanket. Then she placed him to sleep beside her own daughter.

George's eyelids were beginning to droop. He could do with some sleep. He rose from the bench and stepped towards the doorway.

"You'll keep him then? Just for now?"

"Aye," replied Beatrice. "I'll care for him until someone thinks of what's to become of him." Then as George put his hand on the door latch, she remembered: "George, your home... I could only think of the baby... is it all gone? And the smokery?"

"Aye, all gone." He shrugged his shoulders. "I'll patch it up somehow. Until then, we make our home at St Martin's, same as the rest of them."

"You could always...."

"Nay, you've not got the space. and with two babies it wouldn't be right. Besides, it will be warm at the church. I'm going there now to rest awhile."

Beatrice stayed at home that morning. What else could she do with two babies to care for? The newborn needed feeding, then changing, at least every two hours. Thankfully, he was placid and slept in-between feeds. *What will become of him?* Already, her attachment to him grew as they bonded whilst he suckled. Then he slept, and she did her chores as best she could, with her daughter on her hip or lying on a thick rug on the floor.

It was mid-morning when she finally stepped out to the well behind the cottages and drew a bucket of water. It was good to be out in the fresh air, if only for a moment. The well was a meeting place for her neighbours: a spot to pause and hear the news. The yard was deserted today, Beatrice noticed with regret. She would have liked to have spoken about the baby and found out what was being said about him within the town. If only she could take a walk along the High Street, take the child to see her husband, talk to the townsfolk. Then she would feel a part of the community, sharing the stories of the storm. But here she was removed from it all. Trapped in the home by the two babies. Yet, in many ways she was very much a part of it. All the time she had the baby, Beatrice was very much a part of the story of the great storm.

She staggered back into the cottage. The water-filled bucket was cumbersome. Beatrice's desire for company was fulfilled for now: two visitors were in her home. The vicar stood while his sister knelt on the stone floor gazing at the newborn. *Poor Cecily, how she yearns for her own child*. Beatrice saw it in her eyes whenever they met. *What does the vicar mean by bringing her here? Doesn't Cecily suffer enough every time a baby is born to the parish?*

"Beatrice," the vicar stepped forwards. "He looks healthy enough, would you say? I feared he wouldn't survive. But God chose that spot, knowing His child would be found. We can't begin to understand His mind, but what a gift He has bestowed on the people of this town."

So, it was accepted. It was accepted that this baby is a child of God. If that's what the vicar said, it must be so.

"He seems healthy enough. A little small perhaps but he feeds well." Beatrice moved towards Cecily and knelt beside her. "Would you like... Would you like to hold him? He won't stir, his belly is full of milk." She carefully lifted the fragile bundle. "Sit yourself down, Cecily. Hold him on your lap."

Cecily is radiant! Beatrice noticed. *How could I have ever thought her plain?* Her eyes shone and skin looked fresher than it had in years. Then Beatrice realised why they had come.

"Cecily, is he to be yours?"

"This child is special. He brings hope in a time of despair." The vicar spoke gently, "Cecily is ready to cherish him. Her home still stands, and her husband is a doctor. A respectable man."

"Of course. I can think of no one better to love and care for this child." Beatrice smiled. Already she was bonding with the little one, but suspected she was carrying her second child. The baby would give such pleasure to Cecily.

"I can't feed him, Bea. I can't just take him as my own. Would you...?"

"Of course I will. We can share the care until he is old enough to feed from a cup. I'd struggle with the two little ones to look after, but between us he'll fare well."

They were silent for a moment. Cecily looking down at her new son, memorising all his features, eager to report back to her husband. He shifted slightly in her arms and opened his eyes that didn't yet focus on his new mother. She didn't know how she could leave him with Beatrice, to walk away for even a moment.

"I could have him in the days, couldn't I?"

"Aye, just bring him back for his milk. But at night... at night I must have him, just for a few weeks." It would be hard with two babies, but her own daughter rarely stirred through the long hours of darkness.

The vicar moved towards the door. "Beatrice, there's to be a celebration of the new life and his baptism of course. Not at St Nicholas – the eastern wall has collapsed. It will be at St Martin's. At noon."

"At noon?" Beatrice couldn't hide her surprise. "So soon. If it is because you believed him to be a weakling, then there is no need. I am sure he will live."

"Nay, it is because we need this celebration and new hope. The town is stricken, Beatrice, and it will do us good."

"A baptism then, at noon. I must feed and change him." Beatrice looked at Cecily. "Or perhaps his mother will change him?" Then she paused, looking at the baby. "What's his name?"

"Nicholas," replied Cecily. "It must be Nicholas for both the church and the monk who was there when he was found."

"Nicholas," repeated Beatrice. "Aye, of course."

As the two women cared for the baby Nicholas, word spread around the town. There was to be a ceremony of rejoicing and the baptism of a newborn child. Not, any child: this was a child born to bring light and hope to a stricken place. His mother would be Cecily, the doctor's wife and vicar's sister, but he was also a son of the town, and they would all watch him grow and develop. His mother may be a local woman, but his father was God. The holy man had told them and there was no reason to disbelieve him.

In his room, behind the stone walls of the priory, the monk awoke. Now he was eager to begin his report of the night. With his vellum set out before him and quill freshly sharpened, he wrote of the storm and the destruction of the town. However, the monk suffered from pride. He saw a way to have his name remembered through his writing and he had a story to tell that would ensure this happened:

"The storm had ravaged Romney so that no man nor beast, whether their home be of wood or stone, was safe from its fury. The parish church was despoiled with stone, sand and all manner of debris. It was left unfit for the worship of God. Then, as the tide ebbed and the wind eased, the Lord took pity on the people of the town and blessed them with the gift of a baby boy."

As the words dried on the vellum, the monk settled down to daydream. He dreamt of his words being heard as far away as Canterbury, Winchester and London. People would talk about the arrival of a child who came during the storm and about how he, the travelling monk, had witnessed the baby's arrival. The story would be repeated and embellished throughout the land, and every time it was retold his name would be mentioned and remembered.

Once the vellum was dry, the monk set about packing his small collection of belongings. His time in Romney was over. As he slung his bag over his shoulder and descended the steep staircase, the monk failed to see the lone figure of Agnes, mother of the child, turn her back on Dymchurch and retrace her steps as she returned to her home town of Romney.

Chapter Six
Agnes

The monk walked away from Romney, having witnessed one of the worst storms of the century and painstakingly recorded his account. It was time to travel on, to witness new sights and share his experiences. As he strolled, he thought ahead to his arrival in Canterbury and how he would tell the news:

"There was a storm like no other...the sea bounded through the town, leaving destruction in its path... a newborn child was found... a boy... in the church... a gift from God to ease the people's suffering."

Such was his jubilation and pride that he barely noticed a young woman whom he passed on the coast path. Her head was lowered, and she carried nothing. It was Agnes, mother of the child, returning to claim her son. She had walked half the way to Dymchurch, but on reaching an area known as Jesson had turned abruptly and retraced her steps along the coastal track.

Agnes' heart was burdened. She had seen her home and father's boat destroyed and left a newborn child in the hope that some good person would find him. How long could the baby survive, wrapped in a rag and without milk? Guilt gnawed at her stomach. Agnes knew she had no means of caring for her son, yet her maternal instincts drove her to return to him. She had no plan as to how she would begin to claim him, for surely someone had the baby and was taking care of him. There was no thought as to how she would tell her exhausted and defeated family.

Agnes' thoughts strayed to Will, to whom she had been betrothed for the last three years, since she was eleven. She felt some affection for him – he was a good man who had been a part of her life for many years. Her marriage was expected to take place next summer and the thought pleased her. The union would bring security and a decent home. It was a good match for her – many thought it was too good a match. A fisherman's daughter and a tradesman. She had done well. Will had not – he had not done well to promise himself to a girl who would lie with another before they made their wedding vows. She couldn't keep him to those vows now. He would be disgusted by her, and she couldn't expect any more of him. He was a good man, but not a weak fool.

Finally, she thought of the man who was the father of her child. Hugh Alcock – how her heart had soared at the very sight of him strutting around the seafront. She had seduced him and felt no shame, thinking nothing of his wife and child. Thinking nothing of her own dignity. She wasn't the first woman to have come between him and his wife. Perhaps her child wasn't the first of his born out of wedlock, but he was probably the first born to a mother who didn't know she was carrying a new life. There had been no signs: no gentle swelling of her belly, no tiredness or a feeling of nausea. But now her milk was beginning to form, and her breasts swollen. She needed to feed her baby and he needed her.

Would Hugh acknowledge the child as his own? No, he would want nothing to do with the pair of them. In fact, he had tired of her many months ago. He would want her to keep quiet, would most likely threaten her.

He had quite a temper. Maybe he would pay towards the child's upkeep? Pay for her silence.

Now she neared the area where the boat building and repairs took place alongside the smoking and salting of fish. This was Hugh Alcock's world where he reigned supreme. Agnes was exhausted and it was only with a passing interest that she saw the huge shed had collapsed. The storm had even had the better of Hugh, so it seemed. All around it the smaller buildings lay like piles of kindling wood, just as they did in her own area, on the beachfront near the church. Not a soul was there, salvaging what they could or beginning repairs. *They must be sleeping. Even though the sun is at its highest, they'll be resting after the long night. But they should be up again by now. There is so much work to be done.*

Passing by St Nicholas Church, she saw the east end had fallen in and shingle filled every crevice. The tower and west end stood strong though and Agnes felt compelled to check the base of the tower. Tentatively she picked her way over the stones and peered into the open doorway. There was no sign of her baby.

Now she could see all along the beachfront where her father had kept his boat. There were piles of salvaged materials pulled free from the tide which was high again. There was still work to be done... so much work. The rebuilding of boats and homes. Where were the men who had been frantically trying to salvage their livelihoods and cottages? *How can they sleep while their families are homeless? Where is my father? And Robert? And John? They wouldn't sleep while they have no means of going out to fish.* Agnes noticed an eerie silence. They couldn't *all* be sleeping while there was so much work to be done. With mounting horror, she feared Romney had been abandoned.

She turned towards the High Street, anxiety now making her limbs stiff. It was empty too: no traders and no housewives with their baskets. Then from the shadows of a shop doorway an old woman appeared, and Agnes watched as the lone figure carefully picked her way through the debris. She followed as the woman turned towards the priory and then shuffled into the church of St Martin's.

Now Agnes could hear music and the murmur of voices. With interest, she stepped across the churchyard and into the porch. A scene of rejoicing was set out before her. Every space on the stone floor was filled as people jostled for position, every aisle crowded, every windowsill and nook filled. Candles burned, hundreds of them sending out their soft yellow light and bringing warmth to the grey stone walls; incense smouldered giving an aroma of far-off lands to the damp building. What could have happened in the midst of all this storm-inflicted horror? What could have happened to bring the whole town together to celebrate?

Then the voices became hushed, and conversations trailed away. The church was almost silent, save the rustling of clothes and whispers from children. The vicar was walking towards the back of the church, sometimes having to push his way through the congregation. All attention was on him. As he approached the font, he held up a baby, swaddled in embroidered cloth. The child was tiny and, although he was almost within touching distance of Agnes, his features were obscured by both the cloth and the vicar's hands. What could not be denied was that this child was so small. Newborn. Agnes gasped. Her mouth dried and her throat constricted. Then turning to the woman beside her, she somehow forced out the words:

"Who is the child?"

"Where have you been, Agnes? You must have heard the news?"

"I... I was helping... with the salvage. Then I slept," she lied.

"He came with the storm, the baby did," the woman informed her in a low whisper, proud to be passing on the news. "A gift from God to help us through our suffering. That's what the monk said."

"The monk?"

"He was up in the church tower. Watching. No one put the baby there, or he would have seen them. The boy is a miracle. A gift." She nodded knowingly, believing the word of the holy man.

"The baby is a gift from God?" repeated his incredulous mother.

"Aye. God's child has come to Romney. We are fortunate indeed."

The vicar was talking about the child, but Agnes could barely hear his words, just the rise and fall of his voice. Prayers came: words from the vicar and repeated by the congregation. Agnes went through the motions of the responses, as her emotions fought within her. Should she stand up now, take responsibility for her child and deprive the town of its glory? Or should she allow her son to live a life where he was honoured and cared for by the town?

"Who will look after the baby?" Agnes asked her companion.

"The vicar's sister," replied the woman. "She has none of her own and is now truly blessed."

Agnes knew what to do – what was best for the child. Cecily was both the vicar's sister and the doctor's wife. Her house was of stone and would still be standing beside the priory. The baby would have the best of care, and Cecily would love him as her own. As she made the decision, Agnes felt a rush of wellbeing. She had done an unforgivable thing, lying with another woman's husband, but now the town was in celebratory mood and a desperate woman had her own child.

Then the baptism was over, and the clergy moved back to the chancel, taking the child with them. His importance was such that he could enter the domain of the priests. Singing radiated from behind the decorated screen separating the clergy from the worshippers and Agnes's heart felt lighter as her body swayed in time to the rise and fall of the Latin verses. The tension eased from her body now she knew her son's future was secure. The music and the joy of the familiar hymn took hold of her, and she felt carefree again. Selfishly, she realised that her own future was also safe as long as she could hide the signs of recent childbirth. Her young body would soon recover.

As the song ended, the baby began to cry and the vicar handed him to his mother, Cecily, who in turn passed him to Beatrice. Agnes gave the slightest nod of understanding. *Of course Cecily could not feed him; the child needed a wet nurse.* As baby Nicholas latched on to feed, Agnes' own milk began to seep through her shift. It was not going to be that easy to give him up; her heart slumped again, and she turned to walk out of the church.

It was chilly outside, and the day seemed dull after the yellow warmth of the candlelit church. Agnes pulled her shawl tight around her shoulders and walked through the empty streets to the beachfront, kicking at loose shingle. The high tide was lethargic, uninterested in causing any more trouble for the town. At the ruins of her home, Agnes turned her back to the sea and paused to absorb the damage. The end wall still stood, with roof beams and thatch hanging off it. The rest of the cottage's wooden walls and reed-thatch roof lay this way and that, with pieces of furniture peeping through.

Sleep. She needed sleep. Agnes knew she could do no more for now, so she returned to her place of safety – the pig shelter. The old sow stirred a little to see Agnes climb into her snug home then closed her eyes and didn't flinch as the young woman lay against her side and settled down to sleep.

"Agnes... Agnes. Thank God."

Agnes opened her eyes and for a moment her world spun as she tried to make sense of where she was and why. How long had she been asleep? Not long, she was sure of that, maybe half an hour or so. That was it... the storm... the baby... her son... and now she was back and tired. Of course, she was tired, she had not slept all night. It was the same throughout the town, people up all night homeless, and salvaging all they could.

"Agnes, sweeting, where have you been all this time?" Her mother didn't wait for an answer but turned and called to her husband, "John, she's here! Our girl is here. With the sow." Then back to Agnes: "We've been worried, coming back here and you nowhere to be found. We thought you'd be at the church... with the others at St Martin's, but no one had seen you."

Rousing herself from her sleep and barely able to keep up with her mother's flow of words, Agnes struggled with her response. "I was looking for you... you and Pa. The cottage fell down... It was falling when I got out. I'm sorry I couldn't take anything with me. There wasn't time. I just sheltered with the sow." She stood on shaky legs and began to climb out of the pig shelter. "Then I went and looked for you and father but didn't see you. It was so busy of course... and dark."

Agnes' father arrived, his relief visible. "It's a comfort to see you, girl. It's been a terrible night."

"Aye, I know." Agnes replied. "The town is in ruins. Has anyone...? I mean how many... how many dead?"

"You'd hardly believe it! Only the one. That Hugh Alcock. You wouldn't think the Lord would want to take *him*!" John gave a brief grin.

"Hugh?" Agnes began to sway a little. "Hugh? Was he on the beach?"

"By his shed," her father explained. "Helping himself with no thought to the others, by all accounts. The shed started listing and you know the size of it. He couldn't hope to get out alive."

Agnes slumped down on the shingle. Her son had lost his father. Barely a day old, and his father was dead. She shook herself like a dog shaking off fleas. What foolish thoughts; they deserved no space in her head. The child was never going to know Hugh as his father and Hugh would never have known Nicholas as his son.

"Agnes, sweeting, he wasn't a nice man. Feel pity for his wife and child, but don't fret over him." Her mother knelt beside her. Then she put her hand on Agnes' forehead. "You don't look well; I wonder if you are sickening for a fever. It's not like you to look so low." Then taking Agnes by the arm she helped her stand, "Let's get you to St Martin's. There's hot soup and dry blankets."

"You're right, Ma." Agnes grasped at an excuse for her usual lack of vitality. "I was ill last night, and I've not eaten since... since we were all together for supper. I'll take a rest and then help as much as I can."

She was led by her mother back to the crossroads with the High Street. Traders had tentatively opened their shops, but the street remained sparse of people. Agnes glanced up and down, noting some storm damage to roofs and awnings, and the swathes of debris, sand and stones on the road and in drifts against the buildings on the far side. Exhausted, Agnes glanced towards the shoemaker's shop and felt guilt weigh heavy on her small body. She turned away – her burdens were great enough without adding Will to them.

How different the church was from when she had been in it an hour or two before. Where there had been a warm glow from candles, now the only light came through narrow windows, and much of the interior was shadowed. The gentle murmur of prayer was lost, and people no longer faced the altar in rapt attention. They sat in clusters, talking quietly, caring for young babies and shouting sharp commands to lively youngsters. Benches had been brought in to provide seating, hay mattresses were strewn upon the floor and a table near the rood screen had donations of food to be shared.

Mary led the way, with her daughter following. Halfway down the nave, on the right, was Agnes' brother, named John after their father. He was sleeping under borrowed blankets. Nearby, with a child on her lap and one leaning beside her, Robert's wife sat awkwardly on a thin mat. Her hair was ragged and face pale. She looked up at Agnes and smiled but said nothing.

"John was up all night, collecting what he could, him and all the others," Mary smiled down at her sleeping son. "Now, Agnes, you settle down here, put this blanket around you and I'll get you something to eat. They are bringing in soup all hours of the day. We work as long as we can, then eat and rest. It's too soon to live by the usual ways."

"Thanks, Ma," Agnes perched on a bench and wrapped a blanket around herself, as her mother suggested.

All around were the families who lived alongside her at the beachfront and those from the cottages near the boat repair sheds. No seafront homes had been saved and very few families had any other place to go. Generations of the same families lived at the top of the beach and now they huddled, side by side, small collections of their belongings piled up beside them.

"There you are, Agnes. Nice and warm." Mary handed her daughter a bowl of soup and placed a chunk of rough bread in her lap. "That will help and then lie down beside your brother and sleep. You'll feel better for it."

"Thanks, Ma." Agnes tore into the bread and dunked it in the thick soup. As the warmth seeped into her body, her eyelids began to fall. Five minutes later she lay on the stone floor in a deep sleep.

When she woke again, the sky had darkened and some of the candles had been lit within St Martin's. Agnes' first sensation was that of her hip and shoulder feeling stiff and cold; there was only a blanket between her and the stone floor. The mattresses were needed for the old and infirm. Then she became aware of her breasts, full and throbbing. Instinctively, she pulled her shawl around her. The signs of the recent childbirth would subside within the next few days. She had seen enough of life to know that a mother with no child to feed soon stopped producing milk.

Her parents, Mary and John, were there but not her brothers. Seeing her searching gaze, Mary told Agnes: "They are back at the cottage, making some sort of order out of it all. Pa and I have brought back as much as we could pull out." She nodded towards an untidy heap of clothing, bedding, pots and pans. "But, the rafters, the planks – we can't bring them here, can we? They'll be reused through – even the reeds. We'll save what we can. What else can we do?"

"She'll be all right though, our Agnes." John spoke then. He was a man of few words, saying only what was necessary.

"Aye, it's a relief not to have to worry about you." Mary confirmed.

"Not to have to worry about me?" Agnes repeated, fear clawing at her heart.

"Nay, Will has been to see me and he'll marry you within a week." John informed his daughter.

"Within a week?" Agnes pulled herself upright and looked to her parents.

"Aye, he's a decent man and no need to wait until next summer. Fourteen is a fair age to marry and you've blossomed nicely over the last few months. You'll make a fine wife, Agnes." Mary smiled at her daughter with misguided pride. "Aye, William will be pleased to take you as his wife, and we must be grateful."

Chapter Seven
Agnes

"Within a week?" Agnes repeated. "I'm to marry in a few days?"

"It's been planned for years" Mary crouched down beside her. "He's a good man. Ready to give you a home, and he'll take me and your pa too."

"A home. Of course, we need a home." Her mind, usually bright, was befuddled by the events of the last twenty-four hours. "We're all to live with Will?"

"Just for a while, until your pa has built a new home. Then it will just be you and Will"

"That's kind of him... kind of Will," Agnes acknowledged.

The church was becoming crowded: children racing up and down the central aisle, heaps of belongings stacked awkwardly by the areas allocated for each family group, donations to be shared. The air smelled of damp, from both the ancient stones and the piles of possessions which were wet from the storm. Babies crying, toddlers shrieking, women gossiping, men planning... How was she to bear being confined amongst all this? She longed to be free – running errands for her ma or selling fish on the beach – with the wind whipping at her hair and sea-spray on her lips.

"I'm going out, Ma." Agnes stood abruptly. Then seeing her mother's concern, added, "Just for a while. I'll be back before dark." She adjusted her shawl, then stepped over the blanket which had been her meagre cushion as she lay on the floor to sleep.

Drawn to the sea, Agnes ran across the churchyard and down the road leading to St Nicholas Church. At the High Street junction, she avoided looking towards the shoemaker's, not wanting to see Will, to catch his eye. *Foolish thoughts. He won't be standing about outside his shop. He'll be working inside, or more likely, helping out wherever he's needed.*

When she reached the beach, Agnes slid down the bank and onto the smooth wet sand. She paused for a moment to inhale the sea air and to immerse herself in the rhythm of the tide. Now she felt free from the crowding within St Martin's and unburdened by the duties that lay ahead. It was strangely quiet, with no boats either on the bank out at sea. Agnes' favourite moment was when the fishing boats bobbed on the tide, waiting to come in with their catch. She would be there on the beach, ready to help bring in the haul and display it for sale. *Would the gulls notice something was amiss? They would have to work harder for their feed, unable to swoop upon the fishing boats for an easy meal.*

She walked along the shore for five minutes or so, only scrambling up the bank as she rounded the corner where beach met estuary. Just as she loved the beach and the ever-changing moods of the sea, Agnes was drawn to the estuary and watching the Rother move lazily out to sea. The sun was setting in the direction of Old Romney, casting a warm light over the mudflats and river, causing each stone to throw a shadow, and for all colours to be more pronounced.

Agnes paused, her brow creasing as she looked upon a vast shingle ridge which had been pushed across the mouth of the river. She stood, open-mouthed, trying to grasp the enormity of what was before her. The river was blocked, but why did it not rise up and flow over the top? Why did it not force its way through or swell in volume until it formed a great lake that spilled through the town?

"It's gone." Will was standing behind Agnes, causing her to start. "I don't know how or why but the Rother has gone."

"Gone?" Agnes repeated in disbelief, although she saw it for herself.

"I saw it myself this morning, at dawn," Will informed her, as he moved closer. "Not the river. I didn't see the river. I saw it had gone. But I was so tired, and Cecily was here, so I didn't stop to question it. That's why I came now."

"I wonder..." but Agnes couldn't voice her words. Her mouth dried up as guilt swept over her and she tried to force something out. "Cecily? What was...?"

"She was upset." Will saw it now – the desperate woman he had met before dawn. What had happened was between them, not to be shared, not even with Agnes. "It all got too much, the storm... the horror of it all."

"And now she has a child... a baby." Agnes tried to sound bright, as if it were the miracle everyone believed it to be.

"Now she has a baby," Will confirmed. "I can hardly believe it. To think she stood here, so alone, and now she has a son to love and raise."

"Did she want one badly?" Agnes ventured to ask. She was too young, too inexperienced in the ways of life, to understand Cecily's need.

"I think she did." Will wasn't going to tell Agnes about the vision, that Cecily had become so sure she would be blessed with a child. He hadn't believed it at the time, but now... now it seemed that all manner of odd things had happened during that night.

72

"Agnes..." Will reached out and took her hand. His own felt solid, wrapped around hers. She turned to look into brown eyes that in turn gazed back at her. He stood a head taller than her, his features regular and figure muscular, yet slim. "Agnes, I spoke with your father, and we are to marry. Does that please you?"

"I know." Agnes looked back towards the abandoned estuary. "Pa told me."

"Do you feel you're too young?" Will asked.

"Too young?" Agnes reflected on the question. She hadn't been too young to lie with Hugh Alcock, or to give birth to a son who was not yet a day old. She could clean and cook with or without her mother's guidance. But to be tied to the home hour after hour, she felt that she was not too young, but too free-spirited. Yet, at the same time she yearned to hold her baby and be bound to him. She was a mixture of contradictions.

"A little," she conceded, "but I know you'll be kind to me, and your heart is good. You do this to give us a home, for my parents as well as myself."

"I'll be good to you," Will confirmed and turning towards her, he tilted her chin upwards and kissed her gently.

Agnes found herself responding, enjoying the sensation of his firm lips on hers. Her heart began to beat a little faster and she felt regret when they parted. Will looked into her eyes of the darkest brown, and he stroked her face with slightly rough fingertips. She wanted him to kiss her again – how easily all thoughts of Hugh were forgotten. William was her betrothed and she had always been fond of him. *There was never the chance to see him as a lover. We were pledged when I was eleven, and it is as if he became part of the whole family, not part of me. How could I have not thought of him in that way…in the way I saw Hugh?*

Will kissed her again lightly and said: "You'll have your mother to help in the home and will soon become accustomed to living in the High Street. At night, I hear the sea crashing on the beach at high tide, just as you did from your cottage. It's not so different."

They turned, by mutual, silent consent and started to walk back along the track to the St Nicholas Church and then across the High Street to St Martin's. Parting at the church, Will returned to his home behind the shoemaker's and Agnes to the stifling confinement of her temporary home.

By the following morning, the families within the church had settled back within their usual daily rhythms. The men left early, with stomachs full of porridge, and headed to the beach to work on building new boats from salvaged wood. Not expecting to replace every vessel, they worked in family groups, with neighbours or friends. Until they could take to the water again, their families would remain beholden to those who donated food to them, and this was a situation which did not lie easy with proud fishermen. The boats were their priority, and afterwards they would decide on where and how to build new homes.

Agnes spent the whole day trudging between the pump and washtub in the yard behind Will's house and the land around St Martin's. The day was bright and gusty, perfect for drying clothes and bedding. By noon, these were strewn over the ground and across every available tree or bush. When the men returned for their supper that evening, the piles of belongings were more orderly, and the air, which had become increasingly rank from the odour of damp clothes and bedding, was a little sweeter. Mary was pleased – they had retrieved all their clothes, blankets and rugs, and these were none the worse for the drenching they suffered during the night of the storm.

For the church dwellers, some comfort was brought by the farmers from Hope, Ivychurch and St Mary's in the Marsh. They arrived with carts of fresh straw and sacking. It lay heaped in piles, some for each family group, and would bring relief to those who had been sleeping on the stone floor. Despite the air being thick with dust motes from the straw, St Martin's was now becoming a home, and the faces of the wives and mothers were less harassed.

The following day, the third after the great storm, sadness and confusion came in another form to those who had made the church their home. By mid-morning, two families had made the difficult decision to leave Romney. They were neighbours and cousins from the beachfront who expressed their disbelief of ever replacing the fishing fleet with the meagre amount of wood available. The men spoke at length to their distraught wives, offering desperate plans and hopes for the future until finally it was agreed they should leave and take their chances elsewhere.

"It's too soon." Whispers flew between the stone walls of St Martin's, but no sooner than they had broken their fast, the fishermen and their families left. The farewells were brief, and their discomfort great. They carried only a couple of bags each, and departed in the direction of Hythe, with their children trailing behind them.

Agnes felt numb as she watched them leave with their heads lowered. She felt their shame in abandoning the stricken town and feared the news of others leaving. *Who else will decide to leave? I cannot blame them for believing Romney will never recover, but today I will pray to the saints that my father and brothers will never leave our town.*

The mood of the women living in St Martins was low and peppered with resentment. Her longing to free herself from this area of communal living drove Agnes to the beach. Not to the area where her family had lived and worked, but to the east of the town where Hugh had carried out his boat repair business. She felt compelled to see the place where he had died, especially as this was to be the day of the funeral.

No one noticed the dark-haired young woman approach and linger on the edges of the eastern beach. She absorbed the scene with, at first, the huge barn-like construction which had taken Hugh's life, being the focus of her attention. One side lay slumped and, while the thatch had been removed, the carcass of the building was laid bare in a contorted mess of heavy beams and smaller, slimmer supports. The Alcock cousins were clearing the site, placing wood in orderly piles and dragging the tools and materials free.

Nearby, the smokehouses, salting areas and barrel-making sheds were taking shape. Although until the boats were ready, supplies of fish would be limited. In the meantime, several men were hammering stakes into the ground, clearly planning to restore kiddle-fishing. Agnes watched them, setting out the framework of poles, ready to funnel the fish into their trap. A couple of men on the beach were preparing nets to be slung between the frames. If the job was done before the tide rose, there might be fresh fish again by the morning.

Then she saw her – Matilda – standing at the top of the beach, holding her young son by his hand. Even from this distance it felt as if her grey eyes were fixed upon Agnes. Oliver tugged at his mother's hand, but she stood firm. Agnes couldn't see Matilda's features clearly, but she knew that her pale face would be pinched and eyes dull with grief. She wondered where she prayed for her husband's soul, with St Nicholas storm-damaged and St Martin's a refuge for the homeless. Agnes began to back away – aware of her breasts being hard and full of milk for the baby who didn't know her. Her eyes began to fill with tears, and she turned abruptly to walk back along the track towards St Nicholas and her old home, before turning towards the town.

At St Martin's, Agnes told her mother what she had seen: "They've got the kiddle frames up. But the repair shed will take some work."

"Aye, it was a big place," Mary replied. She was feeding her granddaughter some salted fish soup. "Fetch yourself a bowl, Agnes, while it's hot."

There had been changes at the church in the time Agnes had been out. Two fire pits had been freshly dug and young boys were piling wood up beside them. They were to be communal fires for cooking. Until now, local women had provided hot meals three times a day. Now the homeless would cook for themselves but still relied on being given the food. The women could cook for their families, but the men still felt the shame of not being able to provide the food.

Agnes settled down, her hands wrapped around the bowl of soup. She felt compelled to ask about her son. "Have you seen the baby, Ma? The one who came after the storm?"

"I saw him with Cecily this morning. He's a dear thing."

"And is he well after... after being left out, all alone at the church?"

"He looks healthy enough and the Lord wouldn't have placed him there if he wasn't going to guide George to find him. He'll be fine, that little lad will." Mary spoke firmly – she honestly believed that the coming of the child was indeed a blessing for the town.

That afternoon Hugh Alcock was buried, with a graveside service. He had lived in the parish of St Nicholas, so his wife determined he should lie there. Agnes watched his body, heavily shrouded in linen, being lowered into the grave by his two cousins and other local men who had worked alongside him. Hugh had no friends, just those men who feared and despised him. The grave was near the walls of the church. *A man like Hugh needs all the help he can get on his journey through purgatory. Matilda, the priests, and anyone else who cares to, will have to pray hard to help him move on to a better world.*

The priest's words could not be heard. To Agnes they were a constant hum, a muttering whose volume flowed in peaks and troughs, just like the waves out to sea. At times, the small congregation responded to the prayers by repeating a word or two here, a line there. Matilda's head was bowed the whole time and the little boy, Oliver, stood beside her, for once subdued. Agnes stood until her body became chilled before she saw Matilda throw flowers into the grave and beckon her son to do the same. Then the group began to move from the graveside and Agnes shrank away, moving towards the tower.

When the church grounds were clear of mourners and onlookers, Agnes picked her way over the uneven land to the open grave. Kneeling down, she muttered a short prayer:

"Dear Lord, have mercy on the soul of this wretched man who brought great turmoil to my life. Look not on his sins but, in Your clemency, receive his soul in heaven and watch over our son throughout his life on Earth."

Then she stood and flung a small posy of flowers upon the shrouded body before turning away. While watching the burial, Agnes' attention had been focused on the grave and she was barely aware of the damaged east end of the church. Already, it had become acceptable to see the church in its new form. Now something very odd caught her eye, for amongst the rubble a small area had been hastily rebuilt, using both stone and precious wood. It made a booth, with a small window and no obvious door. She took a step towards it.

"Agnes," a whisper came from within.

Frowning, Agnes moved closer and looked at the tiny, barred window. How foolish, there was no one there. Why would there be? But what was this hastily constructed closet? She had heard nothing of it. What was its purpose that it should take priority over rebuilding of boats and cottages?

"Agnes..." the whisper came again, "It is I, Gundred."

Chapter Eight
Agnes

"Gundred?" Agnes recoiled from the booth. "I can't see you."

The window was small, no taller than two lengths of her hand. There was not sufficient light entering the cell to shine upon the old soothsayer. Agnes tentatively took one step and then another towards the booth and gazed past the window bars until her eyes adjusted to the dark interior. Someone shifted slightly and, yes, Agnes could make out the aquiline nose and dark eyes under Gundred's hood.

"You see me now." Satisfaction could be heard in the old hag's voice. "You see me now, Agnes."

Again, Agnes backed away, assaulted by the rank breath and, although she couldn't see them, she visualised the black stumps of Gundred's teeth.

"I see you, Gundred."

"And I saw you, young Agnes. I saw you kneeling at his grave. You who have no business to be there."

"I was just... just saying a prayer for him."

"There need be no secrets between us," Gundred said, and although she couldn't see the smile, Agnes sensed it was there. "You wouldn't want his wife, the godly Matilda, to see you at his funeral. Full of suspicion that one. Shame... shame that she was once a dear sweet girl. Not like you."

"Not like me?" Agnes repeated, her chest tightening.

"You have no secrets from me. The words needn't be said."

Agnes was young and brave; she had never taken much notice of the old woman before. Some people did – hanging onto her every word, giving her a penny to pray for them, or tuppence for one of her remedies. But Agnes' life had been blessed: a loving family, food in her belly, good health and she was betrothed to a decent young man. What did Agnes need of the remedies or good wishes of Gundred? Here she was, blocked up in some form of cell. This woman could not hurt her. Who would take heed of whatever secrets she had to tell?

"What are you doing here?" Agnes ventured to ask.

"Well, there's a story, young 'un... You've got time for old Gundred now, have you?"

"I've got time," Agnes confirmed.

"Well, you go and get me a nice dish of stew and a jug of ale, then I'll tell you. I like you, Agnes, for all your sins, so I'll let you do that for me."

Agnes nodded her agreement. She was curious and it would do no harm to keep the old hag happy. So, she ran lightly over the uneven ground of St Nicholas' churchyard and back to the other church, her temporary home. The new fire pits were both burning steadily, and three-legged cauldrons crouched over the flames. Agnes grabbed a wooden bowl, then ladled salted fish with vegetables into it. From the church porch she filled a mug of ale. Then she scurried back to St Nicholas Church and Gundred in her cell.

The window bars were on a hinge and could be opened from the outside. Agnes slid the bowl onto the stone window-ledge for it to be snatched by the greedy old hag. The ale was then placed on the narrow ledge.

"Why are you here, Gundred?" Agnes asked.

81

"It's that Hugh Alcock..." but Gundred's eyes were lowered to the bowl of soup and she was busy spooning it into her mouth. "This is doing me some good, Agnes."

"Hugh? He can't have got you locked up like this?"

"I'm not locked up," Gundred announced with pride. "I'm bricked up and for good! I've made my home in this anchorhold."

"Bricked up?" Agnes repeated with horror. "Whatever for?"

"To pray for him!" Gundred took a slurp of ale.

"To pray for Hugh?" Agnes questioned. Why must the old woman make such a fuss of all this? Couldn't she just tell?

"Aye! It was Matilda that arranged it and very good of her too!"

Agnes didn't reply. Gundred was enjoying this too much. Relishing the attention. She turned a little, as if to walk away, as if she were bored. Not wanting to miss the chance to tell, Gundred raised her voice a little.

"I tell you, Agnes. It was Matilda who had all this done for me and I'm so grateful, I'll pray for her along with Hugh!"

"Matilda has done this so that you'll pray for Hugh?"

"And, very nice it is," cackled Gundred. "If only you knew, you'd be wanting to be here yourself!"

But Agnes, who loved her freedom, felt waves of horror ripple through her young body. She wanted to run... run as fast as she could and never pass by the east end of the church again. Curiosity forced her to stay and face what the old woman had to tell.

"I've a nice bed of straw and someone who comes daily to take away the spoiled bits," Gundred continued. "I've a window out to the churchyard, looking over the graves... especially his, of course. And a window to the inside, so once the church is repaired, I'll be able to see the priests. And not a job to do for the rest of my life,

82

other than pray for that scoundrel. Now doesn't that beat my broken-down cottage, and me having to do everything to fend for myself? Sometimes I barely had the food to fill my belly or the means to keep warm. No worries at all now. None at all."

Agnes paused for a moment. Could it be true? She'd heard of it... a whisper... a tale of it happening elsewhere. Would Gundred really give up her life in order to dedicate it to praying for Hugh? Would her prayers enable him to gain a swifter path through purgatory? Was the loss of freedom worth the security of this anchorhold, which was but a cell with its bed of straw?

"Well, I've some praying to do. Must not forget my duties," Gundred cackled. "I thank you, Agnes, for the soup. Very tasty. Not my first meal of the day and not my last. People are kind like that, thinking of old Gundred and her prayers. I've never been so well fed as I will be from this day."

Agnes nodded her goodbye, and with a feeling of unease, she hurried back to St Martin's. Her mother was expecting her to help, and she had been gone half the day. She'd not have this freedom once she was married.

Glancing down the High Street, she saw life in the town was gradually returning to normal. Most of the market traders had set up stalls and the shops were open. The streets were still covered in debris, but it had now been swept into piles. Agnes smiled as she noticed a group of small children jumping on the shingle hills, causing them to scatter once again. Would that be her own son in two or three years, she mused? Playing in the street while his mother, Cecily, looked on?

In the churchyard, the homeless seemed to have become settled into their new routines. Clean washing was spread over the ground and trailed across low trees. There was now a third fire pit, and three pans of soup or stew simmering in blackened pots. A group of women gathered at the porch whilst an elderly man hammered a notice to the wooden door.

"Here she is! Agnes, it's your banns!" someone called to her. "On the door. He's just putting them up."

Agnes came closer. It was to be expected of course. Pa had said she'd be married soon. So, it was to be at St Martin's. She should have known... should have shown some interest, but with the storm keeping everyone so busy the subject had been avoided. Not any longer.

"Aye, Pa said it would be soon." She stood and looked at the marks on the thick paper. "I'm lucky to have Will."

"He's a handsome man, no doubt about it." A young mother gave Agnes a knowing look.

"When's it to be?" asked another woman, a neighbour from the beach track.

"I... I don't know. Soon. That's what Pa told me." The marks on the paper told her nothing. She knew her numbers though.

"Sunday next." Mary joined her daughter and neighbours. "That's what your pa and Will arranged. We thought for it to be sooner, but Will has his home to prepare for us all, and that's good of him."

Sunday, and today it was... Agnes frowned for a moment... Friday, today it was Friday. On Sunday week, twelve days would have passed since the storm. Would her body have recovered? Would Will receive her as his wife and be none the wiser? Agnes was unsure, but relief soared through her body. The wedding was to be nine days from now. There was hope that she need not bring dishonour upon her family and humiliation to her husband.

"It's good news, Ma." Agnes said the words her mother needed to hear.

"Aye, it is." Mary looked at her daughter with concern. "I'll help with the chores, Agnes, but it will be your duty to look after Will. No running off to the beach when there's a home to care for."

"I know, Ma. He's a fine man and I'll do my best." She meant it. She *would* try.

On the fourth day after the storm, Agnes and her sister-in-law, Joan, sat on the shingle ridge. The sea was midway up the beach, with the tide slowly rising. The wind was light and September sun warm on their outstretched legs. It still seemed strange for no boats to be at sea, but on the old beach track the remains of several wrecks were being made into two new vessels. It was the start of restoring the fishing fleet, and the men being able to feed their families again. With nets strewn at their feet, the two young women manipulated tough string to repair the tears. As they worked, they chatted idly, Agnes' dark hair close to the beige hood and light-brown curls belonging to Joan. They were both barefoot, but Joan had her leather shoes beside her. Only that morning, Mary had scolded Agnes for going without shoes again. "You'll be married in a week and be casting shame on your husband if you go barefoot, him being a shoemaker and a proper tradesman too." *She is right, but for just this one week, I will do as I wish.*

"There goes George," Joan commented, interrupting Agnes' thoughts. "Him who found that dear baby."

"Oh, aye," Agnes feigned disinterest.

"Looks like he's got something to tell," Joan continued. "He's in a fair hurry."

They watched as George joined the boat builders, and work stopped while there was much gesturing towards the estuary. Then George moved on to tell the news to another group of men.

"They'll be talking about the river," Agnes said with interest. "Doesn't it make you wonder, Joan, where it could have gone?"

"It's gone and that's that," Joan stated.

"But where?" Agnes persisted. "Where did it go, and why hasn't it come back?"

"I'm more interested in my home and Robert getting out on the boat again," Joan said, tossing aside a piece of newly-mended net.

"There's no mystery in that," Agnes replied. "The boat will be ready as soon as the men can fix it and Robert's looking at a burgage plot north of the High Street. Pa is hoping to have one there soon. You'll have your own cottage again and a long strip of land for a pig and chickens. But the river, no one knows where that's gone. It's a mystery."

They worked for another hour. Agnes' thoughts were all on George and whatever news he had told the men. It was to do with the river – she felt sure of it. Hadn't they been pointing in the direction of the estuary? Finally, when their fingers could no longer work the nets, Agnes stood and declared, "I can't do another knot, we'd best get back to Ma and your little ones."

They dragged the nets off the shingle bank and went to tell Agnes' father and brothers that they were leaving.

"You've done a fine job, my sweetings," John said.

"We saw George," Agnes began. "What did he have to say? Did he come with news?"

"Aye, there's been a meeting and men are to go off looking for the river. Your William was there. Very interested, he was."

86

"I'll go along to see him." Agnes turned back towards the town. "We'll see you later, back at St Martin's."

Agnes pushed open the door leading into the shoemaker's. Will sat by the window, stitching leather; he looked up at her and smiled. "How are you? I hear you've been out on the beach repairing the nets."

"Aye, Joan and I have been sitting on the ridge for hours. The men are fixing the boats. Strange for them not to be at sea." Agnes perched on a rickety stool. "They said there's been a meeting with the important men – the bailiffs and jurats – in St Lawrence's Church, and they are talking about the river."

"I was there, at St Lawrence's." Will grinned at her, knowing her interest in the river. Romney had a wealth of churches, with St Nicholas and St Martin's being the largest. St Lawrence was a smaller place between the beach track and High Street.

"You were there!" Agnes replied, her eyes widening. "Tell me about it: Where's it gone? Will they get it back?"

"Come here and give me a kiss first," Will stood and took her hand, pulling her gently towards him.

She responded willingly, enjoying the sensation of his lips on hers. As Will's arms wrapped around her waist and pulled her closer still, his tongue darted into her mouth causing a ripple of desire to run through her body. They parted slightly, his arms now resting on her hips and hers around his neck.

"About the Rother..." He kissed her lightly.

"*Mmm*?" she wasn't so curious about it now.

"There's to be a group of us – some jurats and some others – whoever can be spared. We're going to..." Will leant in and they kissed again, lingering for a moment,

"...we're going to go and see where it's gone. It might take a week or so."

"We? You're going?" Agnes backed off a little. When would this be? Before the wedding? A knot of discontent twisted in her stomach. "When?"

"After the wedding." He looked a little guilty. "They would only wait until the day after."

"Oh."

"This is huge, Agnes." Will clutched at her hands. "The river has gone, and it fills my thoughts as I know it does yours. The river and the sea – you love them as I do. But where is it? We need it. The town needs it, and I have the chance to find it."

"I could come too?" Agnes clutched at the thought. "If we're married, then I could go with you."

"Nay, it's not right." He kissed her again, briefly, as if to pacify her. "Stay here, settle into our new home with Mary and John. I'll be back in no time, bearing news the whole town will want to hear."

But Agnes thought of the freedom, of following the riverbed to Hope and Old Romney and perhaps beyond. How far would they journey before the mystery was solved? Would they sleep under the stars or tents made of sails? Would they pass near the edge of the flatlands or even scale the distant hills and look down across the Marsh? The thought of the adventure engulfed her and with it the knowledge that she, even as a married woman, would be left behind with the cooking and the cleaning. She turned away from Will, releasing herself from his grip.

"I'll see you later, tomorrow mayhap."

Stomping back to her temporary home, Agnes knew she had been unfair. Will and the others were not setting off on an adventure – the future of the town was at risk. With no deep harbour at the river mouth, the merchant ships would no longer dock and trade with the townsfolk. She had overheard a lot of murmurings about that between the men who assembled together in the evenings. Their talk was far more absorbing than that of the women.

They should not be arguing for no good reason, Agnes knew that, so she turned and sheepishly opened the door of Will's shop. "I'm sorry, of course you must go, and tell us all about it on your return."

"I'm being selfish," Will replied. "The most beautiful wife in the town, yet I leave her to chase a river. The others think I'm a fool!"

"No," she grinned. "If I could search for the river, I would. And leave my handsome new husband behind!"

This had been the fourth day after the storm. On the sixth day, two of the men who worked at the boat repair yard left New Romney, taking their families with them. They were bound for Hythe. There was work aplenty for these men, but who was to pay them when the fishermen had no income?

On the seventh day, Agnes' brother, John, left the town. He was done with the sea and decided to walk inland, working as he went, but intent on reaching an inland town. In St Martin's, the remaining families claimed more space for themselves.

Chapter Nine
Agnes

The wedding day came, twelve days after the storm. Time was now marked by that great event. Agnes woke early in the morning. Beside her, Mary snored gently and her father, John, tossed and turned on the hard floor. She could hear Robert's wife singing gently to one of the children, trying to soothe her. Further away, a newborn mewled for its milk and Agnes sighed relief that hers no longer flowed. The air in St Martin's was no longer sweet from fresh straw – it was rank from stale sweat, damp clothes and rotten breath. It would be good to get the family out of here, Agnes reflected. Better if they could breathe the salt air, but Will had a good house. At least it still stood.

Gradually, the families began to stir and soon the church was alive with chatter. Agnes pulled her tunic over her shift. She had no other outfit – her everyday clothes were also her wedding costume. The only difference from this day onwards would be that, as a married woman, she would wear a hood or veil to cover her hair. She had washed and darned her stockings the day before, not wanting to marry with holes in her heels, and now she pulled them on before slipping her feet into boots. The boots were new, well-stitched and sturdy. A gift from Will.

Agnes had washed her hair in a tub of warm, scented water the evening before. She took a comb from a small drawstring bag and sat cross-legged on the floor, rhythmically pulling it through. It was soothing, the dragging of the wide-toothed, wooden comb through her thick mane. Agnes thought of Will and the kisses they had shared within the last week and found herself looking forward to the wedding and festivities that would follow.

The families in the church snatched at a breakfast of bread and fat on a Sunday morning. For six days a week, the church was solely a home for the victims of the storm, on the seventh it was needed for services. St Nicholas was still in a state of disrepair – the task to clear it of debris was colossal – and those who wanted to worship on any other day had to use either St Lawrence's in the trading area of the town or walk along the path of the departed river to the small church at Hope.

Now temporary beds had to be pushed aside, and belongings were carefully stowed in orderly piles. Nothing was to be left near the altar screen. If the sides and back of the church must be used as storage areas, then at least when the congregation faced east, all would be as it should.

As Agnes worked with the rest of them, her glossy hair became tangled, and pieces of straw clung to her tunic. It was only when the local community began to gather for the morning mass, Agnes once more prepared herself for the wedding. She brushed the worst of the debris from her clothes and straightened her stockings. Then Mary handed her the comb, and it was pulled it through her hair again. As the vicar arrived, her sister-in-law passed her a gold cross, studded with tiny red jewels. "I wore it at my own wedding," Joan said, as she placed it around Agnes' neck and tied the ribbon.

John came and took his daughter's hand. "Time to wait outside for Will."

"Thanks, Pa." Agnes looked up into the weather-beaten face of the man who had her own dark hair and eyes. "Thank you for... for being a good father."

John looked down at her and smiled. He was a man of few words and would leave what needed to be said to her mother.

The September sun shone down on the family group, who waited at the entrance to the porch. They smiled and exchanged greetings with friends and neighbours, traders and the important folk from the town. Mary darted back inside and returned after a moment clutching a scented pomander with a ribbon which she slipped over Agnes' wrist. "I had it filled yesterday," she told her daughter.

Agnes raised it to her nose, breathing in lavender and rosemary. The children, her niece and nephew, ran over and she showed it to them. Then she looked up to see Will, turning the corner from the High Street. The men – her father and Robert – went to meet him. He was with his parents, cousin and brother. They were laughing and joking. As they neared the church porch, Will's eyes met hers and he smiled at her, his eyes crinkling at the side.

At that moment the widow, Matilda, and her young son turned the corner of the church. The wedding party fell silent and stepped aside, allowing her to pass between them. She walked with her head lowered, not wanting to make eye contact until she was just about to step into the porch, when she looked towards Agnes with dull eyes and spoke, "I wish you well in your marriage. May no woman put it asunder."

Agnes tried to whisper a response, but no words came. Seconds passed and it seemed time froze, with just the indistinct murmur of voices in the background. Still Agnes said nothing. What could she say? Matilda turned away abruptly and walked into the church, passing the vicar as he came to greet the wedding group. *May no woman put asunder* – the words slammed about in Agnes's mind. She tried to push them aside, but a glance at Will made her wonder if he had heard what had been said. She offered a bright smile and stepped towards him, readying herself for the exchange of vows.

It was an awkward gathering – standing there in the church porch with the occasional churchgoer still wanting to enter the holy building, while others waited outside. Side by side, Will and Agnes faced the church door, with their family gathered around them. The vicar began, "Does anyone present know of any just reason why this couple cannot be wed?"

There was no reason, but at that moment the unmistakable cry of a newborn could be heard within the church. Was it her son, Nicholas? Agnes didn't know, but she was reminded, as she would be every day, of her ungodly ways. Shame weighed upon her. Silently she vowed to be good wife.

"Wilt thou have this woman to thy wife, and love her and keep her in sickness and in health, and in all other degrees be to her as a husband should be to his wife, and all others forsake for her, and hold only to her to thy life's end?"

Will looked into Agnes's eyes and replied without faltering, "I will."

"Wilt thou have this man to be thy husband?" These words were directed at her now, at Agnes, and she must... she must listen and respond in the right way. "...and to be buxom to him, serve him and keep him in sickness and in health?"

"Aye... I will."

Will took Agnes' left hand and carefully pushed a patterned ring onto her third finger. It felt odd to have the band there and for a moment Agnes panicked –

from this time her life was to be restricted and devoted to her husband. She looked up and, as Will leant down to kiss her lightly, she felt herself respond. Again, Agnes vowed to be the wife he deserved.

The children threw rice on the newly-married couple as Mary placed a veil on her daughter's dark hair. "I wish it didn't have to be covered," she murmured to her only daughter. Agnes fidgeted as a band was tied to secure the cloth in place. Then, with Will's hand on her shoulder, they entered the church with the rest of the family following. There was some whispering and movement as space was made and they stood, heads bowed in prayer.

Afterwards, friends, family and neighbours joined together to celebrate the wedding in an informal party. No invitations had been given but those living in the church had become one large family and welcomed Will's neighbours from the High Street along with his family. The three pans standing over the three fire pits accepted gifts of meat, fish, beans and vegetables until they were full to the brim. Benches were dragged from nearby homes, and music came sporadically from whistles, flutes and fiddles, while children bashed upon drums and symbols.

"Shall we dance?" Will reached for Agnes' hand and, setting aside her wine, she smiled eagerly, cheeks dimpling.

"Aye, I'd like to." Agnes loved dancing and had watched the couples' dance with interest over the years.

Stepping lightly over the tussocks of grass and enjoying the sensation of her hand firmly in his, Agnes followed her husband as the crowds parted to make room for them to dance. The light tune of the flute led them through those first steps of coming together and parting briefly, hands clasped, separating, then joining again.

As the fiddle and whistle joined in the melody, so did more young couples. Agnes and Will found themselves as part of a circle, gently bobbing in time to the music, changing places, circling, stepping close and then away, yet still returning to each other, sometimes clapping, sometimes tapping their feet to the rhythm.

Agnes felt the tension of the last twelve days flow from her body as it swayed in time to the music. It was lovely to be sharing this moment with Will, who sometimes held her close and looked at her as if he were thinking of their being alone together. At times they sank to the ground, tired but happy, and after a few minutes Agnes would pull him to his feet for the next dance.

The people of Romney partied on the greens surrounding the church all through the afternoon, thankful for the chance to forget about their worries about the future. Those who chose not to dance still hummed along, tapping fingers or toes.

"Look at how everyone has worked together," Will commented, nodding across to the three fire pits where townsfolk queued with wooden bowls.

"Aye, we'll all go to bed with full bellies," Agnes smiled.

"It's done the town good, this wedding and the baby... given people hope for the future."

Agnes looked across towards Cecily who sat holding baby Nicholas close, rocking him gently. She knew she had made the right choice. Agnes had given a gift to the town and to Cecily, who glowed with happiness whereas before she had looked pale and drawn.

Will saw her gazing at the baby. "Strange how that happened," he reflected. "I wonder if the monk went off to tell the tale about it?"

"Why would he?"

"That's what he was doing. Writing what he saw – travelling along and writing about it. It was he who said the baby was a gift from God, that no one had put him there. He must have written about it."

"And maybe told people... important people." Agnes hadn't thought of the monk, not once since he had gone, not until now. "I hope he didn't."

"Why not?" Will asked.

"It's just that Cecily is happy, and the baby is fine. We don't want people coming and fussing all over him."

"Well, that's up to the doctor and Cecily, and the vicar too. They won't let Nicholas be pestered." Will thought about it for a moment, "No one's going to want to come all this way. They won't come disturbing us all. There's nothing to see, just a load of broken up boats and wrecked cottages. We won't get important folk coming here."

At that moment, Cecily saw them looking across and stood, carefully supporting her son in her arms. She smiled shyly at them both and picked her way through the townspeople who sat or lay on the grass, relaxing after the food and dancing.

"Have you held a baby?" She offered Agnes the sleeping Nicholas. "It's the tradition... and will ensure fertility... so you must."

Agnes stepped back, not sure if she could... if she could bear to hold her son and then return him to his mother. "Nay, Cecily, it's just a silly tale... leave him be while he sleeps."

"Oh, you must," smiled Cecily. "You're young now and mayhap it doesn't worry you yet, but I didn't hold a child, and look how long I waited."

"Go on, Agnes. It won't harm the baby," Will gave her a nudge.

Then her mother, Mary, and Joan, her sister-in-law, were there and Mary was exclaiming, "Oh sweeting, we forgot... we forgot about the baby. You must hold him – it's still your wedding day and not too late."

"Oh, Ma!" Agnes laughed. "I don't need to bother with all that. They threw the rice, so leave him be." But Cecily was intent on handing Nicholas to the mother he didn't know and, as she did so, he opened his dark eyes and it seemed he focused on Agnes' face. She looked down on him. *How tiny he is. Has he changed at all in these past twelve days? Aye, his skin is clearer and he had a little more fat on him. Yet he is still so small. So delicate. If I bend forwards a little, will he still smell as he did? Will they notice?* Agnes lifted the baby towards her face and, as she leaned forward to kiss Nicholas on the forehead, she inhaled slowly and deeply, savouring the moment. *It seems as if it is just us.*

Then from somewhere Mary was speaking. Agnes had to pull her thoughts away from the moment in the pig's shelter when she had held her son to her breast and the moonlight had shone on him, showing his features for the first time. Somehow, she found her voice and responded to her mother: "What was that Ma?"

"He's a lovely boy, isn't he?" Mary was saying. "Agnes looks smitten. She'll be wanting one of her own in no time!"

And there was Will, smiling down at his new wife and looking so pleased with his choice, while Agnes forced herself to smile back. Her arms, now stiff and leaden, reached out towards Cecily and the precious child was transferred back to his adoptive mother.

"He likes you," she said to Agnes. "Now, I'm sure that you'll be blessed with one of your own." As a new

97

mother, Cecily could not help but think that all young women needed their own child in their arms. "The sun will set soon, so I'd best get him home before the air becomes damp."

Cecily turned away and, as they watched her go, someone else caught Agnes' eye... someone who she thought had not stayed for the wedding celebrations. Matilda stood, looking towards Agnes, and Agnes knew she had watched the whole scene – the giving of the baby in order to ensure Agnes' own fertility. She was set apart from the other folk, not only did she stand aloof, but her good cloak and fine woollen tunic showed her as a person of some riches within the town. The sun, which was on its westward path and low in the sky, shone on her chestnut waves, only partially covered by her hood. Her grey eyes were fixed on Agnes and as their eyes met, she made the sign of the cross on her chest before turning away. Agnes shivered.

It's been a long day, let's get you prepared for bed," Mary said. "Joan will come along, and a few of the wenches from the beach track. We'll make you look comely for William."

"She's comely enough," Joan smiled. "There's not another to match her in the town."

"You can come along in a while," Mary spoke to Will. "Get yourself an ale and we'll see you shortly."

"I'll not keep you waiting," Will grinned.

By the time Agnes pressed on the latch and opened the gate leading into Will's garden, they had been joined by half a dozen young women who had lived and worked alongside her at the beach. They laughed and joked as they walked the length of the narrow garden and held back as Agnes opened the back door to her new home.

"In you go, Agnes sweeting." Mary gave her a little push into the living area, and they all stepped in after her.

Agnes led the way upstairs, although it was the first time she had been up the ladder and into the space above. As she emerged into the room under the eaves, she saw that a wooden bed frame dominated it. Tomorrow there would be a screen set up, and her parents would join herself and Will until their home was replaced.

Beyond the bed was a shuttered dormer window tempting Agnes. From it she saw the church tower and western end of the nave, clear over the rooftops of the High Street buildings and although she couldn't see the beach, the sea was there softly sparkling in the glow of the evening sun. Perhaps when the fishing boats were repaired, she could sit at this window and watch them come in, not that she could just sit around, but surely if she had some sewing or darning...?

"Come away from the window, love."

"Aye, your husband will be here soon."

"He'll not be waiting for a comely maid like you."

The fire had long gone out in the kitchen below, but Joan carried a jug of warm water which came from one of the three fires at St Martin's. She poured it into a basin and Mary added a little scent.

"Off with your tunic, wench."

"Don't be shy."

"He's a handsome lad, your new husband,"

"Aye, and a good one too."

Agnes removed her tunic and veil then stood, like a small child, as the woman washed her with soft cloths. Then she lifted her arms obediently to have her shift replaced with a new one.

"A bit of scent."

"Aye and a few ribbons."

"Now where's the comb?"

Finally, Agnes had her hair combed through, and as this last task was completed, she could hear the men arrive through the back door.

"In you go, William."

"She's lovely, give her a kiss."

He entered the room, followed by half a dozen friends. Her own friends and family moved aside to allow Will to reach his wife. Bending down he gave her a brief kiss. The well-wishers turned and one by one they climbed down the ladder. There would be another hour of merry-making before dark.

Chapter Ten
Will

Will woke at dawn and turned to caress the curved rump of his wife. She had been eager and softly yielding the night before. He smiled at the memories. Agnes might be only fourteen, but she was no virgin, he could tell that. She was too knowing, too warm and lacking in timidity. There was something very seductive about her, and the discovery was no great surprise or disappointment. He'd seen men watching her mature over the last year and been proud that one day she would be his. No matter who she had lain with before, he had claimed her now.

Longing for Agnes to wake and rouse his passions again, Will knew he must leave at daybreak, so as she stirred, he moved away, not wanting to disturb her. Silently, he swung his legs out of the bed and lowered his feet onto the wide wooden floorboards. Then he fumbled with his clothing, pulling on his shift, then a tunic of natural coloured wool which fell to just below his knees.

As he knotted his belt, Agnes turned in the bed and spoke softly. "You're off then."

"Aye, I'll just cut some bread and slip away." Will sat on the edge of the bed and stroked his wife's hair. "I'd rather stay. At least for a while."

"You'll be back in no time." Agnes tried to sound as if she accepted his leaving her. "The whole town will be gathered to hear of your travels. I'll have to fight my way through them."

"Nay," Will smiled, although she couldn't see his features. "The others can tell. I'll be at home with my wife." He leant down and kissed her gently. "A week... ten days, and I'll be back, but I'd best go now."

"God's speed, safe journey," Agnes called out as he climbed down the steps to the kitchen below.

A few minutes later, with his thick, hooded cape wrapped around him, a bag slung over his shoulder and a slice of dense brown bread in his hand, Will closed the shop door behind him and saw the others gathering at the crossroads.

There were three of them journeying with Will. Mark Butcher and Richard Stoneman were town jurats – influential tradesmen who had been elected to keep the rules of the town. Then there was Michael Vintner, a wine merchant, who lived and worked in the area of St Lawrence. Several of the fishermen would have loved to come, Will reflected, but they couldn't spare the time, not with homes and boats to rebuild.

They nodded their greetings to Will. "He's left his wife then," Mark Butcher said. "I did wonder if he'd have the nerve to."

Will expected the banter and took no heed. "Come on, we've a fair walk ahead of us."

With their backs to the sea, the travellers set off past the priory and St Martin's, then left Romney behind them. They spoke little, concentrating on the uneven tracks, always expecting to lurch or slip. Their spirits were high though, lifted by the adventure, and the men set a brisk pace. On reaching the small settlement named Hope, the sun had risen clear of the horizon and lent a warmth to the simple stone church sitting on a mound. Scattered cottages straddled the roadside, and from one a young man appeared.

"It's John Hope," Michael said. "He plans to join us." Then to John, "Coming to find the Rother, are you?"

"Aye," John replied. "I'm curious to know why she doesn't pass by anymore."

Now the five of them trudged on, the autumn sun on their backs, and talking a little now and then. The flat fields of Romney Marsh stretched to their right, with the golden stubble of harvested corn and wheat breaking through fertile soil, and ragged green tops of root crops and cabbages in disorderly lines. Grass was closely cropped by clusters of sheep and sturdy lambs. The five men passed labourers clearing the reed-lined ditches of debris, and others pulling weeds from between rows of root crops. It made a pleasant rural scene before the harsh winter set in, and life became a struggle. On the other side, the abandoned riverbed teamed with birdlife.

"Do the people of Hope miss the river?" Mark wondered aloud.

"Aye, the women especially," John replied. "It was fresher than that in the dykes." He inclined his head in the direction of the drainage ditch. "It was the best place for them to do their washing and served us well with fresh water for the animals. We can manage though, not like them in the town who rely on the merchants' ships moored in the estuary."

"I'm done with Romney," Michael agreed. "With no wine to import from France, what use is a wine merchant?"

"There's many a family that make their own wine," Will commented.

"Aye, but the town's master traders, the clergy and such folk, they like something a bit different from our own ale and wine," Michael said. "I'm curious to know where our river's gone and if there's opportunities for me there. If not, I'll be going east, past Hythe until I find a haven that will take a merchant ship, and I'll set up there. I'll be off before the year's out."

The others shook their heads. There was no need to voice their surprise, for there was none. As they walked in single file along the track close to where the Rother had been, there were still vast, shallow pools of water, a sluggish trail and great patches of sodden river mud. Along the main path of the river and the wide expanse of reed-filled marshland, there was Old Romney Church and the cottages.

"Of course, those folk at Old Romney had ships docking there once," Michael commented. "'Til it all silted up."

"Aye," replied Mark, who at forty was the oldest in the group. "It was one settlement all the way from the river mouth at the new part of Romney to the old part inland. Longport, they called it. My grandfather's father remembered those days."

"They lost their port too," Michael reflected, and the others nodded knowingly.

On they went, occasionally passing comment about the demise of the river, but mostly concentrating on their step. With no fishermen present, it was Michael who would feel the loss of the port most keenly. But Will knew they would all suffer from the loss by varying degrees. If the fishermen deserted the town, then the boat builders and their families would follow, and with them a hundred pairs of feet that would give their money to another shoemaker in another town. If the cloth and wine and exotic food traders could no longer reach the port, so the town's merchants would leave and take their custom elsewhere. Will would suffer with the rest of them, he could see that.

Across the sulky water and oozing mudflats, the settlements of Midley and Lydd stood, just about visible in the clear morning light. They were further west than Old Romney and stood on shingle banks, once islands amongst the sea marshes.

"I've never been to either of those places," Richard commented. "Never been to Walland Marsh, yet I see those places over there and it feels like I know them."

"It's a watery place, Walland Marsh is," mused John. "Not like Romney Marsh proper. Nay, it's full of reed-beds and suchlike and the sea... well it breaks through them mud walls whenever it takes a fancy to."

"You been there, have you?" Will asked.

"Not me. Not exactly, but my cousin, he took a boat over several times and told us about it."

Not far past Old Romney they reached the banks of the Rhee Canal, and there came an unspoken agreement that it was time to sit down for a mid-morning snack. The five of them perched side by side all facing the man-made channel. This ribbon of water was straight, cutting through the fields with no heed to the natural winding watercourses of The Marsh. The Rhee was on a quest – to take water from inland and spit it out at the river estuary. It was built to help the Rother, to give some extra force in order to flush away the silt that had been threatening to overwhelm the estuary for some time.

"The water still flows," Mark stood on the bank and looked down.

"Aye, but it's only a part of what's needed." John was pulling bread and cheese from his sack. "It's not enough to shift the silt without the river and the pair of them aren't strong enough to move that shingle bank blocking our estuary."

"I don't see what's to be done about it." Michael was gloomy. "We are in God's hands and even He can't shift all that shingle."

They ate in silence after that. Will wondered what his wife was doing. Was she marvelling at her new home, with its fireplace and upper floor? Or was she, as he suspected, on the beach watching the fishermen repair their boats? Perhaps helping with some tasks such as stitching a sail or knotting a net?

When the adventurers stood and, with their backs to Romney, set off again, their path was different, no longer meandering to and fro alongside the dykes. Now they walked a straight track as they followed the Rhee, marvelling at this structure excavated by their ancestors.

"It was the king who ordered the extra bit of channel from Old Romney to New," Mark informed. He seemed to be the most knowledgeable when it came to the history of their area of the marsh.

"Well, it is a Cinque Port, so he'd have an interest in it," Will commented.

"I wonder what he'll have to say about this," Michael spoke with bitterness, "Mayhap he'll come along and clear the shingle bank himself, for a bit of a canal won't make any difference."

The Rhee took them all the way to Snargate, where John assured them that he had some sort of cousin living there and they would be made welcome.

"I've never seen him, but my brother has and says he's a good man. There'll be a barn and it'll be no trouble for them to fill our bellies." He scanned the area and led the weary group away from the banks of the Rhee. "Over there, behind the church. I'm sure that's the place."

Sure enough, there was soon back-slapping and hand-shaking all round. Will was introduced as being 'newly-wed to a comely wench', followed by much head shaking at his choice to desert his young wife. They crowded into the farmhouse and sat, elbows tight against their bodies, on benches around a table. There wasn't much pottage to share around but cold mutton, cheese and bread was produced and so they enjoyed a fine feast.

As the sun set, there was more talk about the great storm and the loss of the river. In Snargate, the Rhee was of some importance as this was where one of the gates controlled the flow of the water destined for Romney. In fact, one of John's distant relatives was being courted by a young man who tended the gate. Would there still be a need for the Rhee, they wondered, and a job for the gatekeeper?

There was a barn, small but weathertight and each man carried a roll of blankets on his back. So, with some straw on the ground and a blanket wrapped tight around their bodies, the five of them settled down for the night. But not to sleep, not yet. With a newlywed friend amongst them, the urge to tease and question Will was greater than the need for sleep…

"You'll be missing young Agnes?" Mark began.

"Aye." Will grinned into the darkness.

"And she'll be missing you?" Mark continued.

"I hope so," Will replied.

"And she'll be thanking you for Rohesia," John sniggered. "I know my wife did!"

"I've not talked of her," Will turned onto his side as if to dismiss the conversation.

"Did you, John? Did you tell your wife about Rohesia?" Richard asked.

"He must have done," Mark stated. "Or how else could she offer her thanks?"

"Not in so many words," John admitted.

"I didn't lie with Rohesia," Mark said. The others turned towards him. "She was just a girl then. It was her aunt who taught us all the ways of women."

107

"So, it was a family trade," Michael guffawed.

"Aye, and she were a buxom wench," Mark told them. "Very willing for a coin in her purse. She served the whole of Romney. Got herself set up in a stone cottage on the lane to Hope."

Will hardened at the thought of his evenings in the hands of Rohesia. His cousin had taken him along a few years back when he turned seventeen. "That's what you do," his cousin had said, "so as not to disappoint your wife." Will had no thoughts of taking a wife at the time, but he had plenty of thoughts about the young women he saw around the town and beachfront. Most of them married by the time they were fifteen or sixteen, and he envied many of their husbands who could lie by their slender young bodies and touch their silky skin.

For Will and his friends, it was the toughened skin, rippled thighs and sagging breasts of Rohesia. But what she lacked in youth, she made up for in her exuberance and lovemaking skills. She was coarse in manner and had no shame in her trade, claiming to be as important as a doctor or priest, vital to the well-being of young men. She must have been thirty-five or more, Will reflected, but she passed on her experience with relish and now he could pass his on to his own soft-skinned bride.

"And, she was a virgin, young Agnes?" Mark pushed his questioning beyond the limits.

Will felt himself redden and his stomach tighten.

"Of course, she was," snapped his friend, John. "She comes from a decent family does Agnes. There was no need for that, Mark."

"Pretty wench," sighed Richard. "You've a lovely wife there, Will."

"Aye," replied Will, pulling his blanket tighter around him. "Now let's all get some sleep before I leave the four of you and set back on the track to Romney."

Will woke several times in the night. He was used to a straw-filled mattress, and the layer of straw on the earth floor soon flattened to give no comfort. *Should I have come on this journey? I wanted to for my own interest, but I thought it would impress her and that was part of the reason for me being here. Should I have left her? Is there someone else she could turn to in my absence? Nay, whatever she has done, whoever she has lain with in the past, it is over now. Agnes willingly gave herself to me on our wedding night, and before that there were our kisses…* He turned onto his side and drifted off to sleep for another hour.

The five explorers were all awake at daybreak and quickly moved the cloaks used as extra blankets, wrapping them snug around them. Their bodies ached and they rubbed at hips and shoulders which had borne the worst of the earth floor. The air was sharp with cold. Rough planked barn walls offered little protection from winds which tore across the flat land that morning.

"At least it's bright." John stood at the open doorway.

"Aye, I'd rather suffer the wind than the rain," Mark spoke while securing his blanket in a tight roll. "Now I'm going around the back before my bladder gives out."

They left Snargate with the promise of a warm meal and use of the barn overnight on their return. "You'll be welcome here," claimed the distant cousin of John Hope.

Their sacks were filled with apples and pears from the orchards, as well as bread, cheese and a chunk of ham. If they couldn't find a welcoming kitchen that night, then they wouldn't starve.

The route continued to take the five friends alongside the Rhee Canal and across the bleakest, lowest area of the Marsh, known as the Appledore

Dowels. There was nothing much to see, except for sheep, the occasional cottage or shack, and the winding, reed-lined dykes. Cutting through it all was the man-made Rhee, with its banks that raised the five of them several feet above the land. They were nearing the old coastline, the ridge of hills which, in ancient times, had known the sea rolling in and breaking upon the beaches below them. Today these were softened by the early morning mists gently rolling above the Marsh. The men walked in silence for some time. Used to the busy sounds of town life, it was eerie to have only the bleating of sheep and the occasional call of a curlew punctuating the air.

By mid-morning, civilisation had been reached in the form of Appledore, a small town sitting on a gentle rise at the very edge of Romney Marsh and on the former banks of the Rother.

"It's gone and left them high and dry too." Michael gave a nod towards abandoned fisheries and small boats slumped on the thick slime of the riverbed.

Beached boats, tangled piles of rope and netting, platforms and posts listing in the mud – the area already had an air of neglect. There was just one old man, standing ankle deep in the riverbed, bending over the bow of his boat. He turned slowly, his back still bent and matted grey hair hanging around his lined face.

"Where's the river gone?" called John.

"Gone?" replied the man. "What's it to you?"

"We've come from Romney in search of it," Will answered.

"Well, it's not here, is it?" the old man retorted. "Them's all talking about it in the market though." He turned back to his boat.

"We'll learn nothing from him," John said. The others nodded their agreement.

For the first time in their lives, the five men walked up the slope and off the Romney Marsh. They were now in a wide street with market stalls on either side. Beyond these were houses, inns and shops of various sizes. To their right was the parish church, set back from the main street. A group of men sat around a roughly hewn table, supping ale outside an inn. They looked over and nodded at the five strangers.

"You're new here, aren't you?" one of the men said. His tunic and breeches were plain but of a decent cloth, his hair was neatly cut.

"Aye, we've travelled from Romney, down by the coast," Mark informed. "We've come in search of the Rother."

"Oh, have you!" the man replied. "We wondered about you, wondered if the river still came your way. It's gone from here as you see."

"Where did it go?" Will asked. "Do you have word of it?"

"We know something of it and it's not good news for Appledore." The stranger paused and took a sip of his ale. "The river has gone the other side of the Isle of Oxney. Over that way," he inclined his head to the west to indicate where Oxney was. "Folk from the village set off three days ago to find it. Not that they'll bring it back – our port and fisheries are lost."

"We're on the same quest," Richard said. "Do we await their return or follow them?"

"I say follow them," replied Mark with gusto. "We'll have an ale and be on our way..."

The others nodded in agreement, eager to learn more. It was only the stranger from Appledore who seemed despondent: "You'll need to get to the Isle of Oxney and that means wading through the riverbed. It's not easy, I'm telling you."

Chapter Eleven
Agnes

Agnes stood back and surveyed the bedroom. The blankets and rugs had been hauled outside and dust beaten from them. Floorboards were swept and the rafters freed of cobwebs. The mattress had been stuffed with clean straw and linen sheets washed. Downstairs, a pan of pottage was simmering over the fire and fresh bread was on the table. She had done it all on her own, with no help from Mary who was busy down at the harbour, as well as helping Joan with the children. Agnes was determined to be the wife Will deserved, and not to sulk over his journey to find the Rother or to fret for her baby son.

It was now twenty days after the storm and she had been a married woman for eight of those, although Agnes had only spent one night with her husband. October had arrived and with it the relentless mists slinking in from the sea. The air was still, and low clouds hung about the town, sluggish and thick with salt. The townsfolk huddled within damp shawls and kept themselves to themselves, their wits dulled by the swathes of heavy, chilled air.

Agnes felt stifled by the mist. She could barely see the shape of St Nicholas Church tower from her bedroom window and the sea had shown no spirit at all these last few days. She thought of Gundred, trapped in her anchorhold, and wondered if anyone had remembered to feed the ageing hag. Now the thoughts had crept up on her Agnes felt compelled to visit the old woman, although her chest tightened a little with the fear of what she might hear from the soothsayer.

A sheet of woven hemp now hung across the room and Agnes pushed it aside in order to reach the steps down to the kitchen. Her parents had moved into Will's home on the day he left, and her father had put up the curtain a couple of days ago. Agnes glanced at the straw-filled mattress on the floor and felt, not for the first time, a little uneasy that she now slept in a wooden framed bed.

Pulling her cloak from a hook on the wall, Agnes wrapped it around her slender body. Then she stooped over the fire and ladled pottage into a wooden bowl. Next, she walked through the shoemaker's dusty shop and onto the High Street. It was mid-afternoon but the sounds of the market and townsfolk were muted by the lingering mist. Agnes felt alone. She walked along the road which approached the church and then alongside the churchyard wall before turning towards the ruined east end.

To her surprise, Agnes saw that Gundred had plenty to entertain her – the stonemasons had started work on repairing the stricken wall.

"Here you are, young Agnes. I knew I'd be seeing you soon enough." Gundred peeped out of her small barred window.

"I brought you some pottage," Agnes lifted the bowl towards the window.

"Very nice I'm sure, for someone who is in need of a bit of food," Gundred replied with disinterest.

"Have you had plenty to eat?" Agnes asked. Gundred was so difficult to please since being shut up. It was a wonder that anyone bothered with the old woman.

"Aye, the stonemasons tell their wives and there's always a little something for me – a bit of pie or bread and cheese, sometimes a piece of spiced cake. They see that I'm well fed so I can concentrate on my praying."

"You don't need…?"

"I'm not saying that Agnes. Pottage, you say? Warm, is it? Of course it is. Pass it through then." Gundred's gnarled fingers clawed at the bars.

The pottage was devoured in minutes and, while she ate, Gundred kept her beady eyes on Agnes who watched the stonemasons at work and tried to avoid looking at the fresh mound of earth covering the body of Hugh Alcock. *How is his spirit faring*, Agnes wondered? *Does it dwell in purgatory with the other sinners, or was Gundred's praying going to release Hugh earlier than he deserved?*

"You'll be thinking of that no-good scoundrel," Gundred's sharp voice broke through Agnes' thoughts and caused her to start. "He'll take his time reaching our dear Lord."

"But you pray for him," Agnes stated, "to speed his journey?"

"Well, I've hardly got the time," Gundred cackled. "I get so many folk passing by, wanting to see me, wanting to hear the wisdom of old Gundred. It's a fine life, I tell you."

"A fine life?" Not for Agnes, she knew that. How could Gundred bear to be trapped like this, with hardly the room to lie down at night? Was it worth it for a bit of food? "But you are here to pray. That's why we feed you."

"Aye, I am," Gundred replied. Then she looked beyond Agnes and her eyes narrowed. "Be off with you, I see your secrets, and we need no words. You bother my prayers." She started moving her lips as if in prayer.

Agnes turned and saw Matilda, widow of Hugh, and her young son entering the churchyard. While the mist still shrouded both women, and before either of them was forced to greet the other, Agnes stepped away from Gundred with no further words. She lowered her head and walked away towards the outer wall of the churchyard where the boats had been moored. Kicking at the shingle, she wondered at Gundred's words.

How can she know about the baby? Did she see the signs I was with child when no one else noticed? Nay – she is no more than a wicked old woman who wants to trick me into telling her something and I must keep away from her. No good will come from me seeing her. I have no need for any prayers or advice the old hag may throw my way. And as for food – she is better nourished than the rest of the town!

"Agnes, Agnes... there you are." Mary's calls penetrated her daughter's thoughts of the storm and her newborn son. Mary was on top of the shingle bank, waving frantically and Agnes' spirits rose a little – something had happened! There was news to tell! "Agnes, come along... where have you been? Never mind, the men are back. Will is back!"

Agnes scrambled up the bank and onto the old track. "Where... where are they?"

"St Martin's." Mary took her daughter's hand. "Come along. He'll be fretting to see you."

Through the mists, figures scurried. The whole town was gathering to hear the news.

She saw him as soon as they rounded the corner from the High Street to the churchyard. His hair looked ragged, his breeches and tunic were stiff with dried mud, and his eyes were weary, but Will's smile was broad as he picked up his wife and spun her around.

"We're back!" He placed her down again but kept his hands on Agnes' waist. "I missed you, but it's been an adventure." With that he lowered his lips to hers and they clung together for a moment.

"Tell me then," Agnes smiled up at him.

"Michael's going to tell, with help from the rest of us, of course. Not John. He stopped off at Hope to tell folk there."

With their fingers entwined, the newly-wed couple walked into the ancient building where the church dwellers' belongings had been hurriedly pushed aside. In this attempt to tidy up, the smell of stale body odour was in no way concealed by pots of dried, scented petals. St Martin's was still a makeshift home to many families, and it was only on a Sunday it was thoroughly cleared for the church services. However, candles had been lit to recognise the importance of this day. They cast a mellow light over the pale stone walls and gave a welcoming sense of warmth to those who had come in from the swirling mists.

As Mary, Will and Agnes stood for a moment amongst the teeming crowds of friends and neighbours, Agnes found herself being pushed aside to make way for someone who entered in haste and was determined to press onwards to the front of the church. Yet on seeing her husband, the man paused for a moment.

"Ah, William... I'm keen to hear your news... Good man." Lord Craythorne gave Will a friendly pat on the shoulder before continuing to thrust his way onwards.

"Nice that he shows an interest," Mary commented.

"He wants the town to prosper. The river is as important to him as it is to the rest of us," Will replied. "He doesn't want to be Lord of nothing. That won't keep his wife in her finery!"

Will understood life. Agnes reflected on this and it gave her a sense of pride. He talked to the traders and the important men of the town and he understood how things worked... what was important. She gave his hand a squeeze, and he smiled down at her before letting go.

"I'll go and join the others," Will told Agnes. "Not for long, then we'll have time to do our own catching up."

Michael Vintner was standing at the front, just before the rood screen separating the chancel from the nave. The priests were there too, all three of them – from St Nicholas and St Lawrence, as well as St Martin's. Where were the others? Agnes scanned the crowd: there was Richard Stoneman with his wife and brother, and Mark Butcher had just met up with Will. They were all about to join Michael. Now, Lord Craythorne was facing the townsfolk and hopefully the fate of the river would be told.

"Here they are, and I know we are all eager to hear news of our river and where it's got to," Lord Craythorne began. "Silence now, and let's listen to what Michael has to say."

Michael stood and looked down at his mud-encrusted breeches, torn stockings and scuffed shoes. He made a gesture of brushing his hem clean before looking towards his travelling companions and then at the people of the town.

"Well, we're all in a bit of a mess. Been sleeping in barns, and our wives won't be best pleased with us so I'm sorry about that." Michael looked through the upturned faces and spotted Agnes. "Apologies especially to Agnes, who said goodbye to her smart young husband only to see him in this sorry state and them only a week married!"

Some sniggers rippled through the audience, punctuated by a few bawdy comments.

"Enough of that," Michael continued. "You've come to hear of the Rother, and we found her all right, but it

117

will be God's will if she returns to Romney. I doubt even the king himself will shift her.

"We walked to Hope and from there we went along the riverbank, not that there was any river to be seen, just pools of water and mud… mud everywhere, just like you see it here. After a while, we joined the Rhee Canal and walked beside it. Now that had a bit of water in it, a trickle… nothing that was going to shift a bank of shingle. We followed the Rhee all the way to Snargate… you know of Snargate? That's where the gate is, letting the water into the Rhee… but there's no water to be let in, nothing to speak of. We stayed overnight there, with John Hope's cousin and one of the family... well, she's to marry the gatekeeper. They say the water stopped flowing on the night of the storm, just as it did here. Nice folk they were, friendly.

"Next day, we arrived at Appledore, on the edge of the Marsh. It had gone from there too."

The others nodded in agreement and Richard added, "They've still got their boats and nets, but they're just sitting on the mud and the jetties… there's no use for them."

"They were all talking about it there, in the marketplace," Michael continued. "They were wondering about us… if the river still came our way and they told us that where the main body of the river once flowed around the Isle of Oxney and past Appledore, it had taken a fancy to flowing the other way. There was a group of their men, just like us five, who had gone over to Oxney to see what had happened. Now, we could have just waited in Appledore for them to return but we wanted to see it for ourselves and so we had to get across where the river had been, and I'm telling you it's a lot easier to cross a river of water than a river of mud. We did it though, using planks and ropes and the help of those good men, and looked a sorry sight at the end of it!

"We walked up the hill to Oxney, stopping here and there to talk with people, and it was on the other side of the Isle that we saw her. The river had gone the other side of Oxney and was flowing good and proper, but not to Romney. The people there, they reckoned she was going over to Rye and the old town of Winchelsea, but they didn't know for certain. They were waiting for word from those Appledore men who went before us. We had a bed in the church that night and they fed us well. They arranged for an old man with a boat to take us down the river to see where she was going now. We had to see it for ourselves... to see if there was a chance of bringing her back."

Michael paused for a moment. All the attention was on him, even the children had caught the sense of anticipation and stood in silence, faces raised towards him.

"You set off on a boat," Lord Craythorne beamed his approval. "Well, that's nothing to men of Romney and you had to see it for yourselves, not rely on the word of Appledore men."

"It was a small vessel, and we had the use of its owner. They say it's tricky at times to see what's river and what's the flooded marshlands. But you could see her all right – our river, our Rother. There she was, carving out a nice channel for herself through all those wetlands." He paused, seeing it again in his own mind. "It's not like our bit of Romney Marsh you see. Here it's fields and dykes keeping the water in its place. Over there, it's marshland and creeks and walls of earth where they're trying to keep the sea back, but she forces her way in and the whole lot is flooded again."

Agnes saw it all in her mind's eye and longed for Will to tell her more, to say if it was as she had pictured it. The mist, which had dampened her spirits when it hung over New Romney, became magical as it rolled over the marshlands, kissing the tops of the reeds and lending a soft light to the landscape. Did the water dry up beyond the earth walls and did men try to make use of it to grow crops or graze sheep? And what type of people were they – these marsh-men and their families who lived their lonely lives, battling against the might of the sea and attempting to survive on ground that must be salt-laden? Did the Rother destroy homes and farms as it pushed its way through, forcing a new path to the sea? Or did it follow the waterways already waiting to welcome it?

She looked towards Will, standing there at the front, and her heart swelled with pride and a longing to be close to him again. Then the baby Nicholas cried – it must be him, for he was the only newborn in the parish and there was no mistaking the mewl of a tiny baby. Agnes thought of Hugh, his father, and how he had strutted about the beachfront and town, of how attractive he had seemed to her as she changed from girl to young woman. At the time Will had been nothing more than a good man, decent and reliable. Now, he was her husband, the adventurer, with tales to tell of places she would never see. Standing there in his mud-caked clothes, weary yet eager to be a part of this, Will looked more attractive than ever before... more appealing than Hugh had ever been.

"It was a small boat," Michael continued, "but we moved along quite happily, with just a dab of the oar every now and then to keep us from any mishaps. The current was strong, and we could tell that the river was settled in its new route already. We had the old sea cliffs to our right, from the time when there was no Romney Marsh at all. Then, on the other side, there was nothing more than great pools of shallow water with reeds poking through and the earth walls all broken down by the sea.

"We set off early and by mid-morning we'd reached the town of Rye, set on a hill with water all around it. Not just seawater, there's two other rivers coming along to the same place. Rye is all old town walls and gateways, winding streets going up the hillside and houses perched on top of each other. Right at the summit, there's a fine old church looking out over the place. But what I was forgetting to say was that the tide was coming in and pushing its way up the river, so we couldn't have gone any further and we got to Rye just in time to see where the river went."

"What did those men of Rye have to say about the river?" Lord Craythorne asked.

"Well, it didn't matter much to them, one way or the other. They already had two rivers giving them a path to the sea and a decent harbour all set up. They hadn't been using the land as there had already been a tidal creek passing along, which explains how the river found her way so easily. Rye has everything that Romney once had and the river is nicely settled there, there's no question about that."

"Nicely settled?" Lord Craythorne repeated. "Did you see no way of forcing it to turn back?"

"The river's changed its route around the Isle of Oxney," Mark confirmed. "And that was no trouble as it already flowed both ways. Before, most of the water went Appledore way and now it flows the other way. After that, there are creeks and tidal channels aplenty, with nothing to hinder the flow. By the time we shift that wall of shingle over in our harbour – and that's if we ever could move it – there would be no tempting the river back."

"That river is done with Romney," John said, and the others nodded, their faces showing that they had accepted this fact days beforehand.

"At least we still have our town," Will added. "They told us about Winchelsea while we were in Rye, Old Winchelsea, that is. All gone in a storm just before our lifetimes. The sea took the town down and there was no hope of rebuilding it. They built another on the hill opposite Rye and we could see across to it. The sea won't get it up there."

The people of New Romney, with their own storm fresh in their minds, shuddered at the thought of losing the whole town. Although for many, those with their homes and boats destroyed, their fate was not much better.

Part Three
Spring 1288

Chapter Twelve
The Monks

"He gave his permission!" The words were barely a whisper from Brother Gregory as he passed along the line of silent grey-robed figures who sat in the refectory of St Augustine's Abbey in Canterbury.

In return, Brother Nicholas, the traveller monk, gave the most imperceptible of nods. He tried to hold back the smirk as his lips twitched at the sides and eyes shone. Raising a spoonful of vegetable soup to his lips, he lowered his eyes and concentrated on his meal. The soup was good, full of fresh produce grown in the abbey gardens – destined to satisfy his hunger and not his pleasure.

Thoughts darted around but Brother Nicholas allowed no emotion to show on his face. He was one of many sitting in contemplative silence at the long heavy slab of a refectory table. It was cold in the room, not that he should mind, it was not his place to bother about such things. Only the abbot, the prior and the dean sat close enough to the one fire for it to make any difference. Did they not need to pray in the cold? His thoughts strayed to the comparative comfort of the more senior monks: not only did they sit beside the fire, but they had their own rooms and softer bedding. Did he not deserve a few simple luxuries in exchange for his life of prayer?

Suddenly, his fellow monks were rising and he, Brother Nicholas, had missed the cue to leave. He had been wrong-footed but maintained a blank expression while turning and leaving the cavernous stone room. Somehow Brother Gregory managed to move down the line – he was clever that one, and curious about the world outside the abbey gates. You could see it in his eyes, the way they darted about.

"The garden." Again, Brother Gregory's words were no more than a murmur. Brother Nicholas did not respond but nevertheless the arrangement had been made.

An hour later, all the monks were at work, some in the grounds of the abbey, or absorbed with domestic duties, others painstakingly transcribing documents, and letters. Brother Nicholas was breaking up the clods of soil, frozen hard over the winter, when Brother Gregory sidled up to him, spade in hand.

"The abbot says I may go with you." The younger monk's blue eyes shone in anticipation of an adventure.

"This is a serious task," Brother Nicholas said, but his stomach fluttered with expectation. Soon the baby in Romney would be recognised as a child sent by God! He had spent many hours over the long winter recording the tale of the child's birth and now he must return to learn of his first months. There were plans for the child which he would discuss with Brother Gregory on their long journey to Romney Marsh. Brother Nicholas recognised, in those vivid eyes and eager voice, someone who had ambitions and a desire to gain more from his life.

"A child sent by God – it is serious beyond all else," Brother Gregory agreed.

"The weather improves by the week," Brother Nicholas stated. "I hope the abbot will release you within days."

"It is my greatest wish," Brother Gregory lowered his eyes, as if pious to the core.

Brother Nicholas had no need to be released by the abbot; St Augustine's was not his home monastery. He was merely a visitor who had boarded over the winter, awaiting his chance to return to Romney. Having arrived in October, the winter months had seemed longer than ever before while first rain, then ice and snow, confined him to the boundaries of the abbey and cathedral.

As he knocked the clumps of earth about, Brother Nicholas relived his first days in Canterbury. His news had been shared within hours of his arrival in the city. How frustrating it had been to then wait for an audience with the abbot and then the archbishop.

"There has been a great storm!" He recalled his words and how he had uttered them, refraining from blurting out the news which had bubbled away inside him, and remembering to treat his audience with the reverence they commanded. "I watched it all from the church tower... I saw it all and at the end of the night, after the sea had ravaged the town, destroying livelihoods... at the end of the night, God left his son for the people of that town."

They had demanded more explanations and finally the monk had been asked to write his story. Whether they believed him or not, the archbishop and abbot were educated and wise in the ways of the world. Here in Canterbury they were honoured with the first cathedral built in England and the archbishop was the most senior religious figure in the land. Since Thomas

Becket had been murdered in the cathedral, it had become one of the most important centres of pilgrimage in England. But you could never keep your eye on everything, and who knew when another archbishop might be murdered in Exeter or York or Winchester… and the glory shifted from Canterbury? If a child of God were born within the diocese, their glorious cathedral and those connected with it would indeed be blessed.

The finest vellum and a supply of freshly cut quills had been provided and, using his own notes as guidance, the story was written, the facts embellished, and pages decorated. The travelling monk wrote slowly and carefully, taking great pride in the flowing text with its loops and lines. He was a keen artist and sketched the Norman tower of St Nicholas Church, the sea crashing upon the beachfront and the humble priory which had been his place of rest. Finally, the baby was sketched, with his snub nose, dark lashes and perfect lips, cradled in his bed of shingle within the base of the tower.

A leather case was made for the book, and for a short time it was displayed in the cathedral, with two monks guarding it at all times. The people of the city, most of them illiterate, gathered in the cathedral and patiently queued to gaze at the script. For a time, the city became divided between those who had and those who had not seen the story immortalised in ink. Within weeks, nearly everyone had viewed the book, and those who had not were of no significance. After a month, it was locked away in a wooden box within the sacristy. By then the story was spreading by word of mouth, slowly but steadily, reaching the villages and towns surrounding the city. Brother Nicholas was satisfied; he knew the news of God's son was becoming known, and with it the tale of the monk who discovered the child.

Brother Nicholas and Brother Gregory left at first light on Monday of the last week in March. The narrow streets of Canterbury were coming to life as buckets of slops were thrown onto the streets, market traders were preparing to set up their stalls, and street cleaners were tidying away the debris from the day before. As the road became wider and houses more spread out, the city was quieter – the wealthy were still in bed during these early hours. City walls loomed high, and the pair left Canterbury by Postern Gate, then set off in a south-westerly direction.

Their robes wrapped tight around them, they walked into the brisk morning breeze, not yet speaking with ease as they were unused to having the freedom to do so. The road had a steady trail of country-folk coming into the city to sell goods at the market. Some pushed carts of fruit and vegetables, others ushered animals along the road or struggled with baskets of dairy produce. A horse and cart passed by with crates of chickens and another with bales of cloth.

Brother Gregory's eyes were alight and darting from one person to another. Brother Nicholas, the travelling monk, had seen these scenes time and time again, in different towns and cities. People went about their business in much the same way wherever they lived. He noted the gaze of his companion settled occasionally on a peasant girl. Young Brother Gregory was lustful and there was no surprise in that. Confined in a monastery since the age of fourteen, what chance had he had to learn about life and its temptations? He was ripe for an adventure.

"Do you see the curves on that fair wench?" Brother Gregory whispered as they passed a girl with a basket on each rounded hip.

"A touch of her sweet flesh and you've a lifetime of nagging," Brother Nicholas murmured.

"What would we know?" Brother Gregory replied gloomily. His blond hair and dancing blue eyes caught the attention of the young woman and, despite his long, hooded robes, she gave him a cheeky wink.

"Did you see that? Did you see?" Brother Gregory looked back and received a kiss blown through the air. "There's a life outside the abbey. A life I know nothing of."

"Aye, and you'll see plenty over the next few weeks," Brother Nicholas advised him. "Take heed you are a monk first and a man second, no news of improper manners should reach Canterbury."

Brother Gregory bowed his head a little and said no more. They walked for ten hours that day, pausing now and then for some bread and cheese to ease their hunger and ale to quench their thirst. They passed no settlements of any significance and those villages they did see were both small and infrequent. The road was high and by mid-afternoon they were admiring spectacular views across the countryside, towards a distant band of shimmering sea. The road began its descent as the sun became low in the sky, and the monks made their beds in a barn that night.

The next day they continued not long after dawn, and soon it was clear Brother Gregory had something on his mind. "This road – a Roman road, you say. Does it take us directly to Romney? How long did it take you to travel to Canterbury before?"

"I didn't travel this way before," Brother Nicholas replied. "I was set on travelling around the coast, I walked from Romney through Hythe and onto Dover, where I rested for a few days, then to Sandwich. There I followed the river Stour into the city. "This road doesn't go as far as Romney. There is no straight road over the Romney Marsh."

"But this road, this straight road, it takes us a fair way?"

"Aye, it takes us directly to Lympne," Brother Nicholas agreed. "To the old sea-cliffs, from a time before the Marsh was formed."

"I find it a lonely road," Brother Gregory surmised. "The settlements are sparse. There is a need of several inns upon a road such as this."

"A road such as this?" questioned Brother Nicholas.

"Aye, pilgrims need a place to rest. Not that they have need of much comfort, but here there is nothing. I shall seek out some wily folk on our return and let them see the benefit of making some accommodation available."

"But this is no pilgrims' route," Brother Nicholas corrected him. "You are mistaken, this is nothing but a route for the Romans."

"But it *will* be," Brother Gregory exclaimed. "When news spreads, we'll thank those Romans for aiding us in building our pilgrims' route."

"Sometimes, I find it hard to follow your thoughts," Brother Nicholas frowned, and shook his head slightly. "You are so unused to being able to talk at ease that all sorts of words spill out in a jumble."

"Not at all," Brother Gregory gave a rare grin, it being unnatural to show such wicked pleasure within St Augustine's Abbey. "My thoughts are quite in order. We are travelling to see the infant and to write of his progress. But I see beyond this to a time when our news has spread. People will want to see the child and this town which suffered during the great storm."

"You see... you see people making a pilgrimage," Brother Nicholas stated, his sallow face brightening. "To learn of the baby I discovered, mayhap... aye indeed... I see it too!"

It was late morning when the two monks stood on the hillside at Lympne, and Brother Nicholas spread both arms out in front of him, palms raised to the sky. "Brother Gregory, you see before you Romney Marsh and, in the distance, the birthplace of God's gift to the people who suffered from the storm!"

Flat lands stretched in front of them as far as the eye could see. There was a hint of a ridge of hills, but so distant that they were nothing more than an indistinct band between land and soft blue sky. Irregular fields were bordered with ribbons of reed-lined drainage ditches, and crooked wind-swept trees. Cottages and farm-buildings were sparse, and the occasional church tower or spire could be seen.

"It looks to be a dull place," Brother Gregory concluded after a moment's contemplation. "Only the sea cheers it for me."

To the left, a great bay arched and beneath the clear sky, the sea glistened a pure cornflower blue. How calm and inviting it looked. How could this be the same sea that had thrashed grey and menacing upon this very coast?

"A dull place?" repeated Brother Nicholas. "Not at all, it is much the same as anywhere else. Or it *was* much the same. When people hear of the child – God's gift to the town – Romney will be a place of wonder. You are right, Brother Gregory, they will travel to see the child."

"Will we reach Romney today?" Brother Gregory asked.

"I believe we could," Brother Nicholas paused to consider the matter. "But let us rest overnight, perhaps in Dymchurch or Eastbridge, and arrive in the morning. I wonder how the child fares and what else has happened in my absence?"

It had been a long, hard winter for the people of Romney whose bellies ached with hunger and scrawny limbs shivered from the cold. With their boats in pieces and no fishing to be done out to sea, fish had only been caught by line or kiddle net from the shore. This meant there was less to be salted or smoked and stored away for the winter. The farmers could ask a good price for mutton and the meat sold well to those who had pennies to spare. When those coins were spent, there was nothing left for clothing or shoes. Since the storm, no merchant ships had docked at Romney and the town could boast none of the exotic goods from places they could only imagine.

What else had the monk not seen in his absence? An infant's life was fragile, and he had not seen that, despite the hardships, the baby Nicholas had a strong chubby body, a mass of dark blond curls and gorgeous dimples in rosy cheeks. He now lived with his adoring mother, Cecily, through the days and nights, having been weaned from his wet-nurse. Nicholas was bright and cheerful, eager for adventure as he crawled around his home, unaware of his importance within the town.

The widow, Matilda, had been busy overseeing the rebuilding of her husband's beachfront repair sheds and visiting his grave daily. She felt at peace with her decision to install Gundred in a place where, she believed, the old woman had nothing else to do but pray for Hugh's spirit. But at times, when her gaze fell on her son, bitter thoughts engulfed Matilda. She felt sure that her son had a brother born to another woman. That child was too young, his features still those of a baby, but she was going to wait... for she had patience in abundance.

The monk failed to see that Matilda was waiting... waiting to see the features of young Nicholas mature. And if the child had a look of her own son or dead husband, she would expose him for the fraud he unwittingly was. She would shame the girl from the beachfront and shatter the child's pedestal from beneath him. She would not see that child rise to a position of greater importance than her own dear Oliver.

From his vantage point on the church tower, the travelling monk had not seen the river change direction and possessed no knowledge of the impact this had on the town. He assumed that, following the clearing of the debris and rebuilding of homes and boats, life in Romney would continue as usual. He did not know every day the townsfolk were drawn to the estuary and wondered how to bring back the river, to use its force to clear the harbour. They knew this to be a wasted effort, but still they spoke of the river returning and it became a hope to which they clung.

Others, such as Michael Vintner, had packed up and left before the winter set in. They planned to make a better life for their families along the coast towards Hythe and Dover, or inland towards Ashford or Tenterden. Those who were left behind could only wonder if they had made the right decision to stay and they would never hear again from those who moved away.

As the monks, Brother Nicholas and Brother Gregory, neared Romney, Brother Nicholas could feel his chest filling with pride as he recalled the time when the newborn had been found and how it was he who had realised the boy was a gift from the Lord. He was so much a part of the coming of this child, that the townsfolk would recall the moment and rejoice at his return. With his head held high and back straight, Brother Nicholas passed through the deserted boat repair area and walked along the beach track in order to show Brother Gregory the very place where he had discovered the baby.

On approaching the eastern end of St Nicholas Church, it was clear a team of men had worked hard to restore the gable ends, which had been damaged by the force of the storm. The mortar looked to be new, and the stones had been cleaned. But, on closer inspection, it seemed the work was not quite complete – tools and stone were piled up as if work had been abandoned partway through the day.

"Here, it is. The church!" The travelling monk waved his arm in the direction of the fine Norman church. "And there... up there on the tower, I watched the storm... The greatest storm man has ever witnessed."

"A good solid building," Brother Gregory voiced his appreciation. "Plenty of space for the pilgrims to gather. And where, Brother, did you find the child?"

They were walking to the western end of the church, where the shingle still lay deep around the base of the tower and huge piles of sand and stones showed that the church interior had been cleared of storm debris. Brother Nicholas' focus was all on the open doorway into the tower, and he was about to show the very spot where the child had been found when Brother Gregory's attention was shifted to beyond the churchyard.

"Look, over there – a gathering as big as any we'd see in Canterbury Cathedral!"

"Whatever can they be doing?" Brother Nicholas looked in wonder at the gathering. "Surely all the townspeople must be assembled."

Chapter Thirteen
Agnes

Agnes put a protective hand over her belly which swelled gently during her second pregnancy. She always felt vulnerable when she saw Matilda. Not that anything had ever been said about the baby, or Agnes' shameful lust for Matilda's husband, but she was uneasy, nonetheless. Young Oliver pushed past, brushing lightly against Agnes. He had pulled his hand free of his mother's, eager to forge ahead, and now Matilda was there, trying to keep pace with her head-strong son. Agnes saw the young widow dart a look of pure hatred towards her, before turning her attention back to Oliver.

They had no choice but to keep moving with the flow of people surging towards a small patch of land by the church tower and the beach. Will circled his arm around Agnes' waist and guided her through the gathering of townsfolk, towards her parents who stood on the shingle ridge.

"Have you heard what this is about?" Agnes' father, John, asked Will.

"Nay, and I was talking with Adam Stoneman's wife only yesterday. She won't breathe a word."

"Whatever it is, it's important enough to take Adam away from repairing the church." John was repeating what everyone had been saying for weeks.

"Aye, the rest of the masons were still there. But Lord Craythorne, he put Adam Stoneman to work in a barn at the manor house, and not even his son knows what he's been up to." Will retold all he knew. "Richard knows nothing of it."

A whisper flew through the crowds, eventually reaching the ears of Agnes and her family: "They're here, Lord Craythorne and his wife." She could almost feel the anticipation on the salt-breeze as voices dropped and all eyes turned to the two most powerful people in the area. They lived in a moated stone house to the north of the town, beyond Rolfes Road and away from the streets of humble wooden homes. They chose to come into the town infrequently, sending servants to shop and worshipping within their own private chapel. Romney Marsh did not attract the wealthy gentry and in a larger town, such as Canterbury or Tonbridge, Lord and Lady Craythorne would not have been amongst the richest or most influential. But here, in Romney, they were to be revered and the townsfolk bowed their heads in respect.

They came into the town on foot, with Adam Stoneman and the priest from St Nicholas walking a respectable pace behind. Since the storm, Lord Craythorne had honoured Romney with his presence more often than usual. Agnes had seen him many a time, gazing at the lost harbour and blocked river, speaking with the fishermen and traders whose livelihoods had been lost when the storm came. It was whispered that he had written to King Edward about the plight of Romney, asking for royal intervention and guidance as to whether the shingle bank could be cleared, and the Rother directed back to its previous route.

Lady Craythorne chose to keep her distance from the town, and it was believed she spent little time at the manor house, instead choosing to live with family in Saltwood and Dover. *Does she think she is too glorious to be in Romney with the fishermen and all of us who work so hard, but can't dress in luxurious cloth or afford gold and jewels?* Agnes gazed in wonder at the long linen dress, with its decorative trims, worn by Lady Craythorne. *It's beautiful. But too long to be any good for doing a day's work in. She must just sit about looking wonderful and getting others to do all her chores. It would drive me mad to have gold bracelets at my wrists, and you can't gut fish with rings like hers. I know those shoes of hers must be so soft, but I'd rather wear none than worry about getting them wet or muddy.* Lady Craythorne's face, framed by a wimple, was pale and without expression as she glanced towards Agnes, and the young woman bowed her head slightly.

Without pausing to speak to anyone, Lord Craythorne strode along, with his wife gliding beside him, to an area recently cleared of rough grass and weeds. Here, over the last few days, a stone plinth had been erected.

"Look, Ma, I hadn't seen, not with all the crowds," Agnes whispered and tugged at Mary's arm. "They've put something on the stone."

"Aye, a cart came at daybreak, but we've not seen a glimpse of what it held," Mary informed. "It's heavy, I'll say that. It took Adam Stoneman, both his sons and a cousin to pull it into place."

"They kept it covered though?"

"Aye, it wasn't to be seen," Mary confirmed.

Mother and daughter fell silent, as Lord and Lady Craythorne stood looking towards the townspeople gathered. The crowds were now quiet, knowing something wondrous was to be revealed and not wanting to miss a word of explanation.

"People of Romney, it's been half a year since the great storm and we've all suffered for it," Lord Craythorne began, and a murmur of agreement rippled throughout the crowd. "Our fishermen have restored some of their boats and built new homes upon the burgage plots, but the merchants suffer for lack of trade and some of our men have left Romney forever. Amongst all our suffering, we were given a gift from our Lord, and it is this child, Nicholas, who gives us hope that all is not lost to our town. He is our future, our saviour. To honour him and the man who declared him sent to us, I have asked Adam Stoneman to create a lasting memorial to the gift of a child who came to us during the storm."

Agnes' mouth went dry, and her unborn child kicked. Her hand sought Will's and held it tight, as a rough covering was pulled off the statue to reveal the travelling monk and, in his arms, the baby Nicholas. The stone had been carved to show the slender face and lowered eyelids of the monk, looking down upon the newborn child, swaddled in a piece of cloth. The child's wrappings and the monk's robes mingled into one, cascading to the plinth on which they stood. Agnes stood transfixed.

What does this mean? I never thought… never planned for this to happen. All I wanted was for him to be fed and to have a home with a family who would care for him. It was a wonderful thing that happened – Cecily having a baby when she couldn't have any of her own. That was enough. It was enough for me, and the baby and Cecily. It wasn't easy. It was awful, but I made the right choice.

Now he has become a symbol of hope for the town, and they all believe it – they believe my son was sent by God. I thought those stories would fade. But they won't, not with this statue here to remind them. It's too late to speak the truth, and now it will be up to the good Lord to punish me as He wishes when my time comes to leave this Earth.

While these thoughts tumbled to and fro in her mind, Agnes looked away from the statue for a moment. Then she saw him… but not just him, now there were two of them. Standing at the base of the tower, where the child had been found. Two monks. The travelling monk – she recognised his thin face and calculating eyes even from this distance – and another, perhaps younger, monk standing beside him. They were mesmerised by the statue, which was of no surprise, as surely the monk had not been expected. It was likely he knew nothing of the freshly unveiled statue.

As Agnes stared at the travelling monk, a crescendo of whispers built up around her. Like the sea dragging upon the shingle the murmurs rose and fell until they caught the attention of Lord Craythorne, and he was forced to turn and see what it was that took the crowd's attention away from himself. Then the crowd fell silent, staring in disbelief at the monks who had arrived at such a time, and the monks in return stared back at the townsfolk and the statue. The original monk had a bewildered look on his pinched face. As for the younger one – there was no mistaking the look of glee in his eyes.

"This is God's will indeed!" Lord Craythorne was not lost for words for long. "What fortunes shine upon Romney. Now the very person who found the child, Brother Nicholas, comes amongst us again."

The monk bowed his head, apparently overwhelmed in his belief the child had been named after him, rather than the church, St Nicholas, which rose solidly above him. Agnes felt frustrated – irrationally angry that this monk was being given the honour of finding her son. *That is not the way it was. It was George who found the baby... George who laboured long and hard all night before finding him in the base of the tower. The monk watched the storm all*

138

night and offered no help to the townsfolk, then he climbed down from the tower at dawn. But he claimed the child was a gift from God, which is what gave baby Nicholas this position of status when everything else was so awful. It's all wrong.

"Come," called Lord Craythorne. "Come and stand by the statue; do you see it is you with the child? Let us see your likeness!"

Agnes watched the monk move forward slowly and his gaze travel to and fro across the gathering. She did not like the look in his eyes which were small and close-set, and she believed he gloried in the attention in a way a monk should not. *Why have they come here? What do they want with Romney and the child?* Fear twisted in her stomach and again her unborn child kicked.

"Come, Monk," Lord Craythorne urged.

He moved forwards then, passing through the crowds who shifted aside to let him pass. The younger monk glided in his wake, eyes dancing and face glowing. *What is it that excites the younger one so much? What does the baby and its place in the world have to do with this monk?* The travelling monk stood beside the statue, looking up at it. His face was expressionless, it was just his eyes that narrowed as he looked at the details of the carving. He hid his emotions well. Was he calculating how best to respond?

"Here he is… but to arrive on such a day… how did you know?" Lord Craythorne bellowed.

The monk merely stood, looking bemused.

"No need to speak. This is a surprise to you, no doubt." Lord Craythorne reached out to pat the arm of the travelling monk. "And now there are two of you!"

The younger monk bowed his head in acknowledgement and with a modesty Agnes perceived to be false.

"We didn't know of this...," Brother Nicholas mumbled. "We came to see the child... to learn of the first months of his life."

"The Archbishop of Canterbury is most interested in the child," Brother Gregory spoke up, his voice ringing out clearly. "We are to write of his life so far and I wonder – have any other miracles occurred since the coming of this child?"

There was a gasp amongst the crowd, and it seemed as if the onlookers were frantically thinking of anything... any minor incident, which could now be deemed a miracle. Agnes could see it in the faces of the women as they turned to each other with raised eyebrows. There would be a queue outside the priory later, as the women gathered with stories of unexplained happenings.

Now the younger monk surveyed the crowd, seemingly pleased with the response so far. "I wouldn't be surprised... in fact the archbishop told me himself...," Brother Gregory confided to the people, "that he plans to visit the baby, Nicholas."

He is a liar, Agnes thought as she noted the look of surprise flash over the other monk's face.

"That will be a great day indeed for the people of New Romney," Lord Craythorne swelled with pride. "We'll have to prepare rooms at the manor house."

Agnes' attention had been focused on the statue and the monks, but now she turned to look for Cecily and the baby. There was no sign of them. She would be there, of course, but there were so many people and Agnes couldn't spot them. After a moment of searching, she saw Cecily, sheltered within the arms of her husband.

Of course, Cecily would not want all this attention on the baby. All she had ever wanted over the last few years was to hold her own child in her arms, to love and nurture it. Agnes could not see her face, nor that of baby Nicholas as he too was wrapped within the doctor's arms. Like Agnes, the doctor and Cecily would want the child to be raised with little attention thrust upon him. What did this mean – the return of the monk to see the baby?

"Where is he?" Lord Craythorne's voice rang out. "The baby Nicholas should be here too. These monks must see how he has changed from scrawny newborn to fine youngling in the last half year."

With her head bowed a little and the doctor's hand at her elbow, Cecily moved forwards with Nicholas perched on her hip. On reaching Lord Craythorne, the baby reached out, and Cecily had no choice but to hand him her son, who was then held up high for all to admire.

"Is he not a fine child?" Lord Craythorne asked the monks, who were no experts in this matter. They nodded their agreement.

Nicholas did not sense his parents' reticence and was generous with his smiles. Dark blond curls moved in the breeze, his skin was clear, and chubby legs kicked with excitement from under his embroidered tunic. He shrieked his pleasure, causing a ripple of laughter through the crowd and the pain of love to shoot through Agnes' heart.

"You must eat and rest," continued Lord Craythorne, "but later you'll meet with his parents – the doctor and Cecily – and they will tell you of his first months. Then talk with Adam Stoneman about the statue… and with whoever else you like. We are all keen to share the story of this child. He has a place in all our hearts."

The monk muttered something in reply and Lord Craythorne was immediately waving his hand towards the townsfolk. "These men have travelled far. Let them pass through and allow them to rest and take some nourishment at the priory. They'll be amongst us soon enough, wanting to hear of the child and mayhap the other changes in our town over the past months."

The crowds parted to allow the monks a clear path. The travelling monk walked with his eyes lowered and cloak wrapped tight around him. He was a modest figure, apparently taken aback by the attention that had been thrust upon him. But the younger one sailed along in his wake, cloak billowing and smiles for everyone. As he passed close to Agnes, Brother Gregory's blue eyes lowered to her rounded breasts and, as he raised his eyes to her face, there was no mistaking the look of lust within them. This young monk was a handsome man, for all he was wearing his robes, and he reminded her of another man – one who had swaggered round the boat repair sheds and tempted her to lift her skirts. Agnes recoiled, turning slightly to Will.

Chapter Fourteen
Matilda

"Hush now, stay here with Grandma while I visit Pa in the churchyard." Matilda peeled her son's clenched fists from the skirt of her tunic. She turned to her mother, who had a firm grip on Oliver's arms, "I won't be long, but I have a need to be there."

"Have you considered Henry's offer?" The older woman asked. "It's been six months. Long enough to grieve."

"Aye, I've thought of it, and he's working hard in the repair shed, the men like him better than... they like him well enough." Matilda paused for a moment to think how best to voice her concerns, "It's just a little soon, and I still think of Hugh."

"He's a decent God-fearing man," Matilda's mother reminded her. "A regular churchgoer and loyal too."

"Aye, he's worthy enough and fond of Oliver." Matilda shrugged her shoulders. "I'll be off now, Ma."

Matilda walked along the track between Rolfes Road and Fair Field Road. Hugh's cousin, Henry, would make a loyal and steadfast husband. *He'd not be lusting after any girl who shot a smile in his direction, and I'd not be lying awake at night wondering whose bed he was keeping warm. He is handsome enough... good enough for me... but I was spoiled by having the finest man in Romney as my husband.* And so Matilda's irrational thoughts rambled on.

She passed her stone house, walked straight towards the beach and past the wooden cottages which had been rebuilt. Matilda then turned to the right, away from the repair shed which had claimed her husband's life and now stood tall again beyond the high tide mark. The church loomed large in front of her now. The east end was in shadow, but lines of fresh mortar stood out amongst ancient stones.

Matilda knew Gundred's beady eyes were upon her as she picked her way around graves and tussocks of grass. *What had I been thinking of, installing the old hag in the anchorhold? I'll never pray in peace at the graveside until the old woman has died.* But Gundred had lived through one winter, cocooned in her thick bed of straw and as well-fed as Lady Craythorne.

With her back to the church, and more importantly to Gundred, Matilda sank to her knees at the graveside and whispered a brief prayer. "Lord, be merciful on this soul and take him into your arms. He repents his sins... I know he does... let him rest in peace."

Reluctantly, the widow stood. There was no avoiding Gundred now. The barred window was so small and the interior of the cell so dark that Matilda could barely see Gundred's form when she stopped a few paces back from the church wall.

"That you, Matty? I can't quite see you." A cackle of pleasure rang out.

Matilda forced herself to take another step closer. "Aye, it's me."

"It's been like the fair here today," Gundred commented. "I've never seen so many people, with so much to tell old Gundred. They look after me well, the people of Romney do." She paused for a moment, before adding, "I thought you would have been along earlier."

"Aye, I meant to, but Oliver...." Matilda used the well-worn excuse.

"I've been praying as much as I can," Gundred informed her. "As much as I can, with folk bothering me all day, bringing me food and wanting to hear a bit of my wisdom. He's faring well, is that no-good husband of yours. I feel things, as you know, and I'm telling you he's grateful to old Gundred who's helping him good and proper on his journey to our Lord."

"I'm glad of that," Matilda replied. "I pray he is at peace."

"And, talking of your husband..." There was a lift to Gundred's voice and Matilda knew that if she could see her features, those beady eyes would be dancing and lips curling in delight. "I've not seen young Agnes in a while... she used to come by, but not in a while."

"She's well enough." Matilda would not rise to the old hag's mischief.

"Having another baby... a baby, I mean." A burst of laughter was expelled from Gundred, and Matilda put her shawl over her face to protect her from the putrid breath. "Her husband's child. Nice man is that Will, very nice indeed, I've always liked him. He's one who always has a smile and a kind word for a poor old woman."

"Aye, they're having a baby," Matilda confirmed, her mouth dry and throat constricted.

"And there's a new statue, I hear," Gundred made as if she was changing the subject. "Very fine. I'll never see it for real but it's in my mind's eye. There's plenty of folk that were good enough to come earlier in the day and tell me all about it. Aye, some come as soon as they can with news, knowing I'm stuck in here and feeling a bit lonely at times. They bring me a nice bit o' food too – very generous Romney folk are."

"I've brought you some spiced cake." Matilda pushed her offering through the window bars.

"Most kind," Gundred said without feeling, then began to break off pieces with her gnarled hands and push them into her mouth.

Matilda made as if to turn away, but the old woman was not done with her yet.

"And what do you make of the statue of that monk and the baby? Is it a fair likeness?"

"The baby was newborn, I know nothing of what he looked like then," Matilda replied sharply. "Others can dote over him, but I had a husband to bury and mourn."

"Aye, and they change so quickly. Who does he resemble now?" Gundred asked, before adding, "How foolish… sent by God he is, we can't compare him to mere mortals… but if we were to… let's say we were to think of who he looks similar to… what would you say, Matilda? Is he a redhead like the Stonemans, or dark like young Agnes from the beach-front, or fair like… like your Oliver?"

"Oh, I don't know," Matilda shrugged her shoulders. "He is neither one nor the other, not a redhead, but fair or dark… they change so quickly."

"So, he's not got a head of curls like your Oliver? You'd notice that."

"I don't have the time to notice. He is nothing to me." Matilda's stomach twisted and she stepped back from the cell window. "It's getting dark, I must get back… for Oliver."

"Aye, I'll see you soon," Gundred called out. "I've not heard your impression of the monk yet, but it will wait for when you have a little more time for an old woman."

Matilda scurried around the edge of the church, still strewn with debris from the storm. At the base of the tower, she carefully slid down the mud and stones, which had settled into place over the last six months, and into the entrance of the church. As stones rolled onto the floor, Matilda reflected that if the townsfolk couldn't clear the entrance to the church there was no hope of clearing the harbour mouth.

With the sun low in the sky, it was dark in the old church. Just a few candles flickered near the altar. But, even in the dim light, damp stains could be seen, rising up the pillars to the height of where the storm debris had settled. Knowing that Gundred's eyes were still upon her, for the cell had a window to the outside world and one inwards to the church, Matilda lit a candle. Then she knelt and muttered a quick prayer for her husband's soul:

"Blessed saints, in your infinite kindness, look with favour on your servant Hugh. May he rest in the peace of your love. Amen."

As she rose, Matilda sensed she was no longer alone and, turning sharply, her heart lurched. Standing a few paces before her was the monk, not the original one, the travelling monk, but the other one. He was in his habit of a grey-brown wool, a simple hood over his head and a plain leather belt at his waist. But for all that he was dressed as a monk, he did not look at all monk-like from his dancing blue eyes to the curl of amusement on his lips. This monk looked like someone who enjoyed life and took every opportunity to gain pleasure however he could. His hood was slipping back slightly, and a crop of wild golden-brown curls were on show. There was no sign of that round, bald tonsure monks usually had. Matilda felt a blush stain her cheeks and her heart tightened, for this monk had an air of Hugh as he looked down upon her, boldly holding her gaze.

"Did I startle you?" he asked.

"Not at all, Brother." *Why must this meeting, this uncomfortable moment, be played out in front of*

Gundred who was surely pinned to the bars of the inner window of her cell?

Matilda turned away slightly, intending to step past him and leave the church. Her colour was still high – the attraction to this man was instant and it was an attraction that no godly woman should allow. But instead of allowing her to go on her way, the monk turned and kept pace with her as she walked down the nave.

"A fine church," he commented, "but a little damp I fear."

"It was the storm, Brother. It filled with mud, sand and shingle from the sea."

"It will dry in time then," he smiled his optimism. "It's an honour to be here, to finally see the Port of Romney and meet its people."

"And what…," Matilda faltered, she shouldn't ask, shouldn't pry, "…what brings you to Romney?"

"The child, of course," he grinned at her. "This child Brother Nicholas speaks of."

"Brother Nicholas?"

"Aye, he is here with me. He has told all of Canterbury about the baby."

"Of course, he was here last autumn, but… his name, I didn't know his name." Matilda felt the heat rising in her cheeks again. *This man, this monk – I shouldn't be talking with him in this way.*

"He is Nicholas, like the child who is named after him. What pride he must feel to learn this today!"

"Oh no!" Matilda could not help smiling at the misunderstanding. "The child was named after the church where he was found, this church – St Nicholas!"

"He will be disappointed!" the monk exclaimed, clearly finding enjoyment in the tale. "If only the child had been named Gregory, I would have liked that."

"Gregory?"

"Aye, for myself. Brother Gregory."

"If he had been Gregory, it would not have been for you who have only met him today." Matilda felt young and playful, as she had before her marriage. "It is a common enough name."

"True." But his eyes still danced at the thought of such an honour.

They had reached the base of the tower now and faced the bank of storm debris at the open doorway.

"So, you are here to see the child?"

"To learn of his life," Brother Gregory told her. "He may be young, but it must all be told and recorded. The tale of this child will be shared throughout the land."

"He's just a baby – what is there to tell?" Matilda's tone was soft and belied the bitterness she felt.

"I know nothing of babies," Brother Gregory admitted. "I know nothing of women either, but I believe they like to talk and the woman who cares for the child will happily speak of his character."

"Perhaps." Matilda had spoken enough of the baby. She looked down at the stray pebbles scattered across the floor. "It's getting late. I must go." She nodded briefly in his direction and turned her back on him.

The sun was about to set as Matilda walked along the edge of the churchyard and across the top of the beach. *How odd to be talking with a monk as if he were… as if he were a man, which he is, of course, but not a man who has thoughts about women. Not a man who should have thoughts about women.* Matilda sensed Brother Gregory was not quite as devout as a monk should be and her curiosity was aroused.

Later, when Oliver slept, Matilda knelt before the altar in her bedroom. The secret void in the floor of the room was now empty. The wax doll representing Agnes was gone. Matilda had buried it behind the house on the day of Hugh's funeral. All her ill-wishing and attacks on the body of the wax figure had done no harm to Agnes, who was now happily married, whilst Matilda mourned her husband. The girl from the beachfront had tempted Hugh, there was no doubting that, but in turn Matilda had committed a great sin in wishing harm to her. God was all-seeing and knew of Matilda's sins.

I must pray more fervently than ever if I am to have a peaceful passage to heaven. She knelt for some time in front of her plain altar, until her knees became stiff, and the candle burned low. When Matilda finally rose and checked on Oliver before going to bed, she felt a sense of peace she had not known for some time.

The following morning, Matilda sang softly as she cleared out the fire and re-laid it. Oliver watched in surprise and babbled his own tunes. Together they sang and laughed through breakfast, and while Matilda helped her son into his tunic and stockings.

"See Cousin Henry," Oliver demanded as his mother laced his shoes, and placed a coif over her hair, securing it under her chin.

"Aye, we'll see Henry in a while, but first we'll go to the town. We need bread and cheese and wine."

"Bread and cheese and wine and biscuits." The child took advantage of his mother's good humour.

"And biscuits," Matilda repeated.

They shut the sturdy wooden door behind them and stepped out onto the Fair Field Road.

"Cousin Henry!" Oliver cried out, waving to a man working outside the boat repair shed on the beach. "Ma, look – Cousin Henry."

"Aye, there he is," Matilda gave a nod in Henry's direction and, with her basket under one arm, and Oliver's hand in hers, turned to walk along the road.

Matilda walked swiftly, her attention no longer on Oliver's chatter. As the priory came into sight, her heart gave a foolish lurch. She admonished herself: *Brother Gregory won't be standing about outside – what purpose would that serve? But… he may be in the church visiting those poor families who still have no home and will have stories to tell of the storm.*

"We'll see how those people are in the church," Matilda told Oliver. "Some of them are the families of men who worked for your pa."

It only took a moment to see Brother Gregory was not in St Martin's. Matilda spent a few minutes exchanging words with the women, asking how the fishing fared and if their new homes were nearly complete. Lord Craythorne had marked out burgage plots in the south-west of the town, beside a track which was now known as St John's Road.

"Aye, we'll have our own cottage on the roadside and a nice long plot of land for growing food and keeping chickens," one woman informed her, but Matilda's interest had waned and she didn't hear a word.

"Come on, Oliver, we must get to the market." Matilda left St Martin's with her son in tow.

She was not to be disappointed that morning, as after filling her basket with food and putting a biscuit in Oliver's chubby hand, they walked to the new statue. A few people had returned to see it now the crowds had waned, and among them was Brother Gregory. Matilda felt her cheeks glow as she saw him, and he turned towards her with a smile of recognition.

"I have seen the child," Brother Gregory announced with glee.

"Was he as you expected?" Matilda asked, while loosening her grip on Oliver's hand.

"I had no feeling of what he might be like," Brother Gregory replied. "He smiled at me and made some curious noises."

"Like any other child," Matilda smiled. "He is no different."

"We'll have to wait to see if he performs miracles or shows himself to be saintly in any way," Brother Gregory paused, and ran his eyes from Matilda's face to her neck and the soft curves of her breasts.

How long had this monk been closeted away? He had a man's desires, that was clear enough, and if it was not for his monk's habit, he would fulfil his needs soon enough. There were plenty of wenches happy to please a wholesome young man. Released from the abbey, he seemed inebriated by his new experiences.

Matilda turned her attention to the statue of soft grey stone. She looked without seeing at the faces of the monk and child, and the beautifully carved folds of the monk's habit. While she did so, her cheeks burned in shame for the thoughts she had about this monk.

"There is no need for the child to grow any older before people travel to see him and the place of his birth," Monk Gregory voiced his plan.

"Travel to see him? What is there to see?"

"This church and the place where he was born... the cloth he was wrapped in... a lock of his hair... people will come in their thousands to this holy place."

"They'll travel to Romney to see those things?" Now Matilda was looking at him again. Bitterness and resentment towards the child gnawed at her stomach, while her attraction to the monk deepened.

"Aye, at this very moment Brother Nicholas is praying for guidance; he asks how our Lord would best like His son honoured."

"I wonder what message God will give," Matilda replied. "For only he knows the truth of the child."

Chapter Fifteen
Matilda

As he stood here on the night on the storm, did Hugh know he was living his last seconds on Earth? Did he hear the creaks and groans as the wooden uprights capitulated and slumped down upon him? Did he think of her and Oliver in his final moments?

Unable to settle, and with her son fast asleep, Matilda had left her stone house and walked across the track to the beach. Perhaps it was due to the south-westerly breeze, or perhaps it was the need to remain concealed, that led to her being huddled in the shadows of the repair shed. The moon was huge, still hanging low in the sky and sending a glittering pathway across the sea to the shallow waters at the shoreline. The colours of Romney were limited to a palette of silver and grey, while the sky was black, covered in sharp white pinpricks of stars. Standing there, leaning slightly against the wooden plank wall, Matilda found a peace previously lost to her within the confines of her home. The sound of the sea slapping down on the sand and the rhythmic pull of the retreating tide on the pebbles and seashells, lent a harmony to her turbulent mind.

Matilda had a plan, but how to make it come about? She had to rid herself and the town of the bastard child spawned by her husband and the wench from the beachfront. *Agnes should suffer for this. She has tricked the town and all the good people. Every day, I have to endure the reminder of Hugh's lust for other women, and the people of Romney are made to look fools by their belief that the child was gifted to them. Not for much longer. Cecily will face great sadness – she who is nothing but good… and will grieve the loss of a much-loved child.* But Matilda had seen the tell-tale swell of her belly. Cecily was to be blessed with a child of her own before the year was out – *one baby will soon be replaced with another.*

Matilda gave a brief smile – a plan was forming in her mind, but how to make it happen?

As the night air chilled her, Matilda stood watching the tide reach its peak and then retreat, before realising that the repetitive sounds of the sea and the gentle creaking of the willow boughs behind her, had been joined by new sounds. A soft giggle… gentle murmurs… a movement of pebbles underfoot. She had no want for company and was about to retrace her steps around the back of the shed when there was a clink of metal against stone and a dull thud. Something had been knocked over within the shed. Most likely it was one of the men finding shelter for a bit of fun with a young woman, but if it were thieves then she would have to rouse Henry.

At the front of the shed, Matilda found one of the huge doors ajar and, as she cautiously peeped around the corner, she saw that she was not mistaken in her initial thoughts. A tall young man had his arms wrapped around a woman, who giggled before he silenced her with a long kiss. Matilda couldn't make out their features and was about to move away when the cloaked figure stepped backwards into the light of the moon, his hood falling back to reveal curls that shone in the soft light.

She stood, held to the spot, whilst a claw clutched at her heart, and still the moon shone upon the monk and his lover. As if born to please women rather than serve God, Brother Gregory nuzzled the neck of the

154

wench as she wound her arms around him. Then deft fingers unlaced her tunic and he reached for smooth, young breasts while mumbling his pleasure. After a moment, the woman whispered in his ear and pointed at something in the dark shadows of the shed. The monk nodded his agreement and reaching down to the hem on his habit, he pulled the garment up and over his head, revealing muscular legs and a fine, honed torso. Matilda gasped to see him standing there in just his thin shift falling to mid-thigh. His habit was thrown into the shadows on the floor. Before he joined his lover on their bed of loose sacking, Brother Gregory turned towards the open door.

Still locked in her own private horror, Matilda remained frozen, and their eyes met. Then, as there came a soft call from the darkness, he turned and stepped out of the ribbon of moonlight. What did this slattern have that could tempt a monk from his vows? Matilda knew the answer; Brother Gregory was ready and waiting to taste the forbidden pleasures a woman could offer. With a longing that was ridden with sin, Matilda stumbled back to her home. It was a long time since her husband had wanted her in the marital bed. She would never find peace that night, but she now knew what was to be done, how to persuade the monk to be a part of her plans and welcome them as if they were his own.

"I was talking with that monk this morning," Matilda's mother commented as they drank wine, and Oliver played with his wooden knights at their feet.

"The monk?" Matilda's colour rose. "Which one?"

"Brother Nicholas who was here during the storm," the older woman told her. "Not that he does much talking, being a monk, but he wanted to hear about the baby."

"I thought he knew about him," Matilda spoke with bitterness. "He was the one who saw the storm and claimed the child was sent by God."

"He *was* sent by God," her mother's voice rose. "You cannot utter those words with doubt. May our Lord forgive you, Matilda. Brother Nicholas was there – he saw it all from the tower."

"Aye Ma, I know."

"He is asking everyone. Has he not spoken with you?"

"Asking what?" Matilda snapped. She hadn't seen the monks in the last two days and was becoming agitated. Time was running out.

"They want to know if we have any memories of the baby coming. Did we see him in his first days? I told him I was supporting you with your grief, and we thought nothing of the baby at the time. I hope that didn't sound uncaring – I am as devoted as our neighbours and the child brings hope to our town."

"What can the child do for Romney?" Matilda wondered. "A fine statue doesn't stop folk from leaving because their homes and boats were lost, and the river mouth blocked."

"There's going to be a display in St Nicholas," her mother stated. "They say that Brother Gregory is gathering anything that has a connection with the child."

"I've not been to Hugh's grave today." Matilda stood suddenly. Then turning to her son, "Oliver, sweeting, do you want to come to where Pa sleeps, or sit with Grandma and your knights?"

"Stay with Grandma," Oliver replied, without looking up from his wooden knights and horses.

"Matilda..." her mother called as she stepped out of the cottage. "I'd be thankful if you'd collect my shoes from the cobblers as you go by."

"Aye, I'll do that," Matilda responded.

156

The day was fair, with just a slight chill to the air and the sun shining boldly in a pale blue sky. In St Martin's churchyard, those children whose homes had been destroyed played amongst the graves. Damp washing was strewn over trees, bushes or laid on the rough grass. The number of church dwellers had dwindled as people left the town or moved into new homes, so now only the two fires burned with a cooking pot straddled over each one.

As Matilda passed by, a mother squawked her disapproval at a group of toddlers, then called out, "If it isn't the pots and fire, it's the clean washing they're messing with!"

Grateful to have only the one child, Matilda nodded and smiled her understanding, but her attention had drifted to the priory. There they were, the two of them, walking with their heads bowed, deep in conversation as they stepped out into the street and closed the priory door behind them. Matilda scurried along, turning the corner of the churchyard in time to see the hooded figures walk straight across the High Street. They looked to be going to St Nicholas, and she followed, for she was heading in that direction anyway.

Bound by her duty to her dead husband, Matilda scurried to the east end of the church, having seen the monks enter the building at the base of the tower. Without a glance towards the small, barred window in the newly-repaired wall, Matilda knelt at the graveside and muttered a prayer in haste:

"Oh God, by whose mercy this departed man will find rest, send your holy angel to watch over his soul, through Christ our Lord. Amen."

Then, as a frisson of guilt shot through her body, Matilda took a few steps towards the old hag in the church wall. "Are you well, Gundred? Ma said she brought you some pie and fruit earlier and I'll be back

157

later with your supper." Then, having given the cunning old woman no chance to reply, Matilda turned and was gone, out of the old woman's view.

In the church, the monks were poring over a collection of fragments of cloth and other oddments spread out on a plain table. Matilda merely nodded in their direction as she swept past them and onwards to the shrine of the Virgin Mary, where she knelt for a moment moving her lips as if in prayer. She could hear the sounds of Gundred shifting position within her cramped cell but resolved to keep her eyes lowered and not to turn in the direction of the old hag.

As she retraced her steps along the nave, the travelling monk, Brother Nicholas, looked across at Matilda. Clearing his throat, he spoke without making eye contact: "Would you mind… a little of your time?"

Matilda nodded without encouragement. She had not come here today to speak with Brother Nicholas.

"We've come to learn… to hear about the child. The child born on the night of the storm."

Matilda looked at him blankly. She did not choose to help this monk but let him stammer and fumble his words as he tried to express them.

"Do you remember the storm?"

"Of course," Matilda answered coolly. "I suffered with the rest of the town's people."

"And then the child came." Brother Nicholas stated. "He brought joy to the town of Romney."

"I have my own son to care for. He made no difference to me." Matilda turned a little, as if to end the conversation.

She didn't look in his direction but sensed that Brother Gregory was no longer picking through the collection of what she presumed to be mementoes of the baby Nicholas' short life so far. The monk before her was lost, unused to talking to strangers and particularly women. Forcing himself to look Matilda in the eye, Brother Nicholas tried once more.

"Do you have any memories of the child, Nicholas?"

"I have none. He is a baby, like any other."

Matilda turned and walked towards Brother Gregory. He stood in the weak light which came through the thick, uneven glass of the arched Norman window. There was a rag – a piece of sacking – in his hand. Even in the dim light of the church, Matilda could see that he reddened a little and shifted uncomfortably as she approached him.

"What do you have there?" she asked.

"This is the cloth that the baby was wrapped in when Brother Nicholas found him over there, in the base of the tower."

"It's sacking," she remarked. "A piece of sack that perhaps had grain in it."

"God has no need to wrap his son in fine cloth," Brother Gregory replied.

"Of course," Matilda replied. "He comes to live amongst us in this ravaged town, not within a palace or abbey." She paused and then continued, "Although he would not be out of place in an abbey… it would be just the place for him." Again she hesitated, making a show of looking though the items in which baby Nicholas had once been wrapped or had perhaps touched in his first months of life. Then abruptly: "I'd like to speak to you about the child."

Brother Gregory looked at her expectantly.

"Not now, not here." Matilda smiled slightly, encouraging him to agree. "I'll meet you tonight… in the barn… where I saw you…."

He knew very well what she had seen and nodded slightly, seemingly unable to reply. Still looking into his eyes, Matilda ran her tongue lightly around her lips, moistening them slightly, before turning away.

"I've been a widow since the night of the storm," Matilda held his gaze in a way she had seen other young women entice men. "I've not had a man in all those months… and you… you're learning fast about life outside the abbey walls."

Brother Gregory gulped and dropped his gaze to her breasts, which swelled gently against the loose ties of her tunic. Matilda pushed back her hood and let long waves of soft brown hair fall down her back, and over her shoulder to caress skin which shone pale in the moonlight.

"Tell me, what have you learned about the child, Nicholas?" Matilda smiled encouragingly.

"I… we… we've spoken with people and are recording his arrival… and baptism." Brother Gregory shifted uneasily. "We talk of a pilgrim's trail."

"A pilgrim's trail?" Matilda repeated, her tone light. "What is there to see here... in this stricken town?"

"To see? The baby of course, the place of his birth… and as he develops, the cot he outgrows, his shawl, his small clothes." Brother Gregory, who had grown so confident with his talk, struggled to think what Romney and the child did have to offer, so uncomfortable was he under the gaze of this woman.

"What a bother, to make the road good across the Marsh and provide places for travellers to rest and eat." Matilda paused for a moment as if deep in thought, then continued, "And the townsfolk here, they think of fishing and nothing of welcoming travellers."

"They would welcome the money brought by the pilgrims," Brother Gregory replied.

"Everyone welcomes money," Matilda replied. "But we still have families living in the church, so where is the space for pilgrims to rest?" Her voice was low and hypnotic to the monk who was so inexperienced in the wiles of a woman. "I'm sure there is a better way and I'll help you think of it. In fact, it will be your very own plan!"

Matilda took a step closer, so he only had to reach out to touch the sweet flesh on display beneath the loose ties of her tunic. Did she tempt him? She believed she did and so great was her need to rid Romney of the child that she thought again of the wenches from the beachfront and the inns. How would they treat this monk who was finding himself as a man?

"Let me see you as I did a few nights back, your hood fallen back… but I saw more than that… here in my shed." Matilda put her arm up and gently pushed back his hood, allowing her fingers to brush across his face."

"Your shed?" he frowned, not knowing.

"Aye, it was my husband's and now it's mine until Oliver becomes a man. Hugh died… in the storm."

"I'm sorry." Brother Gregory remained lost amidst the confusion of having a woman so close.

Matilda knew the young monk was ambitious and her position within the town gave her more allure than the girl he had lost his virginity to just days before. When this moment was over, he would calculate what use she could be to him, Matilda was sure of it. For the moment she would satisfy his needs and take him under her control.

"It was the same storm that brought the baby to Romney," Matilda spoke softly. "The child came but Hugh died in the storm, leaving me a widow."

Helpless and lured by the soft tones of her voice and the curves of her flesh, Brother Gregory's voice was gruff, "I'm sorry for your loss."

Matilda bowed her head in acknowledgement of her grief, and he reached out awkwardly to pat her hand.

She took his hand in hers and again their eyes met. "I get a little lonely now..."

He could wait no longer and bent down to kiss her hard on the lips. Matilda, surprised by his lust, stepped back a little. "Gently, Brother Gregory, I am no whore from the beach-front. There's no rush..."

Chapter Sixteen
Agnes

Agnes stood beside the beach track, looking at the place where her old home had been. Most of it was gone, taken apart bit by bit, to be reused as building materials for the new home, or as fuel for the fire in Will's kitchen. The little that remained took on a new, humbler form as a shed for nets, fish knives and baskets.

Today her parents, Mary and John, were moving to their two-room home in St John's Road. The road ran between St John's Hospital and its burial ground, before reaching the old merchants' quays. All day, Agnes had been walking to the new cottage with arms full of bedding, clothes and kitchenware. At first it was with a spring in her step, eager to be a part of the next adventure in her parents' lives, but now she trudged, weary and aware of the baby pushing on her ribs. She slumped down on the shingle bank, but for once Agnes had her back to the sea and faced inland.

It was a fine day, mild with just a slight chill in the air. The sea rolled in, pulled on the shingle and coiled back again. It had no malice about it. The air carried a hint of seaweed and salt on the light breeze. Agnes found herself relaxed and content with her new life, while looking at the remains of her childhood home. Strangely the old pig shelter still stood. It was probably the only shack or shed which had remained untouched by the storm. The old sow had gone, butchered within a week of the storm, having kept Agnes warm and safe during the terrors of that night. The sow's meat then nurtured the family in another way. Her replacement had been living on her parents' burgage plot for the last three months. No doubt the old pig shelter would be dismantled soon, to be reused for a chicken house or a store.

Agnes closed her eyes for a moment... not for long... she needed to get back to prepare supper. This was the last meal they would eat as a family in Will and Agnes' home before her parents went to the new cottage for their first night. It was the baby that made her tired, so just a moment on the shingle... listening to the rhythm of the sea.

It had only been a few minutes, but she awoke with a start on hearing her brother's wife. "It's a new life for all of us, away from the beach." Joan sat down next to Agnes. "But we've all got fine homes in the town and the men have their boats back, or bits of boats put back together."

"Aye, and they are better homes, no distance from the boat and the beach." Agnes shifted on the shingle – it made an uncomfortable seat. "I can still hear the sea at night, rolling in and out. You must hear it too, Joan, now you've moved from the church."

"Aye, we couldn't hear the outside world from within those thick walls, not with all the snoring and grunting and babies whimpering."

Agnes' brother, Robert, with his wife and the two children had moved into their new home just a few weeks before. The whole family had worked together to finish the cottage and finally move the young family out of St Martin's. Then all the attention had been on the home next door and, at last, John and Mary were able to move out of their part of the room above the cobbler's shop. Only that morning, Mary had pulled down the curtain separating the room upstairs, giving Will and Agnes their bedroom back for themselves.

The young women stood, pulling tunics into place and taking one last look at the area where Agnes' home had been. As they turned to face the church, the two monks appeared from the direction of the town and followed the track towards St Nicholas. The younger one carried a sizeable bundle.

"They bother poor Cecily and her family every day," Joan said, the scowl on her face showing disapproval. "It's been two weeks since they came – what more can she offer them? The child is barely sitting, he needs his shawls and his linens and what he doesn't use, she'll want for the next one."

"She just wanted to be a mother," Agnes said, her thoughts on her own unborn child. "She just wanted a child to love, without all this fuss."

"The vicar has spoken with them, asked them to leave her alone," Joan informed her. "But she told me just this morning that they still want stories of the baby's life. There's some folk that will tell them anything, just to know their words are in that book they are making."

"They'll be back to Canterbury soon with tales of the child and sitting down to write his story on their fine vellum in the abbey, or wherever fine folk sit and write," Agnes said. "Cecily will have peace then."

"Aye, they will, and we can't complain. People will come and see the child. They'll stay in our inns and buy food from our shops." Joan reached out to give Agnes a friendly pat on the arm. "They'll even need their shoes repairing after all that walking."

"They will," Agnes grinned. "There's some folk who will have wished they stayed. Romney's fate is changing again and those who are left will become wealthy through the baby – if they are wise enough."

Yet she thought of the child she had given birth to in the pig shed and although she had grown to accept he was Cecily's son, she didn't like to think of him growing up to be spoiled. She worried about all the attention he would have if Romney became the focus of a pilgrims' trail and he at the very centre of it all. "Let's hope that the doctor and Cecily can bring him up to be like any other child in the town and not give him a sense of too much importance."

"Aye, they are sure to fill his head with sensible thoughts and set him up with a suitable trade. Perchance this will come to nothing. How many people will want to trudge across Romney Marsh to see a child and a motley collection of the items touched by him in his life?"

The two women had reached Romney High Street now and so they separated, Joan to her cottage in St John's Road, and Agnes to her home behind the cobbler's shop.

With John and Mary finally in their new home, Agnes and Will settled down in chairs by the fire. The sun was low in the sky, blazing orange light came through the back windows and into the kitchen. Agnes had some darning on her lap, but her hands were idle and she watched Will gazing into the fire. Did he have something on his mind, she wondered? He had been strangely quiet during supper time, and now, when they should be celebrating having the home to themselves, Will was reluctant to be drawn into any conversation.

"Do you think they are settled, that they have everything they need?" Agnes' thoughts strayed to her parents.

"If they don't, then your ma has Joan next door."

"Aye, of course they do." Agnes stood up, dropping the unfinished darning in a basket. "Do you want some ale or wine?"

"I'm fine."

What was it with Will this evening? He was usually so easy to talk with, so tender and thoughtful. Had he tired of her as a wife and now that her parents had gone, felt he had no need to make the effort? Agnes opened the back door and went to check that the chickens were secure for the night. She paused and stood to watch the sun setting. Streaks of red and orange had the sky ablaze as the fiery ball began to blend into the horizon, then, as it slumped out of sight, Agnes turned back to her husband.

"Those monks are bothering Cecily, so Joan said."

"Aye, so I hear."

Agnes didn't want to darn under the flickering light of a tallow candle. Apart from her wedding night, she'd always had her ma close by and now she felt a little lost. She'd not expected to feel like that, not with Will to share her life. Perhaps he would like to take her upstairs to their bed... to the room they had shared with her parents for several months. She bent down and kissed him lightly on the forehead.

"Shall we go up to bed?"

"Is that what you want?" Will asked, looking up at her, his face serious.

"Why not? It's not the baby, is it? Does it bother you?"

"It's not the baby." Will looked towards the fire, then turned back to his wife. "Did you want to marry me? Was there someone else you preferred?"

"Why ask that now?" Agnes' reply was sharp, sharper than she meant it to be.

"Sometimes I wonder... was it because of the storm? Because you needed a home?"

167

Agnes felt her husband was slipping away from her, that Will hadn't realised how much he had come to mean to her. She was fifteen years old, pregnant with her second child and unable to acknowledge her first-born. Of course, she had been scared to marry Will. Afraid that he would realise that she wasn't a virgin and worse than that – petrified that he would recognise the signs of recent childbirth on her young body.

But now, if she could make the choice again, Agnes would marry Will gladly. She had grown to love and admire him, yet she couldn't find a way to say those words to him. Weighed down by the guilt she carried, Agnes picked up her cloak and wrapped it around her shoulders.

"I'm going for a walk," she said. "I can't settle this evening."

At first Agnes thought to go to her mother and walked quickly past the priory and past baby Nicholas' home with the doctor and Cecily. What would Ma have to say about this? Her second night alone with her husband and already they were quarrelling. How could she explain to Ma that Will had asked if her thoughts were with another man? She couldn't... she couldn't speak to Ma about it. Agnes walked past the row of new cottages and onwards to the deserted estuary.

It was quiet at the river mouth. The tide was low and did not slap against the shingle ridge which had been swept there on the night of the storm. Sea birds had settled for the night and didn't mock or scream at her as they did in the daytime. Agnes wondered about the people who lived on the other side of this expanse of thick, oozing river-mud. Did they come to gaze at it and had the absence of the river led to great changes in their own lives?

She wanted to talk to Will about it, about those people who lived nearby in Lydd and Midley, but whose lives they never touched, so impossible it was to journey over the expanse of riverbed. She wondered about Rye, with its riches in the form of three rivers, and about Appledore – how did that place survive without the Rother? But Will wasn't there. He was distant in his manner and tonight she was without the companion who had come to mean so much to her.

Agnes turned away from the abandoned estuary. If she couldn't share her thoughts, she didn't want to remain there. Instead of going back through the town, she walked along the beach track without any thought in her head as to where she might end up.

While Agnes walked, she retraced her experiences during the night of the storm. Past the site of her home which she had fled from as it fell, and the pig-shelter in which she had given birth. Then she plodded alongside the church, in which her newborn had been left to God's mercy. Finally, to where the story had begun – the repair sheds beside the beach in which she had given in to the desire she felt for Hugh Alcock.

Agnes had avoided this area since the night of the storm, not wanting to meet Matilda or to see the place where it had been proved that Hugh was not unvanquishable. But now she felt compelled to go closer to the spot where her first-born had been conceived – to allow the feelings of guilt to gnaw at her stomach and to repent the loss of her innocence. The sky was black now; the last of the sun's rays were no longer able to touch the night sky and the moon, a fraction of its full self, was hidden behind a meandering cloud.

The Alcocks' boat repair shed was huge, standing on the shingle ridge above the beach, with its wooden planked walls and reed-thatched roof it towered above Agnes. The very size of it was menacing: its great bulk upright once more and stronger than ever since the recent repairs. Sending shingle scattering, she half crawled up the bank and stood by the opening, unable to see inside without the light from the moon. Slowly, her body tense with nerves, Agnes stepped towards the entrance and into the shed.

Gradually, the outline of a boat took shape and stacks of timber showed themselves within the shadows. Then the piles of netting and rope formed on the floor or hung from hooks on the walls. Agnes stood, inhaling the once familiar smell of damp wood and the sickly-sweet smell of iron nails and fixing plates.

Suddenly, all her senses were alert to the sounds of the night. Footsteps... footsteps on the shingle and coming closer. Agnes stepped back so she was flat against the wall, a tangle of nets hanging to her side, stiff with salt and smelling of the sea. Steadily the steps came closer, and without hesitation a hooded man entered the shed, taking several steps inside before he too stopped and stood listening.

Agnes tried to steady her breathing, a hand against her heart which thudded uncomfortably. She shrank further back against the wall when, to her relief, the man turned as if to leave… but no, he stood at the doorway, gazing out as if waiting for someone. Agnes studied the figure, trying to recognise… there was something familiar… of course – the monk, Brother Gregory.

And then, before her thoughts could form any reasonable explanation as to why the monk was there and who he might be waiting for, there came a lighter, quicker footstep. An exchange of whispers aroused Agnes' curiosity further and, as the cloud slipped away from the half-moon, silver light-beams showed the chestnut hair and slight figure of the widow, Matilda.

There was no opportunity for Agnes to ponder over the strangeness of this apparently planned meeting for the reason was immediately clear. The monk, tossing back his hood, clasped her around the waist and kissed Matilda before even a word had been exchanged between the two of them. Then, as she gasped her pleasure, his fingers were on the ties of her tunic and his lips were on the smooth skin of her breasts.

"Not yet, Brother," Matilda's words were soft as she gently pushed him away.

This was no dismissal – Agnes was sure of it. The rejection was just part of the act.

"Tell me about your plans… what did Brother Nicholas have to say? Did you tell it as if it were his very own idea?"

"Aye." The monk's hands were on Matilda's hips, her buttocks…. "Aye, the child should be amongst holy people. He sees the sense in it."

Matilda gasped her pleasure and wound her arms around Brother Gregory's neck, kissing him at length. Pausing, she shook off her hood and let it fall from her shoulders.

"And… he will act on it?" Matilda whispered.

"There is no doubt," the monk confirmed.

"Then you can fulfil your desires tonight, Brother." Matilda's voice was low but riddled with meaning as she took his hand and led him further into the darkest shadows of the shed.

Silently, Agnes slumped to the floor. To move from her hiding place to the open doorway would put her in the light of the moon, which was weak but, if noticed, she was sure to be recognised. So, she became the unwilling audience to their lusty murmurings and animal-groans as Brother Gregory's vows of chastity were forsaken. She wasn't surprised at the monk's full-blooded desire for a woman – he had cast his eyes on her own plump curves. But his choice of woman surprised Agnes. Had he chosen her, or was it she who had lured him to taste her flesh?

Once more a cloud covered the moon and Agnes sighed her relief, slowly standing to her full height. Then swiftly, without looking back into the shed, she sped out of the doorway, scattering shingle but confident that she would not be recognised.

Desperate to be in the circle of Will's arms and to feel secure in his love, yet nervous of how to speak of her devotion to him, Agnes opened the back door. The fire had burned low, and she climbed the wooden steps to their room. By the light of the candle, she could see the outline of her husband's body in the bed. He didn't stir, yet she sensed that he was awake. Agnes removed her stockings and tunic, then freed her hair from its coif before slipping into the bed.

"Will?" Agnes put her hand on his back which was turned towards her. "Will, I'm sorry. I should have stayed at home."

Will rolled onto his back, "I don't want to just be your anchor."

"You're not," Agnes whispered, stretching her arm across his chest.

"Did we marry too young?"

"Perchance we did, I felt too young," Agnes acknowledged part of her fears. "I liked you very much, but now I love you and am proud of you. Proud to hear your stories about your search for the Rother." Agnes moved closer, her curves moulding around his outstretched body. "I love you, William."

Will turned his head and kissed Agnes lightly on the forehead, then moving to face her, he wrapped an arm around her. She relaxed, her head against his chest, listening to his heartbeat.

After a few minutes, thoughts of the evening began to disturb her peace. What was it that Matilda had asked of Brother Gregory? What was it that he had done to please her so much? Perhaps Will could make some sense of it.

"I saw something strange tonight," Agnes whispered. She waited for his murmured response, but there was nothing, just the steady rise and fall of his chest, then a slight snore... Will was asleep.

Chapter Seventeen
Cecily

Nicholas rolled across the floor to his mother and a wide toothless smile spread across his round face. Cecily sat down on the rug, shifted into a comfortable position, and held out her arms to scoop him up. Her eyes shone with love, yet fear weighed heavily upon her. She was five months' pregnant, but that was of no concern. Cecily had been favoured with an easy pregnancy: her skin was clear and her brown hair lustrous. She had suffered only a little nausea and, when tired, it suited her to sleep when Nicholas had his nap.

Her worry was that, as Nicholas' adopted mother, his belonging to her was fragile. Not in the eyes of the town. Here he was accepted as her child to raise as she wished, although he did attract more attention than other babies, due to his unusual entrance into the world. The statue commemorating his arrival troubled Cecily and her husband, who worried about how a child honoured in this way could grow up as an equal to the others of his age. But it was the return of the travelling monk, along with his companion, which led to these feelings of unease about the child. It seemed they had some unspoken claim on Nicholas, and Cecily feared the power of the church. Not their own church here in Romney – it was Canterbury she feared.

Nicholas climbed onto his mother's lap, and she put a cup of creamy milk to his soft lips. His eyelids drooped while she allowed him small sips and, as the cup emptied, he lay his head against her breast and fell into a deep sleep. Cecily turned and lifted him into his basket and, as she covered him with a soft blanket, there was a rap at the door. Her heart clenched and mouth went dry as, wearily, she stood and walked to the door.

"Greetings, Cecily, my dearling." It was a scrawny fellow whom Cecily recognised as being a Romney man. A person who had no particular trade but went from place to place within the town earning a penny here and there for odd jobs.

Cecily forced her face into some form of half-smile but couldn't even bring herself to return his greeting. She stood, waiting to see what he wanted.

"How fares young Nicholas?" His tone was over-friendly, as if he were open to confidences. "Keeps you busy, I'll be bound. And now there's these monks wanting to hear everything about him. It was a lucky day when you choose to look after the baby, what with him being so special."

"He's just like any other child," Cecily tried to discourage any further talk about her beloved son.

"Now, Cecily, my joy, there's these monks come to learn all about the baby and people are to come visiting Romney, so they say."

"So they say," Cecily repeated. "But I'll not have them bothering him."

"Of course not, no need to distress the boy." Pleasing words dripped like honey from his lips, and his mouth twisted in a smile. "So, if you have a few little things of interest – an old shift, a swaddling cloth, a feeding spoon – then the pilgrims needn't bother you when they are wanting to see these small things that have been a part of his life."

"Did the monks send you?" Cecily knew the answer – this desperate man was not the first who had thought of a way to make a penny or two through her son.

"The monks? Aye, they did." His stance was uneasy, his eyes flickering from side to side as he sucked on the blackened stumps of his teeth.

"You can tell them that I've already given all I can." Cecily's voice grew stronger as her confidence grew. "My baby needs his clothes and his linens and his blankets, so farewell to you."

She closed the door, and when her husband, Luke, returned later that day, he was surprised to find it barred. Cecily opened the door, tear-stained and exhausted by the demands of an unusually fretful baby. A loaf of burned bread was in the chicken coop, and the fire needed wood.

"Go to bed for a while," Luke advised.

He didn't need to ask what was bothering his wife. In the last two weeks, since the arrival of the monks, she had been increasingly uneasy and not without cause. Every patient he saw, no matter how sickly they were, wanted to speak about his adopted son and the pilgrims who would come to visit him. For Cecily, every time she left the house, she was hunted down by either the monks or the poor and desperate of the town, wanting to hear about baby Nicholas... wanting something of his.

As both her husband and her doctor, Luke was concerned for Cecily. For five long years, she had longed for a child of her own. As the months passed and new babies were born to friends and family, her spirits had slumped and she had despaired of ever being a mother. Then Nicholas had come into their lives and, as his mother, Cecily was brighter and more interested in life. Now she was fast becoming withdrawn, reluctant to leave the house and relying on other people to do her daily shopping.

"Go and have a rest," Luke repeated.

"I'll just…," Cecily reached for a clean cloth in which to swaddle Nicholas.

"I'll do that," he took it from her hand. "You look exhausted."

When Cecily woke, Luke poured her a cup of wine and put some spiced biscuits on a dish.

"Thank you," Cecily smiled at him. "I feel much better now."

"I see the chickens are feasting on today's bread," Luke grinned back. "Let's all walk to the High Street and see if there is any left in the shops. Is there anything else we need?"

"Aye, some fish from the beach and oats, beans… honey. I'll fetch the basket.

The walk to the town and then the beachfront was uneventful. Cecily was warmed by the afternoon sunshine and felt her body relax. From his position, perched on his mother's hip, Nicholas looked around, curious about the world. It was quiet in the town, and those people they met demanded nothing of them.

They returned to the cottage, and Cecily set Nicholas down on the rug. "I'll make a start on supper," she said.

"I just need to check on Ann Butcher," Luke replied. "I'm concerned about her breathing and said I would call by this afternoon."

"Give her my best wishes," Cecily replied. Her face was now free from the signs of strain.

It was not long after, as Cecily had put the vegetables in a pan over the fire, but had not yet prepared the fish, when there was a loud rap at the door.

"Now, who can that be at this time of day?" she smiled down at Nicholas, who was chewing the corner of the rug, and went to the door.

On opening the door, her smile fell, and all her fears returned. It was Brother Nicholas, his eyes lowered, and a smile fixed on his slim face. Cecily thought, and not for the first time, that he looked a little sly, as if his thoughts were less about serving God and more about adding to his own list of achievements. Standing behind him, blue eyes shining and a wide smile showing good white teeth, was Brother Gregory.

"Greetings to you! There he is..." Brother Nicholas stepped in and looked down at baby Nicholas. It was a smile which did not reach his eyes.

Cecily scooped up her son, holding him tight against her chest.

"May we sit down? A cup of wine perchance, for we have news to please you." Brother Nicholas led the way to the table and settled down on the bench.

"Wine... aye." Cecily, keeping one arm wrapped around the baby, took two cups from a shelf and poured wine. Reluctantly, she sat, her son perched on her lap, and looked at the monks in expectation.

"What a tale to tell the people of Canterbury, Winchester, London and beyond," Brother Nicholas began. "The storm and the newborn found in the church tower. I wonder what distance the news has already spread. There is not a soul in Canterbury who has not been to hear of the child."

"He is a baby, with all the needs of a baby, and that comes first." Cecily's grip on Nicholas tightened.

"And a fine job you are doing," Brother Gregory tried to smooth the way.

"We have been talking of a pilgrims' way, for there will be those who want to see the child and it cannot be denied," Brother Nicholas continued. "But to travel

178

across this Marsh... there is no clear access from the west and from both the north and east, it is no easy feat."

"The mists... the water-filled ditches... Aye, mayhap many will not want to bother," Cecily's spirits rose as she spoke.

The monks were not done with her son. Brother Nicholas had gained recognition for his story-telling skills and gloried at the attention he had received from the people of Canterbury. Nothing had given him more pride than seeing his curling letters spreading in brown ink across the finest vellum. The story of the child sent by God – told in the monk's own words – what could be more glorious? Since being back in Romney, he had spent hours drawing a likeness of the statue, secretly determined that a Canterbury stonemason would be instructed to create an exact copy to stand in the cathedral grounds.

Brother Gregory had relished the freedom this journey to Romney had provided for him. Enclosed within the abbey walls, since the time a soft golden fluff had formed on his upper lip, he was eager to learn about life beyond St Augustine's. His vows of chastity were long forgotten – the wenches of Romney pleased him very well. But it was the widow, Matilda, who acknowledged his ambitions and suggested a way in which the child, Nicholas, could be honoured as befitted his birthright.

"We have a new plan, new opportunities for you," Brother Nicholas offered a thin-lipped smile. "This child will come to Canterbury, to be brought up within the city walls, and raised in the way God ordains through the archbishop and the abbot. Brother Gregory and I will be leaving Romney within days to share the good news in Canterbury."

179

"But he's my son... my child." Cecily stammered, her face drained of all colour, and a feeling of nausea rising in her throat. "He lives here with me and his father. Here in Romney."

"He is a child sent by God for the people of Romney, and Canterbury will see that Romney is not forgotten." Brother Nicholas could only state the facts as he saw them. He was unused to the emotions displayed by women. "We'll find you a house, a good stone house, within the cathedral grounds and you may come with the child if you wish. You can care for him as you do now, and your own children will be as brothers and sisters to him."

"He is my own child!" Cecily cried out in desperation. "That is how I… that is how we see him."

"Of course you love him, we see that," Brother Gregory spoke now. "You will hold him and nurture him and watch him grow. You will be as Mary was to Jesus. But as he grows, he must be under the supervision of holy men, and you can be honoured to be a part of his life."

Cecily did not reply. Tears rolled down her face. She knew that she had no power over the might of the Church. They would have to leave Romney as soon as the monks had gone. Where would they go? How far could she travel, with a baby in her belly and one on her hip? She must appear resigned to her fate, lest they should snatch the child from her now and carry him away to Canterbury immediately.

"I daresay I'll become used to it," Cecily forced the words out. "I expect it is a fine place. How grand the cathedral must be compared to our own humble places of worship."

"You will be well rewarded for your care of Nicholas and be respected within the city" Brother Nicholas told her.

"My husband will be pleased, no doubt," Cecily used all her wiles to convince the monks. "He will gain more recognition for his work as a doctor in Canterbury and will thrive amongst the more educated people."

What little they knew of Cecily. Her life in Romney was secure, with her husband, family and friends embracing her in their love. The baby had brought a happiness she had feared would never be achieved and now she felt a new life stirring within her. She had no need for fine materials, exotic foods or prestigious company. That was not Cecily's way, and it was not the life she wanted for her children.

"You're going within a few days, to arrange things in Canterbury?" Cecily's voice was steady, and she looked Brother Nicholas in the eye.

"Aye, and what a reception we'll have. All of Canterbury will be eager for our news!" He could see it now: look-outs on the city walls, noting their arrival, going ahead to give tidings. An audience with the archbishop and abbot, both eager to hear tales of the child. Then the announcement – the boy, Nicholas, would be coming to Canterbury!

"God speed. Safe journey." Cecily opened the front door for the monks.

"God bless you," Brother Nicholas spoke with all the sincerity he could muster.

Cecily felt like giving up, collapsing upon the floor for Luke to find her, with Nicholas clasped to her breast and tears running down both their faces. But from somewhere within she found strength and a knowledge of what must be done. There was no reason for it, and Cecily was not prone to seeking help from people who claimed to have special powers, but now she knew to whom she must turn. If she had paused to reason with herself, or if Luke had been at home, then she would have thought of no way in which the old woman in the church could have soothed her. But Cecily did not pause to reflect. Instead, she gathered Nicholas to her, and wrapped him in a shawl, then left by the back door to find Beatrice, the dear friend who had been Nicholas' wet-nurse for those first months of his life.

It was late afternoon, and the streets of Romney were quiet. Nicholas was left on Beatrice's lap and Cecily, secure in the knowledge her son was safe, scurried to the church. Her hood was low over her forehead and her eyes looked to the ground. She was determined to encourage no talk with the few who passed by. Within minutes, she was approaching the east end of St Nicholas Church.

"I had a sense you'd be along soon," Gundred's voice was low, forcing Cecily to stand close to the window of the anchorhold. "There are storm clouds brewing, and I know you have fear in your heart. You've done the right thing coming to see old Gundred."

"How did you know? They've only just been," Cecily replied in wonder. "The monks, I mean."

"Oh aye, there's one of them sly and with so much pride you'd think he gave birth to the child himself!" Gundred cackled at her little joke. "And the other… he's got a weakness for the flesh of a woman. More than is decent for any monk."

"How do you know?"

"Those young women, and those not so young, they come along here, talking to old Gundred and I feel they say one thing and think of another. I know things and sometimes I know things those foolish women don't see for themselves." Gundred paused and shuffled closer to the bars. "I told you that you'd hold your own child one day, didn't I tell you?"

"Aye, you did," Cecily muttered, sure that the gift of the child was to be snatched away from her.

"So, you can trust me, because I said you would have what was most precious to you."

"I can trust you," Cecily confirmed.

"And I'm talking about your son, that one they say was a gift from our Lord. He's your child, and you're going to keep him, along with your baby girl that's growing strong within you."

"A girl?" Cecily smiled at the old woman and the strain fell from her face.

"Aye, a girl." Gundred paused and reflected for a moment before continuing. "Now, I see you've only brought yourself and don't you worry about that. They look after Old Gundred, especially that Matilda, her who's up to no good, but that's a different matter. I'm not in need of feeding and I have warm feelings for you, Cecily. I can help you."

"I need your wise words," Cecily began. "They want to take Nicholas to Canterbury. They say that I'll go too and care for him as a mother should. What do I want with being in Canterbury? I fear that if I refuse, they'll take him anyway. If I went, then they would slowly make him theirs. The Church has such power."

"The Church does have power," Gundred agreed. "More than sits comfortably with me."

"I fear that we'll have to…" Cecily dare not voice the words.

"Nay, child, you have no need to run. And it doesn't come easy for you, I see that. You are wanting to ask your husband to leave, but him a doctor… he is needed here in Romney..." Gundred voiced Cecily's worries.

"Aye, and we can't wait… they leave for Canterbury within days and when they return, it will be to take my baby."

"Let me think. I sense I can help you, but all this talk… it's bothering the messages." Gundred retreated within the cell and all that could be heard was a low muttering. It rose and fell, as if the old hag were conversing with herself until, after several minutes, she returned to the barred window. "The person to help you is close at hand. Don't run, Cecily. It wouldn't do you, nor the baby, any good."

"There is someone who can help me?" Cecily whispered. "But not even Lord Craythorne is more powerful than the Church."

"Nay, it's not Lord Craythorne, nor your brother, the vicar. You'll have to trust me now, Cecily…" Gundred paused, and Cecily stood, barely breathing, not wanting to miss the name when it was uttered from within the cell. "…Agnes, young Agnes who was from the beach-front and now married to Will Cobbler. She's the one to help and she may be afraid to do so, but she can help you and your family."

Chapter Eighteen
Agnes

When the rap came at the back door, Agnes could only think that it must be Mary, although the hour was still early. Will had only just gone into the shop, and surely Mary had her chores to complete. Anyway, her mother would have knocked and stepped in, and the door remained closed. So, with a mild curiosity, Agnes opened the back door and, to her surprise, Cecily was standing there.

She had been in the shop once or twice, with Nicholas bound to her body in a carrying sling. And, of course, Cecily passed her in church or in the town and the two women would smile and nod, but Cecily had never called on her. There was no reason for her to do so. There was ten years' difference in their ages, and Cecily had been a married woman for as long as Agnes could recall. Cecily was a woman, while Agnes little more than a girl.

For a moment Agnes froze, her throat tight and the colour draining from her face. There was Cecily, at her doorway, with a slight frown on her face, noting Agnes' distress.

"Are you unwell?" Cecily queried. "The baby?"

"Aye… I become a little giddy sometimes, but it passes." Agnes held the door wide open. "Come in. Lovely to see your little mite. Greetings, Nicholas."

How he had grown, his limbs now plump and cheeks rounded. His hair, which had been dark at birth, was golden and his eyes were a clear blue. And, as she smiled at her son by birth, he smiled back at her for the first time – a dribbly, toothless smile.

"He's beautiful," Agnes spoke with awe.

"Aye, he's a fine baby," Cecily smiled.

Her face shows strain. This isn't how it has been over the last few months. Then Agnes recalled the unveiling of the statue and how, when she had searched the crowds for Cecily and Luke, she had noted the look of discomfort on the woman's face. And how Cecily had stood, with her arms wrapped protectively around her baby and them both within the doctor's arms. *There is trouble and it has something to do with Nicholas, but what brings them to my door?*

"I've barely slept all night," Cecily began. "I can't make any sense of it, of how you can help me… and you'll think me foolish, but I was upset, so I went to speak with Gundred…."

"You're not foolish," Agnes soothed. "She hears things and sometimes she just knows. If you are in trouble, then there's no harm in finding out what she has to say."

"It made no sense at all."

Yet it did. Agnes knew that. Whatever Gundred had hinted at or told, it would make perfect sense to Cecily – if Agnes had the courage to tell.

"You are being bothered by those monks," Agnes started the story, prompting Cecily to say more. "You are worried for Nicholas, that he will not grow up as a boy should but will be filled with self-importance."

"Aye," Cecily looked surprised that the younger woman could voice her thoughts so clearly. "But it's more – they came to me yesterday… They came and said that he is to be taken to Canterbury."

"Canterbury!" Agnes was stunned. This was not how it was meant to be when Cecily took the baby as

186

her own. She reached out and stroked the fair skin of his arm and then his cheek. "Nay, they can't... he's yours...."

"But they can. They say that I am to go with him... that I'll be... that I'll be as a mother to him."

"What right do they have to say what you are to do?" Agnes' voice was high, and she saw Nicholas' face crumple. "Oh, little sweeting, I'm sorry. Silly me, getting cross."

Cecily lifted the baby up high. "*Woooo*, up you go, baby," she sang, and peace was restored.

"They plan to take him to Canterbury?" Agnes was careful to keep her tone even. "To see the archbishop? And you are to go with him?"

"If only it were that. They say that we are to live in the city, that they'll prepare a house for us and Nicholas is to be brought up under the eyes of the archbishop and the abbot. I'll lose him, Agnes. You can see that. They have such power and even if I am with him, he will be lost to me."

Agnes frowned as memories came back to her: The planned meeting within the shed, Matilda's questions and her joy at Brother Gregory's response. What was it that Matilda had asked of the young monk? Was it if Brother Nicholas had agreed with his plans? That was it – and Brother Gregory had said the baby was to be amongst holy people. Matilda had asked if Brother Nicholas believed it was his very own idea, but it wasn't his nor Brother Gregory's idea. It was Matilda's plan. For some reason, she had thought up an arrangement to remove Nicholas from New Romney.

"I went to see Gundred," Cecily continued. "I told her. But it was as if she already knew. She said you could help me, but I don't see how... I can't imagine what you could do."

"It's strange as I've not seen Gundred in weeks," Agnes began. She spoke slowly, not wanting to tell too much... careful of holding her secret close. "I did see something, just a few days ago. It was that monk, the young one and he was talking in private with someone. I could make no sense of what I heard, but now I am sure it was about your baby. I need to think about what to do and if I can use my knowledge to stop the monks from taking Nicholas."

"It wasn't foolish then? Gundred knew... somehow she knew that you could help." Cecily looked at Agnes with wonder. "You saw Brother Gregory and he was speaking of Nicholas?"

"I saw him, but he didn't speak of Nicholas by name. The monk didn't know that I was there, but what I saw made me uneasy."

"What can be done?" Cecily's desperation showed in her face. There was an eagerness for Agnes to explain.

Agnes was thinking, not wanting to make a mistake and it was a moment before she spoke again. "I've got to make sense of this, Cecily. It was only a few nights ago, but I need to think about what I saw and if anything can be done about it. Nicholas has to be saved and if I rush at this, mistakes may be made. Give me today... not even a day... I'll come to see you this afternoon. Let's not speak of this to anyone. There are people who cannot be trusted, and not just the monks."

"Aye, I'll wait for you Agnes, and if you can help... well, I'd be more grateful that you can imagine."

The need to save her son enveloped Agnes. She plunged her hands into the washtub, hoping that the rhythm and moving water would bring order to her thoughts. If she were to claim Nicholas as her own, the town would rise in fury against her. The tempest would be as great as any storm which had hit the town in the last few years. The townsfolk of Romney had taken Nicholas to their hearts, believing his presence was a gift to ease their suffering. How low would their spirits slump if they learned the truth?

But if it were the only way to save him from the monks, she owed him that... Now Agnes squeezed water from the clothes, and the scene in the repair shed ran through her mind. It was Matilda who wanted rid of Nicholas – but why? Was it that she suspected he was Hugh's child or was it that she wanted no other boy to usurp her own son?

The answers did not come to Agnes and, with the washing laid out to dry behind the house, she stepped out of the back gate and into St Martin's churchyard. She hurried along as best she could, the growing child within her causing her body to sway. In the High Street, she hurriedly bought a pie from a market stall and made her way to the east end of St Nicholas Church.

"Cecily's been to see you then." These were Gundred's first words as her beady eyes spotted Agnes.

"Aye, she has." Agnes said, not wanting to tell, but waiting to see what the old hag had to say about it.

"She's upset, Cecily is," Gundred replied, then leaning forwards, so her face was pressed upon the bars, she continued, "What's that you have there, Agnes? It's hungry work all this praying for that scoundrel. Still, he's on his way to heaven – it's what I tell his wife."

"A meat pie." Agnes offered the food and a gnarled hand slipped out from between the bars to snatch at it.

Gundred retreated to savour the pie.

"Does the praying help?" Agnes asked. "Is his journey swifter than it would have been?"

189

"That's what I'm saying, and God knows Hugh Alcock needs all the help he can receive. And, if it helps his wife, she who's up to no good, then we are both happy. I'm kept nice and cosy here and she knows she's done her duty to him, good and proper."

"Up to no good?" Agnes was curious as to what Gundred knew.

"Nay, you won't catch me telling tales, young Agnes. What I know stays here with me and goes no further… you wouldn't want me betraying your secrets, would you?"

"Cecily's frightened. They want to take the baby to Canterbury." Agnes looked at the ground and kicked at the loose stones.

"Aye, and we wouldn't want that. *You* wouldn't want that." Gundred found some pie stuck between her teeth and picked it out with her long fingernails. "And you wouldn't want Cecily and the doctor taking that poor child and running off before the monks return, would you, Agnes?"

Agnes said nothing. She hadn't thought of that, but she could see, if she were Cecily, then she would do anything to protect her child. Agnes herself had already taken chances to protect her newborn son from a difficult life and enabled him to live within a loving family. Now she had to use her wits to save Nicholas from being under the control of the Church.

"What should I do?" Agnes asked.

"Think Agnes, think of what you've seen and what you know. Cecily must keep the child who has become hers. You know that – I see it in your eyes. There's someone here in Romney who wants to make trouble for you – beware of that person. And there's someone who is being led into plots and schemes to remove Nicholas from the town.

"Take care Agnes, for the person who strives to harm you is more desperate than you may believe. The monk is nothing but a playing piece, moved around at the will of the person who holds power over him.

"Above all, protect Cecily and the baby, and all will be well for you. Do not sacrifice Cecily for your own gain. She is good, and the good must come through this unharmed."

"I can't see how... what can be done?" Agnes could tell no more help would come from Gundred. "I'll go and think now, Gundred. Somewhere quiet where I won't be bothered by folk." She looked the old woman in the eye, "Thank you, I'll pass by soon... tomorrow, bring you some food and pass on the news."

"Aye, well only if you have time for an old woman..." Gundred's reply came as Agnes turned away.

Agnes set off towards the abandoned estuary. Determined not to be drawn into any talk as she passed the fishing families, she looked neither left nor right. She passed the shallow harbour, which the newly-formed fishing fleet called home. Then, turning away from the coast, she walked by the shingle bank which had been formed on the night of the storm.

Before long, Agnes was sitting on some rough grass, gazing out over the wide mudflats. Already the warmer weather had tempted seed-heads to fertilise in the rich mud and tiny sprigs of green showed where once the tide would have swept in and out. The huge skeleton-like wooden structures, against which the merchants' ships would have moored, were gone. In fact, two of these mighty beams made a strong frame for her parents' new cottage, and it was the same in most of the new homes in St John's Road. They had no use as relics of a bygone age, stuck in the mud of a former riverbank.

It was peaceful watching wading birds probing the mud, while gulls swooped and squealed above. The air was filled with the persistent dull roar of the sea, the high tide was throwing shingle upon the bank, then dragging it off. The air was mild, scented with the tang of salt and seaweed. Agnes' mind emptied of its tangled thoughts, her baby shifted within her, and she began to feel at peace.

It became clear that although Matilda had provoked the decision to remove Nicholas to Canterbury, the arrangement was now in the hands of the monks. There was nothing Agnes could do to persuade Matilda to stop this plan which was causing such distress to Cecily. It was Brother Nicholas who would make the final decisions which were to affect the lives of these good people.

Agnes would find Cecily and tell her she would speak with Brother Gregory. She would say no more than that she, Agnes, knew something. Gundred was right to say she had seen things, which meant there was hope that the young monk could be persuaded to rethink his schemes. There must be a way of giving Cecily some peace, but without revealing her secrets. This much was clear in her mind, and so Agnes walked a little further inland along the former riverbank, before turning into St John's Road, then walking to the far end where Cecily's cottage could be found.

It seemed as if Cecily had aged ten years in the two weeks since the monks had come to Romney. Agnes looked at the dark rings under her eyes, the lines around her mouth, and hoped that this ordeal would soon come to an end. Cecily smiled weakly and held the door open, her eyes hardly daring to show hope.

"I've been to see Gundred. She didn't say what must be done," Agnes began. "It's as if she knows things but means for me to think it through for myself."

"What did she say?" Cecily poured Agnes a mug of ale and pushed it across the table.

"She says that the monk, Brother Gregory, is being controlled by someone else. It wasn't his plan, nor Brother Nicholas', but now they think of it as their own." Agnes sat down on the bench, but her eyes were roaming around the room. "Where's Nicholas?"

"He's sleeping in his basket by my bed." Cecily smiled and continued, "Poor baby, he has no idea of what's happening all around him. Who within Romney would want him taken away, do you know?"

"I believe I do," Agnes replied, wary of sharing her knowledge, but knowing that she had to give Cecily something to grasp onto. "I couldn't settle… it was just a few days ago, and I went for a walk, along the beach track and towards the repair sheds. I had a peep inside the Alcock shed, just wondering what they were working on and not expecting anyone else to be about. The monk came along… the young one. I stepped back into the shed, not wanting him to see me, and then *she* came along… It was Matilda Alcock and it seemed as if they had planned to meet."

"To meet?" Cecily questioned. "She's been widowed these past six months, but he's a monk."

"Aye, you could tell what was on his mind… what was on both of their minds. But first – now this is what is important, Cecily – she asked him about his plans, and he said the child would be amongst holy people." Agnes took a sip of her ale and looked Cecily directly in the eye, "It was Nicholas she spoke of. It had to be."

"But what does Nicholas mean to Matilda?" Cecily asked. "I can't make any sense of it."

"I thought nothing of it at the time, but she was pleased with him and showed it…."

"Nay! With a monk?" Cecily's eyes widened. "His vows?"

"Brother Gregory is a man first and monk second," Agnes replied. "He's had an eye for the women since arriving in Romney."

"And Gundred knew of this?" Cecily questioned.

"I told her nothing of it, but she seems to know. Mayhap she reads the guilt in Matilda's eyes, or she watches the monks in the church and hears things she shouldn't. Gundred seems to have the gift of knowing."

"And she thinks you can shame Matilda into stopping the monks?"

"Nay, not Matilda, I feel that she won't change her mind. It's Brother Gregory who can be forced to change his. There's something else, Cecily, something it would do you no good to know, but I can use it to force him to see reason. At least I pray that I can."

"Don't tell me then, if it is best I don't know… but perchance one day you'll be able to. All I can do is pray you can help me."

"I'll do my best, Cecily. Nicholas *must* stay in Romney. I have to find Brother Gregory and make him agree that the baby can stay in his home. And if pilgrims come and bother us, then we will thank God they come to see him at Romney and not Canterbury."

"Aye, I shall not complain about the pilgrims if we can remain at home."

"I'm sure you will!" Agnes gave a brief grin. She stood and stepped towards the door. "I'll seek out Brother Gregory and hope he sees reason."

Agnes sank into the hay mattress, exhausted and frustrated. The baby was active, as was Agnes' mind. How late had she been – an hour or two? It hardly mattered how much distance the monks had covered before she realised they had gone. It was done now, and she must wait for their return, although her task would be all the harder when they came with their plans set in place. Canterbury would be awaiting the child.

"Is it the baby? Does he make you uncomfortable?" Will asked, reaching out to rub her back.

"Aye, she's making me tired today," Agnes smiled at the well-worn joke over the sex of the child.

That night was a restless one as Agnes agonised over time lost. *Did I waste time speaking with Gundred, or pausing to reflect at the river mouth? Should I have spoken to Cecily before searching out the monks? All these slowed me down, and if I had missed just one of them, I could have seen Brother Gregory before he left.* But in her heart, Agnes knew she had to take her time in order to make the right choice.

Morning came at last, with the sun pouring warm light across the bed. She had slept little, and was five months' pregnant, but Agnes was young and if her head ached a little and her skin was dull, she would soon recover. She swung her legs out of the bed and pulled on her woollen tunic before climbing down the ladder from the bedroom to the kitchen, then going out to the privy.

Chapter Nineteen
The Monks
May 1288

The abbot turned the last page of vellum and nodded his appreciation. Then he looked up from the book laid out before him. Behind him a fire blazed. In May the rooms within the thick stone walls of the abbey were still cold. Before him Brothers Nicholas and Gregory stood, their heads bowed a little and eyes lowered.

"Very fine. This is a work of art," the abbot summarised. "You have captured the progress of the child's life. He is shown as both himself – a baby – and as a gift from our Lord within the community of Romney. Through your words I feel that I know this child and his family."

Brothers Nicholas and Gregory nodded slightly as they acknowledged the praise.

"The people of Romney have erected a statue to honour yourself, and the child they named after you," the abbot addressed Brother Nicholas. "You tell this without pride. You tell it well."

Brother Nicholas eyed the abbot through narrowed slits.

"You gathered items from his life and you, Brother Gregory, have recorded an inventory of these. The people of Romney trusted you to do right by the child and gave you these small things."

"Aye, they were pleased to be a part of celebrating the coming of the child," Brother Gregory replied, with no hint of a gleam in his eye or a smile on his lips.

"Now the child, Nicholas, is to come here, to Canterbury," the abbot concluded. "He will be very welcome. People will come to see him and to learn of his life and he will need to be protected, lest he becomes proud."

"Aye, his mother is a plain and sensible woman. She will see that he remains steady," Brother Nicholas spoke without emotion.

"You have done well and shown great commitment to Canterbury. Brother Nicholas – will you remain here once the child has come, or do you plan to continue travelling and writing of your experiences?"

"If you would allow me, then I will stay to watch the child grow," Brother Nicholas replied. "And, if I may be the one to record his life, it would be an honour. The greatest honour."

The monks stood in silence for several minutes, while the abbot looked back through the book, pausing to examine some of the illustrations.

"This will please the archbishop," the abbot said as he closed the book and carefully laid it in a wooden box. "You must leave without delay to fetch the child. His family will have prepared for this, and their home here is almost complete. God bless you both." He stood and turned away from them. They were dismissed.

The monks walked in silence down the stone corridor from the chapter house, through the cloisters and towards the workshops. They were both deep in thought, emotions running high, yet carefully showing nothing of this in their faces or manners. It was only when they entered the workshop and saw it was empty, that Brother Gregory spoke freely.

"We are to leave for Romney within days to see those good people who have suffered much."

"You think of satisfying your needs as a man, not a monk," Brother Nicholas replied. "You think nothing of those people and their suffering."

"Do you?" Brother Gregory looked at him in surprise.

"I was there," was the reply.

"The beams have gone," Brother Gregory changed the subject.

"They were to be fitted this morning, and the roof will be tiled next week. Young Nicholas is to have a home suited to his status, and within the cathedral grounds." Brother Nicholas picked up a chisel, "Now enough of your talk, I want to carve in peace and have to complete a bedframe."

The work suited the travelling monk – it was an orderly occupation in which he could exercise his love of art as shavings fell away from the wood and the plank took on new shapes. Chiselled leaves grew on curving stems which, in turn, grew out of the oak bed frame. It would look fine in the child's home.

Brother Gregory was more reckless in his labours, carelessly chipping away, without heed to the grain of the wood or the symmetry of the finished piece. He was shaping table legs and thinking of the wenches he would seek out on his return to Romney. Away from the abbey, his days would follow a pattern which suited him, not restricted by the tiresome recitation of divine office, as ordered by the Book of Hours. He longed to be on the road to Romney Marsh.

A bell tolled within the abbey and tools were replaced neatly on the workbench. The two monks moved swiftly, side by side, back to the cloisters where they were joined by other silent, robed figures, all moving, two-by-two towards the church for the service of Nones. They knelt down with heads bowed, and prayed, their lips moving yet no sound escaping them. The lector entered and stood, ready to read the lessons for the afternoon service.

Brother Gregory listened to the lector's monotone voice – a steady rhythm of words which were heard but whose meanings went undigested. He knelt, he murmured responses and, after the final 'amen', he followed Brother Nicholas out of the church. They became part of the seamless movement of grey figures, who came together in a line and, at the door of the church, separated to go to their own areas of work.

"When will we set out for Romney?" Brother Gregory asked, as soon as they were back within the stone walls of the workshop.

"When this bed has been carved." Brother Nicholas picked up his chisel.

"Two days? Three days?" The younger monk asked.

"When the bed is carved," Brother Nicholas repeated. "It is for the parents of the baby Nicholas. I want to do a good job."

Brother Gregory grimaced at his companion's back and picked up his own tools. Turning to the table legs he chipped away, recklessly causing one to be less shapely than its neighbours. How had he borne all those years, closeted within the ancient walls, following the footsteps of long-gone monks? Now he longed to be free of the abbey and to carve out his own life. But he had no family, no home nor profession, so he must seek his freedom within the confines of the Church. When he was successful in bringing Nicholas to Canterbury, his worth as a messenger would be proved.

It was six days before they finally left the abbey, and six weeks since they were last in Romney. Brother Gregory had become feverish in his desire to be gone from the abbey and Brother Nicholas was tiring of the younger monk's impetuous nature. But despite misgivings on the part of Brother Nicholas, they set out together as soon as Mass and the office of Terce were done with.

As they left Canterbury on the old Roman Road, the countryside was lusher than it had been two months previously. Hedgerows buzzed with insect activity while birds swooped and soared. The day was gloriously warm.

It was on the evening of the second day when they walked into Romney, weary yet jubilant. They strolled into the town, along the High Street, rounded the corner and entered the priory undetected by any of the townsfolk. Having eaten a plain but nourishing meal, Brother Nicholas fell asleep on his straw-filled mattress. Once he was snoring soundly, Brother Gregory left the room, stepped softly down the stairs and left the priory in order to seek out the tavern wench for whom he had enjoyed an unfailing lust during his first time in Romney.

An hour later, Brother Gregory slipped through an alley between the tavern and the High Street, then turned into a side street and pushed gently on the latch of the priory door. At that moment, a young woman, wife of the town's cobbler, was walking back from her parents' cottage. She saw and recognised Brother Gregory, lit up by a beam of moonlight which was cast upon him. He didn't see Agnes, nor hear her heart, which thudded uncomfortably at the sight of him. He didn't know that his return to the town marked a time when she must risk all the security she had built around herself, in order to save her birth son.

Brother Gregory crept upstairs, feeling his way along the rough stone walls, and pushed open the door of the shared room. He cast his habit upon the end of his bed and slipped under the coarse blankets. Within minutes, he was asleep, smiling his satisfaction – he was back in Romney!

The following morning, while Brother Nicholas remained deep in conversation with another visiting monk at the priory, Brother Gregory once again left the building. He was keen to be within the town, experiencing the calls of the market traders, smelling the salt in the air and smiling companionably at the many townsfolk he had grown to know during his last visit.

A young woman was sitting on a tree stump at the roadside, with the grounds of St Martin's Church behind her. She was attractive, with dark hair peeping out from her hood, luscious brown-black eyes which were fixed upon him, and curves that would have tempted him, had she not clearly been with child. Momentarily discomfited by her gaze, he threw a quick nod in her direction and turned away. All too soon she was there behind him.

"I have words to say to you, which you will not want to be known about the town. Follow me into the church… this one here. The last of the homeless have gone now."

Brother Gregory followed the young woman, who opened the heavy, studded door and entered the church. She walked down the aisle and dropped to her knees in front of a shrine, where she muttered a brief prayer. The monk did the same, but his words were said without thought or feeling.

St Martin's Church had changed since his last visit. Then he had taken time to visit the last of the homeless families and to hear about their experiences during the storm. The floor had been strewn with wisps of straw and the air pungent with body odour and bad breath. Now, it was empty of people and their belongings. The building was plain – with birds in the rafters and damp stains on the stone walls. These Marsh people seemed disinclined to make their churches overly ornamental – just a few pieces of carved stonework, colourful tapestries and decorative candlestick holders seemed to satisfy them.

Agnes moved slightly away from the shrine and faced the monk. Her face had a look of determination about it, rousing his curiosity further. What did she want with him? He waited for her to speak first.

"You have returned to take the baby Nicholas back to Canterbury with you?"

"Aye. It is all arranged."

"I waited for you, as you must be told the baby will not be going to Canterbury. He is to stay here in Romney."

Fear clutched at Brother Gregory's heart. This woman looked so young, yet she spoke with such a certainty that it unnerved him. "It is all arranged," he stated the facts. "His mother, Cecily, has agreed to it."

"She felt that she had no choice, but she is desperate to stay here, in her home. Her husband is a doctor. He is needed in Romney." Agnes paused, satisfied that she had the monk's full attention. Some of her anxiety eased, and she spoke with confidence as she continued, "There are things you do not know of, and when you do, you will see that the baby, Nicholas, must remain in Romney."

"The Church has ordained…" Brother Gregory began pompously.

"The Church does not know the truth. I'll tell you, and you will see that this plan must come to an end.

This was not your idea, I know that, but it is you who must undo the harm that has been caused."

"Not my idea?" Brother Gregory questioned. He saw it as his very own.

"Nay, it was Matilda who fed it to you, while you satisfied your desires in the shed. It doesn't matter. She is desperate to rid Romney of the child, but that is not of importance now."

"You'll have your own child shortly, and the baby and his family will settle in Canterbury. Life will be good to them. It will be easier than being in this town which is made poor by the loss of its harbour." Brother Gregory smiled down at Agnes. There was nothing to concern him here. This young woman wanted to help her friend and had come to him all fierce and spitting her orders, but what did it matter to him that he had been seen with Matilda in the shed? And if she told Brother Nicholas, then he would merely shake his head, frown a little and mutter about the sacred vow of chastity.

"I have something to say, then you will see there is little option but to change your plans." Agnes ignored the monk's last words. "But, if you are clever, and I can see that you are, then you'll find a way to celebrate the coming of the child while he remains here, with his family."

"Tell me and then we are done, and I must return to the priory." Brother Gregory was becoming bored and turned to examine a roughly-hewn statue, placed in an alcove.

"The child is mine."

Brother Gregory turned back, "He is not yours. He lives with the good woman Cecily. Go back to your husband – you have nothing of interest to tell me."

"He is mine by birth." Agnes stated, looking him straight in the eye. "And I will not allow him to be taken from Romney."

"How can that be? The child is a gift from our Lord. He arrived on the night of the storm, and no one was seen to put him there. Brother Nicholas was at the church. He saw it all from the tower and he saw that no one put a baby there."

"Climb the tower and stand on the roof." The scorn was clear to hear in Agnes' voice. "Then look out to sea. Will you see me if I walk along the beach track in the dark, and place a bundle at the base of the tower?"

Brother Gregory stood looking past her, imagining the scene. "No, I will not."

"But Brother Nicholas could see it all. How could that be?"

"He is perceptive."

"He is a story-teller. He imagined the words across the page and thought nothing of what was real. Brother Nicholas did not see the baby being placed there and that does not mean he was sent by God."

"But he could have been."

"Isn't it more likely that in the chaos of the storm, the baby was placed there, and no one saw it happen? You've seen the shingle piled up at the church tower. You've seen the stains on the pillars of the church – they show how deep the floodwaters came. People were fighting for their lives, trying to save their homes and their livelihoods. Who is going to notice a girl with a bundle walking amongst them?"

Brother Gregory *could* see it all. Standing here, just steps away from where the devastation took place, he could picture it clearly. Frowning, he tried to put the events of that night in order.

There was one thing which made no sense at all – it was the only argument he had, and he voiced it now:

"Why did the people of Romney accept this? Did they not question the coming of the child? And your husband – he allowed you to place the newborn there? To cheat the people of this town?"

Agnes lowered her head in shame, "The baby was not my husband's. We married shortly after the storm. He knows nothing of this." Then, as if she knew she had done wrong, Agnes continued in haste, the words spilling out quickly: "But he will. I will tell him in order to save my son from being taken to Canterbury."

"So, you have no proof…?"

"My husband knows that I had been with another man before we married. He knows it and two others know that the child is mine. They keep their silence but will speak up if needed."

"You gave birth to a son during the storm and left him to die in the church tower?"

"I left him to be found." Agnes looked up at Brother Gregory. "I had nothing to offer him – our home had gone; the boat was destroyed. I left him to be found. He was well wrapped up."

"Then he became a symbol of hope for the town."

"He did," Agnes agreed. "What was I to do? Cecily had the baby she longed for, and the people of Romney believed the monk's words. But now you come to take him from us, and you must stop this self-serving deed. Leave him here. I will not tell, and the pilgrims can visit. You can record his life and be a part of it, but only if he remains here."

"And his other mother, Cecily – does she know?"

"Nay, but I'll tell her if I must."

"We have a house prepared for them in the cathedral grounds. The archbishop and abbot await the arrival of the child. They will not be pleased. I cannot imagine…."

"You will make it right," Agnes replied as she turned away. Brother Gregory watched her walk down the aisle, her hips swaying gently.

Alone in the church, Brother Gregory slumped on the floor, his back against a stone pillar. He saw his life ahead of him and there was no hope of redemption. This was his doing, his ambition, to bring the child to Canterbury. It was all his plan, and it had been acted upon in the city. He would suffer for its going wrong – banished to a life within the abbey. He would garden and pray, and carve and pray, and never would there be hope of rising to senior monk. His involvement with the child was done. It would be Brother Nicholas who saw the pilgrim's trail come to life and diligently record the child's life. And if it became known that the child was the mere son of a fisherman's daughter, Brother Gregory's shame would be all the greater.

Chapter Twenty
Brother Gregory

"What are you saying? The air of Romney has made you lose your reason. I should have left you in Canterbury!" Brother Nicholas snarled.

"The child cannot come to Canterbury. You made a mistake – he is nothing but the son of a local wench."

"I made no mistake. I was there." Brother Nicholas stated, his tone cold. "I have my wits about me, while you are more interested in pleasuring yourself with tavern whores."

"You were there, but you didn't see." Brother Gregory was determined to shift the blame. He would not take sole responsibility for the undoing of the plan to take the child to Canterbury.

"I saw it all from the church tower," Brother Nicholas repeated his well-worn words.

"I've been told by a local woman that she gave birth to the child. She was unable to care for him – the family home had been lost in the storm, and she was unmarried. She was desperate. What could she do? She left him where he could be found." Brother Gregory took his chance to discredit the other monk: "You were there, and you saw no-one leave the child. That is the truth. But you were looking out to sea and didn't notice a young woman with a small bundle. And what if you had her? How could you know that the bundle of rags was a child? It was before dawn, and you were up in the tower."

"I saw…"

"You saw nothing but the chance to write about the storm and suffered a pride so great, all you thought of were your words upon the vellum, and the archbishop reading them."

"Keep your voice down and let me think," Brother Nicholas snapped. "This will not bring the child to Canterbury."

They were in their small room under the eaves of the old priory. A crooked window faced St Martin's Church and, from his bed, Brother Gregory looked across the churchyard. Women were going about their morning tasks, baskets in their arms and children at their feet. The day was becoming warm, and they had discarded the thick shawls and capes which had smothered their figures during his previous visit. The women of Romney came together, exchanged a few words and parted – it made a companionable scene.

Brother Gregory also needed time to think. But his thoughts became erratic and dangerous – should they snatch the child and take him to Canterbury? It would be of no difficulty to pick up an impoverished woman as they passed through Dymchurch or Burmarsh – someone to care for him. But why take Nicholas and run the risk of men from Romney coming to claim him back? If they were to go to another town and take a child of a similar appearance, then no one would imagine he was a replacement for Nicholas. But one day a pilgrim would feel the need to visit his place of birth and find the true Nicholas there. He could think of no way that they could return with the child as arranged.

Every so often, Brother Gregory glanced towards his companion who was hunched on the bed, his head in his hands. Finally, Brother Nicholas spoke. "We have the word of this one young woman. Let us speak with the doctor and his wife. Perhaps they are willing to travel with us and all this will be for nothing."

"Aye, we must do that," Brother Gregory replied. "but I fear she speaks for them."

"But first we pray and then eat," Brother Nicholas stated.

It was an hour later when the monks rapped at the door of the stone house a few steps away from the priory.

Luke answered the door, "We were expecting you."

The monks bowed their heads slightly in acknowledgement of his words and Brother Nicholas spoke, his voice forced into a friendly tone. "Have you prepared to come to Canterbury? We've been away a long time, but your house is ready. I supervised the building of it myself."

"You have wasted your time," Luke replied, still standing in the doorway, blocking their entrance to the house. "We felt that there was no choice – what strength did we have to stop the power of the Church? The boy is *our* son, and he *will* grow up in Romney. Our town needs him, and we wish him to remain here."

"But... to grow up in Canterbury... within the cathedral grounds...."

"Romney is our home, and he is well cared for here. Set up your pilgrims' trail and bring wealth to our stricken town. Surely that is why God sent him to us. Romney needed him. Canterbury has wealth aplenty."

"I understand," Brother Nicholas nodded. "But Canterbury awaits the child. It would be a good life. I'll pray for Nicholas and hope the right choice will be made. We'll speak of it again soon."

The monks turned away and walked, without purpose, along the road to the abandoned river mouth. On reaching the mudbanks, now lush with fresh green shoots thriving in the moist, alluvial soil, they paused and stared out towards the huddle of buildings which was Lydd.

"I don't want to hear your talk," Brother Nicholas said, before words had even formed on Brother Gregory's lips. "Let us think over the next few days. We have been hasty in our choices so far, now we take the time to reflect and learn from our mistakes. I suggest you pray for guidance, as will I."

Brother Gregory shrugged his shoulders and heaved a sigh of acceptance. Who knew what schemes might enter his lively mind over the coming days?

"The child is to remain in Romney!" Matilda took a step back and looked at the monk in distaste. "How can that be? Canterbury welcomed him, surely it did?"

"Canterbury did. A house is being built for him, within the cathedral grounds. I helped with the construction myself. The abbot was most pleased with our tales of the child and the archbishop is eager to have him amongst us. It is all arranged."

"Then it will go ahead, and all will be well," Matilda concluded.

"The problem is here, in Romney," Brother Gregory reached out to touch the partly uncovered swell of her breasts.

"There is no problem here that cannot be dealt with." Matilda pulled her shawl closer to her body, covering the exposed flesh. "Romney has no say over what has been ordained by your archbishop. He has power over us all if he chooses to."

"Circumstances change – it is not as we thought."

"Not as you thought?" Matilda repeated, her tone sharp.

"I can say no more," Brother Gregory replied.

Matilda stood, silently watchful. Brother Gregory could see that she was thinking it through, trying to make sense of it. He needed to pacify her, without telling of his conversation with Agnes. He felt that if a name were mentioned... any hint of what had gone wrong, and Matilda's fury would soar. Enough had been said, and she would draw her own conclusions with no more help from him. He was not here for talk, yet talk he must in order to sweeten her.

"I thought of you while I was away," Brother Gregory smiled. "We recorded the child's life in a book of the finest vellum. Both the archbishop and abbot were impressed. We carved furniture for the new home. This is but a small delay. We'll pray for guidance and our Lord will find a way."

"You will make it right. I am sure of it," Matilda smiled sweetly and took a step closer. Reaching up, her lips touched his lightly. It would do no harm to indulge in a little fun while he was here.

Brother Gregory still had the taste of the tavern wench on his lips – he had been in her arms as soon as dusk had fallen on the town. The girl had been willing enough to gratify him, but Matilda pleased him too. She had a want for power and that excited him. He knew that she used her body to influence him, yet he didn't care. She was obsessive, he could see that, but what reason did she have for such interest in the baby Nicholas? Brother Gregory was intrigued by Matilda, yet he sensed she was dangerous. He reached out to her breasts again and this time she didn't recoil. They kissed, she with a passion which was desperate, before retreating further into the shadows of the boat repair shed.

The monk didn't know that Matilda's monthly bleed had not arrived while he had been away, and already his seed grew strong inside her. She chose to keep this from him and had hastily agreed to marry Cousin

Henry. The wedding would take place within the week, but until then…

That evening and throughout the next day, Brother Nicholas shared none of his thoughts. Brother Gregory strode around the streets and along the seafront, his habit flowing, and head lowered. Where before he had been charming and attentive to the local people, now he was reserved. He made a show of praying every now and then, but not once did he dare to ask God for a solution. The monk did once visit old Gundred in the church, but she unnerved him with her knowledge, and he moved on.

It was at the end of their third day when Brother Nicholas rose to his feet before the altar at St Nicholas Church and spoke. "I wish to hear this woman speak for herself – the one who claims to have given birth. Arrange for me to see her."

"Very well," Brother Gregory replied. She is bound to go shopping in the morning, so I'll wait and bring her to you.

"I'll be at the statue," Brother Nicholas said. "It is a fitting place to meet."

The following morning, Agnes trailed behind the monk. Six months' pregnant and her mind filled with concern for her firstborn and his family, the bloom of youth had left her young face. At the statue, she barely raised her head to mutter a greeting to Brother Nicholas. And he gave no recognition at all before launching into the subject which was bothering him.

"You asked to speak with Brother Gregory when we returned from Canterbury, having prepared for the child to live there amongst holy people."

"Aye, Nicholas should stay here, with his own folk."

"And what reason did you give Brother Gregory?"

Agnes shifted uncomfortably, displaying none of the bold confidence she had shown when telling the younger monk. "I gave birth to a baby on the night of the storm. My home was ruined, and I was alone in the pig shed. I wasn't married... but I was due to be, and I knew it would cause worry for the family. So, I put the baby where he could be found."

"And what does your new husband think of this? Does he not want his child?"

"The baby was not his – the father of the baby is dead." Agnes raised her face to look at the monk, "But I will tell him, and I'll tell everyone. The child should stay in Romney, and his new family should not be forced to leave for Canterbury with him."

"What's to stop me from telling all of Romney?" Brother Nicholas asked.

"Because then you'll have nothing to write about and tell those folk in Canterbury. Leave him be and you can still tell your tales."

Brother Gregory couldn't help admiring this young woman for her judgement. She had probably never left this town, yet she could see the importance of the child and the impact he had on the life of the travelling monk. The three of them stood, enveloped in their own thoughts for a moment, before Brother Nicholas gave his dismissal of the young woman.

"God will guide me in this matter, and may you pray for forgiveness, as your deception is great."

"I do," Agnes replied as she turned away.

Brother Nicholas turned and walked towards the sea, picking his way over pieces of driftwood and tangles of seaweed. Brother Gregory watched from a distance as the older monk stood, just feet from the retreating ripples. The two of them were there for some time, the younger one looking on and wondering what thoughts meandered within his companion's head as he gazed out to sea. It was only as the tide turned and the older monk was forced to retreat, that he shared his thoughts.

"The Lord has guided my thinking, and I now see the error of my ways. However, the child came to be in the base of the tower, God chose to let him survive and be found. He put me there at that moment, and the people of Romney turned to me, asking for my wisdom. When they chose to believe the baby had been sent to ease their suffering, God gave them hope.

"We did wrong in planning to remove the child from Romney. The people of the town have suffered greatly from the storm. Their homes and boats can be repaired, but nothing can be done to bring back the Rother to flush out the channel. Their deep harbour has gone and with it the merchants' ships. The people of this town face poverty and many have already left.

"In the night, a vision came to me – I saw pilgrims following the route we discussed, visiting the place our baby was found, looking at mementoes of his life. Then this very moment as I stood on the shore, an angel came to me!" The monk looked to the sky and smiled at the wonder of the moment when he had been blessed with the visitation. "He said to me that the child must remain in Romney, and he will do good for the town. The pilgrims must eat and sleep and pray somewhere. They will spend their money and Romney will again flourish.

"The child will grow into a man and he will have healing powers. People will come to see him with their ailments and bathe in the sea which he will bless."

"I saw no angel!" Brother Gregory responded.

"He was for my eyes only."

"It was a good vision, nonetheless," the younger monk admitted. "And in your vision what place did you have in the child's life?" he asked.

214

"I shall write of his progress through life, and travel to spread word of him."

"And myself?" Brother Gregory wondered.

"You were not in my vision," the older monk stated. "I imagine you will return to Canterbury and live a humble life within the walls of the abbey. In time you will repent your sins. It is as God ordained for you."

"I thought as much."

"Tomorrow we return to Canterbury and explain that the baby will stay in Romney." Brother Nicholas declared.

"But the archbishop and abbot… it was their wish for the child. The house has been built." Brother Gregory slumped onto his bed, his head in his hands.

"It is God's will we all follow," Brother Nicholas replied. "We must be grateful for his guidance in this matter."

"Very well." Defeated, Brother Gregory turned to leave the beach. He could not remain in the company of his fellow monk.

The sun was on its descent and the air chilly. Brother Gregory walked briskly along the Fair Field Road, with no intention other than to stamp out his fury as he walked. Recklessly, he kicked at stones and debris on the street as he passed Matilda's cottage to his left and the repair sheds on his right. Then, without any plan in his mind, he turned away from the coast and strode along Rolfe's Road. Here was another area of new building – homes for fishermen and those who had lived on the beachfront. Brother Gregory trudged on until, as he neared the lane which led to Hope, his attention strayed to a collection of clothes left out to dry in front of a low cottage, with a roof of reed-thatch. He paused for a moment, reflecting on the lateness of the hour and the fact that the clothes would become damp in no time.

The monk continued for a few steps past the cottage, made an abrupt turn-about and retraced his steps, his eyes flitting from side to side. The area was deserted, and so he darted towards the clothes and grabbed at a woollen tunic and a cape. As he scurried away, he gathered the clothes into the folds of his habit. Not ready to return to the priory, he turned into St Martin's Church and, having seen the place was empty, shoved the bundle of clothes into a dark corner beyond the altar.

As the skies darkened over Romney, Brother Gregory sat lost in his own thoughts, which took no lucid form but flitted from impetuous plans with no sense to them, to reflections on his time spent in Romney. The moon was sending shafts of soft white light through the windows when the monk finally stood, cold through but resolute that a worthy plan had come to mind. He walked slowly towards the doorway and out into the starlit night.

In the priory, the monks ate their supper in silence before retiring to bed. Brother Gregory lay on the mattress, listening to Brother Nicholas' breathing change to a slow, steady rhythm, punctuated by the occasional snort. He felt himself falling asleep, then waking with a nervous jump. It was time to go before he too was asleep until sunrise.

Taking care over every movement, Brother Gregory, slowly shifted his body until he sat on the edge of the bed. He pulled on his shoes and fastened the laces, then stood and pulled on his habit. At the end of the bed there was a small sack with his writing instruments, his Bible, some stockings and a clean shift. He took the sack in his arms and crept from the room.

He had never been in the kitchen, but a candle still burned low in the hallway, and Brother Gregory was able to use its feeble light to guide him through a series of small rooms to the kitchen and then the pantry. He took a loaf of bread, some cheese and a few soft apples, and placed them in his sack. Then he filled a small, stoneware flask with ale and, having slung the bag over his shoulder, he carried the flask in his hands. As he finished, the candle gave out its last light and so it was in darkness he felt his way through the ancient priory, to the doorway leading to the street.

The outside world was lit by the gibbous moon and millions of shimmering stars in a cloudless sky. The air was cool and, as he stood in the priory doorway, Brother Gregory could hear the gentle pull and release of the sea on the shingle. The tower of St Nicholas made a clear outline against an inky sky, marking the place where this story began on a vastly different night.

The monk crossed the street to St Martin's Church and slunk inside. Here, soft light came in shafts through the windows and lit up the irregular stone floor, sturdy pillars, and tapestries. The shadows were a dense grey-black and it was within one of these that the stolen tunic and cape were found. Brother Gregory swiftly discarded his habit, pulled on the tunic, then reused his own belt.

Brother Gregory still had the habit in his arms as he approached the altar. He dropped it on the stone floor, and it fell into a pool of material, with the hood still slightly raised in the middle. The monk looked down on it for a moment and the sight of it amused him. He would leave it just like that. When the people of Romney came to church, it would look as if he had slipped away into the ground, leaving his habit behind him. It would cause mystery and intrigue for these ignorant people who believed they had a holy child amongst them.

Fumbling under his tunic, Brother Gregory pulled out a gold cross on a long leather lace. He placed it on top of the habit, then adjusted it to appear as if it had remained around his neck until those final moments. Still smiling at the effect caused as he shed the trappings of a monk, he turned towards the altar to pray. "Lord, as I step out into this world, I pray that Christ may walk beside me on this new path."

With the moon high in the sky, Gregory left St Martin's and then New Romney behind him as he set out on the road towards Hope and Ivychurch.

Chapter Twenty-One
Agnes

Although her home was on the High Street, with the cobbler's shop opening onto the road, Agnes was in the habit of leaving by the kitchen door. She enjoyed those few minutes of peace, after pressing the latch on the back gate, when she walked through the churchyard. When was it that she had fallen to walking in this slow, ponderous way? Before her marriage she had run and skipped about, like the carefree young woman she was. To friends and family, it appeared that the pregnancy was cumbersome to her young body and had drained her vitality. But the depression cloaking her was nothing to do with the new life within her – it was fear for baby Nicholas' future enveloping her.

Yesterday, the older monk had questioned Agnes about the birth. Did he believe her? She was unsure, but true or not, if she were to declare the child was her own, then his plans of taking the baby to Canterbury would be hindered. If this thin-faced monk, who claimed Nicholas was named after him, were to continue with his plans she would have tell her husband, her parents and then Cecily and Luke about the deceit surrounding the baby. All her efforts to give her son a better life would have been wasted and her family shamed to a greater degree than they would have ever believed possible.

The monk was right – whatever the reason, her deception was immense and one day, when her life on

Earth had passed, Agnes knew she would suffer for her sins. She prayed daily for redemption, begging God to see the good that had been done in offering the child to the town and in giving Cecily the chance to have her own child. However, you couldn't barter with God. Agnes knew that. He was all-seeing and He knew that she had abandoned her child to save her family from disgrace, enabling her to marry well within days of his birth.

These thoughts ran around her mind, sucking the little energy she possessed, as she plodded through the dew-drenched grass of the churchyard. In the past few weeks, Agnes had become so isolated from the people around her, so engrossed in her own worries, that she barely noticed a woman come from of the church porch and made no effort to give a smile or greeting.

However, something had happened – there was news to tell, and it was to be shared with the first person this woman saw. The women of the town knew that gossip and speculation needed to be spread as fast as the sea breeze could carry it across Romney and beyond.

"Agnes... Agnes, come and have a look. I don't know what to make of it and I'm sure you won't either."

Agnes heard the urgency in the woman's voice and as she turned the depression shifted slightly, allowing her to move her body with ease and for her to lift her face as she replied: "What is it, Bel?"

"I don't know! You'll have to see it for yourself... in the church... It's as if he's sunk into the stone of the floor. It gave me such a fright, like I've not had since the night my roof started breaking up during the storm."

"Sunk into the floor?" Agnes' curiosity was aroused as she stepped over stones and tussocks to join Bel at the church porch.

"Aye, you'll think I'm foolish until you see it for yourself. Not that I want to go back in there, I was set on finding the vicar… but as you're here…"

The day was bright, and so it took a moment for Agnes' eyes to adjust to the contrasting light within St Martin's. Dust motes danced joyously within shafts of light emitted though windows, while the shadowed areas became all the more unfathomable with shades of grey piled upon each other in corners, against pillars and across much of the cool stone floor.

Bel was marching with purpose towards the altar, and Agnes was forced into a scamper in order to keep pace. "There! Down there – what do you make of it?" Bel demanded of Agnes, who was fearful of what she would see and could only decipher a pile of blankets, netting, or something similar.

"I can't… I'm not sure." Cautiously, Agnes bent over the heap of cloth and saw there was something else amongst it – a belt or chain?

"Here, take this." Bel offered a candle. "I was in here lighting this for Gilbert, God rest his soul, and that's how I came across it."

With the flickering yellow light held close to the bundle on the floor, the gold of a cross immediately came to life, shining out and revealing its shape to Agnes. She frowned, recognising it, but unsure of where to place it. Where had she seen this cross recently? Now the weave of the grey-brown woollen cloth came into focus and there was the shape of a hood, with layer upon layer of fabric folded upon itself. And the cross on its leather lace, was looking as if it had fallen with the cloak as it sank to the ground.

"It's a monk's habit. I'm sure of it," Agnes announced to the enthralled Bel. "And that cross, I saw it only yesterday. It belongs to the young one, Brother Gregory."

"And there he is, just sunk away into the ground. Whatever made this happen, Agnes? What could God be thinking of to allow this to happen to someone as holy as a monk?" Bel's words were spoken with equal measures of wonder and horror.

Agnes thought of Brother Gregory and his plans to take Nicholas to Canterbury so he could bask in the glory of the child. She remembered crouching in the shadows of the repair shed, while he pleasured himself with the widowed Matilda. A smile came to her face and her voice was lighter than it had been in some weeks as she replied, "Things like that don't just happen. There'll be another reason and we'll find out soon enough."

"Don't just happen?" Bel repeated, still in awe at the revelation that it was the monk's habit and cross before her. "Perhaps not, at least not in the past, but things do happen in Romney. We've the child sent by the storm – and that makes Romney a holy place! There's no doubting it."

Only a part of Agnes heard Bel's words, so absorbed was she in the mystery of the habit and cross. That they were Brother Gregory's, there seemed little doubt – but what reason could there be for them to be abandoned beside the altar?

"We'll hear what it's about soon," Agnes advised Bel as they stepped away from the bundle and moved towards the doorway. "In a town as small as Romney, it won't remain a secret for long."

"Aye, you're right and by the time I've been up and down the High Street, I'm sure to have some news."

However, further tidings came their way sooner than expected. The two women had no need to walk further than the edge of the churchyard before angry words were thrown in their direction by a woman who, with her basket under her arm, was making her way to the market.

"God's bones, my John is in a temper this morning. I had to get out to avoid his tongue, he's got so much of a fury on him!"

"What's been happening?" Bel asked. "And after you've told, I've got my own tale that will take you by surprise…"

"Not stolen clothes I hope?" came the reply.

"Clothes, but not stolen..." Bel replied.

"You've not come by my John's cloak and tunic?" the woman asked. "What a relief that would be."

"Not unless John has become a monk!" Bel sniggered. "Nay, I can't see that."

"A monk? Not likely. His cloak and tunic have gone from where I left them drying, and after I'd gone to the bother of cleaning them."

Agnes' imagination, awakened from its slumber by the events of the morning, slowly and steadily began to pick up speed. The monk's clothes left at the altar and now the stolen clothes… they began to come together in a series of possible events in her mind. Agnes pictured Brother Gregory, his plans defeated, and reluctant to return to a life restricted by the boundaries of the abbey walls. Perhaps he had wandered the streets of Romney and, on noticing the clothes set out to dry, had seen a chance to make new plans for his life.

Moving away from the other women, Agnes walked to the market stalls on the High Street. Her body felt lighter than it had been in weeks, and she took more notice of the people about her as inside a flicker of hope took told. With her basket filled with milk, cheese and vegetables, Agnes strolled back home, this time entering the house through the cobbler's shop.

It was dusty in there and smelt of leather – a smell which had caused her to feel nauseous during those first months of pregnancy. Will sat at his workbench by the window, stitching a child's boot.

"What news is there in the town?" he asked.

"I met Bel, who was fussing about a pile of clothes in St Martin's, and it was very odd – when we went to take a look, I was sure it was a monk's habit."

"Not something you'd expect a monk to leave lying around," Will grinned.

"Nay, and with John Cooper's clothes stolen from where they were laid out to dry, there's plenty for the women to gossip about."

"Aye, there's always something."

"I'm going to bake some bread now, then go to the beachfront, ready for when the boats come in." Agnes moved through from the shop to the kitchen behind.

It was early afternoon, while Agnes rested by the fire, that Cecily tapped on the back door before pressing the latch and letting herself in.

"Thank the Lord, our prayers have been answered!" Cecily exclaimed, as she lowered Nicholas to the floor.

"Have you seen them? The monks?" Agnes pulled herself to her feet.

"Just the one – Brother Nicholas – he came on his own, talking about messages from the Lord. About our Nicholas, of course. It seems as if God has said that Nicholas is to stay here in Romney. Oh Agnes, I won't mind about those pilgrims now we can stay."

"And you are sure? It's all settled?" Agnes poured them both some wine and handed Nicholas a crust to chew on.

"Aye, he seemed sure enough. Nicholas was a gift to Romney he said… come to ease our suffering. What use was he to Romney if he was taken to Canterbury? He had seen it all, Brother Nicholas had, in a vision of our future. My Nicholas must stay here, and Romney will grow wealthy through visits from pilgrims who will spend their coins in our shops and rest overnight in rooms we'll build. That is why the baby was sent – this is his vision for us and the town!"

Cecily's eyes, dull for so many weeks, now shone as she told the news. She rubbed her rounded belly.

"And, the doctor, what does he say?" Agnes was eager for the news.

"Luke said we would never have gone, but he's pleased not to have to fight it anymore. I tried to believe that we could stay, but how could I when all those powerful people wanted him?"

"Aye, you were right to be worried, but it seems that they've seen sense now. Mayhap you'll not be bothered by too many pilgrims. Will they really come all the way to Romney to see a child, when the roads are so poor, and we are so far away from any large town?" Agnes couldn't see it – a pilgrims' trail to Romney. They'd just have to see what happened as the months passed, and Nicholas grew from child to man. Then she recalled the pile of clothing in the church. "Cecily, was Brother Gregory there?"

"Nay, there was no mention of him."

"Have you heard, there's a strange thing happened in St Martin's?"

Agnes told Cecily about the clothing on the floor, and how she was sure she recognised the cross as Brother Gregory's. "And he's not been seen this morning," she said.

"Well, I didn't see him, but that's not to say he's not somewhere in the town."

"Aye, he could be," Agnes admitted. "But the habit left in the church… and John Cooper's clothes gone. I'm sure he's left Romney. You could see it in his face that he wanted to live his life as man, not a monk."

"Let's hope he doesn't regret it," Cecily replied. "What's he going to do with himself, I wonder?"

"We'll never hear from him again, I'm sure of it." Agnes said.

At nine months old, Nicholas was soon pulling himself up, using the benches or Cecily's knees for support. But, with his crust eaten, he turned to Agnes and pulled on her tunic. His blue eyes looked into hers, and for Agnes the likeness to Hugh was obvious. She reached for a cloth and gently wiped dribble from his lips.

"He's teething," Cecily said. "Poor boy."

"He's cheerful enough," Agnes commented. She reached down and pulled him onto her lap. The boy didn't object, happy to pull at the beads Agnes wore around her neck. Holding her son close, Agnes felt a wave of contentment wash over her. She couldn't be his mother but now, through her unexpected friendship with Cecily, he could be a part of her life. With their new babies due to be born within weeks of each other, the bond between the two women would soon strengthen.

"I don't know what you saw or what you knew, that made those monks see sense," Cecily said. "And perchance I'll never know, but I know you had a part in keeping Nicholas here with us in Romney and I'll be forever grateful."

"I may be big with child. I can no longer run about or clamber up the shingle banks, and by evening I am wearier than I ever felt in my life, but today my body feels lighter, and my mind is livelier." Agnes tried to express the pleasure she felt for being a part of keeping Cecily's child in Romney. "I feel better today for knowing Brother Nicholas seems sure that your baby must remain here. Mayhap his message came from God, or did he come to see that Romney would not allow the baby to be taken? We'll never know for sure."

Agnes held tight onto her birth son as he pulled himself up to stand on her lap, his fists holding onto her black hair, causing her headscarf to become dishevelled.

"I've a curiosity to see if the habit still lies on the church floor," Cecily stood to help untangle thick hair from little hands. "Shall we walk over there and then take Nicholas to the harbour? He loves to crawl on the pebbles and splash in the water. I wouldn't be surprised if he grows up wanting to be a fisherman, rather than a doctor like his pa!"

Chapter Twenty-Two
Gregory

Gregory crouched on the steep edge of a drainage ditch. Reeds, strong and green, pressed against him, and not far below algae floated thick and spongy on the surface. A twisted willow tree shaded him from the afternoon sun and only the gentle hum of insects, the call of birds and bleating of distant sheep filled the air. No men toiled upon the flat land which he could see from his hiding place, and no one had passed along the lane in the time since he had claimed his hide.

As a monk, Gregory had lived a solitary life, yet surrounded by men. During his time in Romney, he had gladly welcomed any company on offer and learned that he was a man who easily succumbed to lustful desires. These last three days had been lonelier than any in his whole life – he would walk for hours and barely see a figure in a field, or a person to greet as they passed on a countryside track.

Having lived his adult life ruled by the toll of St Augustine's bells, Gregory now had no order to his days. After sleeping in a barn, he would scavenge grain from a store or raw vegetables from a cottage garden. The bread and cheese he had stolen from the priory had been eaten sparingly and lasted until the end of the second day. If only he had the means to make fire, he could cook eggs from the birds' nests accessible from the hedgerows.

His aim was to reach a town or large village in which he could look for work. Gregory had laboured on the land in the abbey and, more recently, learned wood carving skills, but these would not be his choice of employment. Gregory knew that his greatest accomplishment was that of being able to write and hoped in a town he would discover a way to benefit from this talent. There were no towns of significance on Romney Marsh, other than Romney itself, so Gregory was determined to reach those distant hills which bordered the flat lands. Once on high land, he was convinced a town would soon be found. However, the tracks twisted and turned, and those hills became lost within a heat haze, until he could only guess which direction he should be walking. He often found himself tiring and there seemed to be no harm in lying down on the long grass at the side of a field and sleeping the early afternoon hours away.

It was after a sleep, and a fruitless search for food, Gregory had come across a cottage, and it seemed that he had no choice but to lie in wait for an opportunity… He had been there for a while, eyes and ears trained upon the cottage across the track. The door was open, and a woman could be seen, passing to and fro across the slant of sunlight falling within the room. Sometimes he heard a few lines of a song, or the clatter of pans as the woman kept busy within her kitchen. Once she left the cottage, and he wondered if this was his chance, but she went no further than the log pile across the yard.

Finally, with a basket slung over her arm, the woman walked through the doorway and turned towards the back of the property. Gregory took his chance, pulling himself out of the ditch and in a few steps he had crossed the rough track. Glancing from left to right, he scampered along a short path and entered the kitchen of the cottage, then paused, his eyes adjusting to the dim light and ears alert to danger. Soon enough, he focused on a table laden with the day's baking and, taking no more time to look at his surroundings, Gregory snatched at a loaf of bread, a pie and a cake. Arms full, he sped across the road and threw himself into the ditch, clinging to the reeds as he crouched.

He dare not put his head above the bank but listened for some sound other than the cacophony of nature's music, while placing the bread and cake in his sack. The pie was moist and would have to be eaten as soon as the thief had moved to a safer hide. His mouth watered at the smell of meat juices, and he snatched a mouthful before moving on.

The ditch was deep, but narrow, and on the further side there were several willows and hawthorns, whereas the side alongside the track was open to view from the cottage. If, on surfacing from the ditch, Gregory remained on the roadside, he would have to run for several minutes before he reached shelter. He threw his sack across to the other side of the water; it caught on hawthorn and rolled to the edge of the field. Then he looked at the meat pie, crammed some more in his mouth, and reluctantly threw the remainder after the sack. It would break up, he knew it, but he was determined to salvage the pieces of the meaty treat. Gregory steadied himself, and jumped, throwing himself forwards and clinging to the reeds. Without pausing, he scrambled up the bank, grabbing at a stray piece of pie as he went. Heart racing, Gregory flung himself flat at the edge of the field and listened again for the sounds that the theft had been discovered. Nothing came from the area around the cottage, other than the yap of a dog and the *bwok bwok* of contented chickens. His sack was just a few feet away, but the pie had fallen amongst the reeds. He shuffled forwards, on his stomach, and started to search amongst the stiff stalks. Luck was with him, the greater part of the pie was within easy reach, and he pulled it towards him, not hesitating to cram some more into his mouth.

It was time to move on and, with his eyes fixed on the cottage, Gregory slowly moved to his knees, then raised himself a little higher. Still chewing the meaty treat, he broke into a run, his body hunched in the form of a primitive man. Within seconds, he was sheltering by a cluster of hawthorns, but without hesitating, he raced on to the next sturdy bush.

As Gregory straightened himself, and took another bite of the pie, he heard a shrill cry come from the cottage. And, through the dense branches, he could just about see the figure of the furious woman standing at the cottage door. She moved to the roadside, looking one way and then the other, before hurrying to the side of the ditch and looking down into it. Her cries drew the attention of a man, who joined her at the ditch-side. The woman pointed at something, possibly a piece of stray pie, or the trail of trampled reeds. But Gregory was triumphant and, cramming more of his tasty prize into his mouth, he moved on.

With no great plan in his head, other than the intention to reach a town or large village, Gregory followed the field edge, then scrambled across another ditch. He stayed level with the road for a while before reaching a wider ditch which he couldn't cross. Not being able to retrace his tracks, he was forced to follow it away from the road. The afternoon sun beat down upon him, and with his belly now full of pie, Gregory stepped into the shade of a windswept willow and sat for a while on the dry grass.

He was lost – there was no doubt about it. For three days, Gregory had followed tracks which seemed to lead in no particular direction. They twisted and turned with the drainage ditches – in fact, they were no more than banks of earth which had been excavated as the ditches were cleared. In turn, these ditches had been formed from tidal creeks and so, apart from eventually leading to the sea, they meandered with no obvious destination in sight.

Once he had left the road, his path was ruled by the ditches, and he could not set himself in any particular direction. All he could do was follow the waterways circling fields and hope to come across a road leading off the Marsh. The afternoon was becoming evening and although the sun was still high in the sky, a low-lying mist began to roll across the land, bringing with it a sharp chill to the air. Gregory's spirits, raised by both the meat pie and the excitement of his adventure, had now slumped. Fearful of spending the night in the open, he had no choice but to keep moving, and prayed he would come across shelter. His pace was forced to a slow trudge, as he became unable to see any further than the next tree.

When Gregory stumbled upon the wide plank bridge, he felt sure that it would lead to a road of some significance. The bridge was made of good, solid timbers, and was sturdier than any other he had crossed. His optimism was rewarded as the road which he stepped onto was clearly wider than any other he had walked upon since he left Romney. Surely two carts could pass each other with ease, and a road such as this must lead to a settlement of some importance.

His back was now a little straighter and his strides a little longer as Gregory turned to his right with no clue as to where the road would take him – but he was certain his destination was near. Before long, the varied shapes signifying a cluster of buildings emerged through the swirling mists. Standing before them, Gregory spotted a cottage, with smoke rising sluggishly from a chimney, and faint light showing at the windows. Beyond it, a small barn looked to be inviting him to settle for the night and, as he peeped in, he was greeted by the satisfying smell of grain and hay. But before he rested, he must drink and an animals' trough in the yard was good enough.

Inside the barn the light was very weak, but Gregory was able to pull at the hay and form a snug bed, which he lined with his cape. Understanding that food was precious and with his hunger still satisfied by the delicious meat pie, Gregory merely ripped off a small chunk of the fruit cake. Then he lay his head on the pillow formed with the hood of the cape and before long he was asleep.

Morning came early with the crowing of the cockerel and the knowledge that the traveller must move on before the farm came to life for the day. His body felt heavy and if he could have sunk back into the hay for an hour or more, then Gregory would have welcomed the respite from his tiring journey. What would this day bring? Mile after mile of flat land, with no company nor sight of a significant settlement, or the town this wide road promised?

He stood and pulled his tunic into place, picking off sprigs of hay. Then he pulled his stockings straight, before slipping his feet into the plain leather shoes. The light was weak, so he fumbled at the straps on the sack and, having felt his way past the bread and cake, Gregory pulled out a leather drinking flask. With the sack slung over his shoulder and the flask in his hand, he moved towards the open doorway of the barn and paused. The early morning mist swirled thickly, and he could only just decipher the shape of the farm cottage. His world was silent, other than the persistent crow of the cockerel and gentle clucking of his hens.

Gregory filled his flask at the drinking trough and took a long draught of cool water before refilling the bottle. It seemed that the occupants of the farmhouse still slumbered as he picked his way along the rough farm track and onto the road.

Which way to turn? The mist hung in swathes above the ditches, and although the sky was becoming lighter to the east, the sun had not yet broken clear of the horizon. His world was still in shades of grey, from the softest swirling mists to the iron-grey of hedgerows and distant fields. His spirits were low and, without pausing to consider which direction would suit him best, Gregory turned towards the faint glow promising the sun would soon rise and a new day begin.

It was as if he walked in a tunnel between the mist-topped ditches, but before long the sky was a blue-grey and the sun appeared a soft yellow through the clouds. Then a cottage appeared at the roadside, and another shortly after, then another on the other side. A man passed him on the road and gave a cheery 'good morning' and, as the sky became still lighter, other figures appeared and more houses took shape on both sides of the road…

Gregory's pace quickened in anticipation of what he was to find. He became less absorbed in his own morose thoughts and more inclined to listen to the sounds around him – a distant shout, the cry of a child, a bark of a dog, the grunting of a pig and clucking of chickens – and then that low, steady rhythm of the sea hitting the beach and its pull on the shingle. At that very moment when Gregory recognised the familiar sound of the sea, he realised the air he inhaled was now rich with the scents of seaweed and salt. There he was, with the beach before him and the cottages now behind. To his right was a huge beachfront shed, and further along the coast, the sturdy tower of St Nicholas Church.

Those roads which twisted and turned, the ditches which coiled and confused… along with the mists they had taken him back to where he had begun. Gregory was meant to be in Romney. He understood that now. Despite the mists, his future was clear. He returned to the town as a man, not a monk, and here he would make his life, amongst the people of Romney.

He had drifted for days without any particular plan in mind, but now Gregory strode out along the end of the High Street, until the shops became more densely packed together and he reached the crossroads. He didn't even think to glance towards the priory and wonder about the monk whom he had abandoned. So impetuous was his nature, he had moved on from that life and gave it no thought.

It was at the further end of the High Street that he slowed down before a tavern and then stood back from it, eyeing its proportions and the open land to its side. This would suit Gregory very well indeed. From here he would carve his new beginnings.

Part Four
The Summer Storm

Chapter Twenty-Three
Matilda

"Your husband's seed grows strong inside you," Gundred cackled. "Henry, is it? Is that who you married?"

"Aye, Henry."

"You were with child soon enough. What are you – three or four months? I see a fair bloom on you." Gundred pressed her face up to the bars in order to examine Matilda the best she could.

"Nay, I've only been married two months," Matilda replied, her tone firm. "I married in May and it's July now." *I will not have this woman hinting these things. The child is my husband's. It will be my husband's.*

"I'd have thought more than that," Gundred said in her all-knowing way.

"I've got some bread and cheese," Matilda offered the food, "and a nice piece of apple cake."

"Very kind of you, Matilda, and I know you pray for old Gundred, stuck in this cell, doing her best for your Hugh."

"Aye, I do." Matilda turned to look at the grave.

"It's been quiet hereabouts recently," Gundred reflected, while chewing on a piece of crust given by Matilda and keeping her eye fixed on the woman standing on the other side of the barred window. "Wouldn't you say it's been quiet, Matty?"

"Aye, it's been quiet enough."

"And that young monk, him who disappeared and came back again. Handsome he was. What do you say, Matilda?"

"He's handsome enough, I daresay," Matilda shrugged her shoulders. She kept her distance from him now. Sometimes she wondered… if he had known that she was expecting his child and if she had known that his monk's vows were about to be overthrown… would he have wed her? Foolish thoughts. He was no better than Hugh – Matilda knew that. No sooner than they were married, and probably beforehand, he would have been lifting the tunic of some tavern whore. There would have been no peace married to him.

"I thought him to be a particular friend of yours. Even though he was a monk at the time."

"A friend?" Matilda replied, her voice deliberately weary. "I thought nothing of him."

"Is that so? He came to visit me two or three times and thought I was good and holy giving myself to stay in here and pray for your Hugh. He didn't bring me any food, with him being a monk and probably he had no money to buy any, but he spared a little time for Gundred, which is more than some folk would do."

"That was kind of him," Matilda said. She turned to watch a shiny black beetle scurrying up the stone wall. "There's another new boat on the beach now. It's ready to go out to sea."

"Aye, that storm couldn't keep the Romney folk from fishing," Gundred nodded her pleasure.

"It stopped us from trading though," Matilda replied.

"You're none the poorer for it," Gundred declared. "That new husband of yours, what's his name?"

"Henry."

"Aye, Henry. He does all right in that shed repairing the boats, like that other one did." Gundred flashed a glance towards Hugh's grave.

"He looks after it for Oliver." Matilda went to turn away but was stopped by the old hag's next words:

"It was that monk, the one you said was fine-looking, who had the idea to take the baby to Canterbury," Gundred informed her. "Now what do you think of that, Matilda? It didn't seem right to me."

"If he were that holy then he should be among people of his kind."

"But he was meant to be holy here in Romney. I don't know what that monk was thinking of, do you?" Gundred paused for a moment and chewed on a piece of cheese. "Nay, the baby was a Romney child and it fair upset folk. Of course Cecily was bound to fret over it, and young Agnes, she had words with him."

"What do you mean, Agnes had words? With whom?" Matilda's tone was sharp, and her eyes narrowed as she looked into the cell.

"Did I say that?" Gundred cackled. "What do I know of things that happen hereabouts? Poor old Gundred, stuck in this cell, praying all day. What do I know of life past this little patch of graveyard I can see through the window? And if I turn around, I see a little of the church and those folk who come and go about the altar."

"You said that Agnes spoke with the monk about the child?"

"Nay Matilda, you're that busy in your mind, you've got in a muddle. I've not seen Agnes in many a week. They say she's worn out with carrying the child. It will be a girl this time – that's what I see."

Matilda turned from Gundred, unable to tolerate her for a moment more. *What was I thinking of, putting the old woman here in an anchorhold? Did it matter if Hugh sped on his path to heaven or lingered in purgatory? I thought it did at the time. But since she was put there, there is never a moment when I can kneel at the graveside without those dark eyes watching. God forgive me for wondering if she prays in order to ease Hugh's journey to heaven, or does she spend her time cramming food into her wizened mouth and gossiping with those who pass by?*

"Matty," Gundred called out, forcing Matilda to turn back towards the cell. "I've not got a taste for apples nowadays." The apple cake was pushed out through the bars and fell upon the ground.

Scowling, Matilda picked it up. There were poor children who would snatch at it in desperation to fill their empty bellies and not complain if it were a little stale, or even that it had already been chewed at. As she turned to walk away, Gundred's voice reached her.

"A bit of your spiced cake, nice and fresh, now that would be good for poor old Gundred. When you have the time, Matty..."

Oliver had been busy playing with his grandmother all morning and within minutes of Matilda taking him home, he was curled up beneath a blanket on his bed, fast asleep.

With a scowl fixed upon her face, Matilda pulled a bag of flour from her shopping basket and some butter. Then from a cupboard she took a pot of honey and several jars of spices, slamming them down on the table. Reaching into a basket, she withdrew three brown eggs. A wooden bowl was lifted from a shelf and, with little care, Matilda began spooning in butter and honey, which she beat to a glossy consistency. Eggs were cracked open and added, further enriching the soft yellow colour of the mixture. She began to find the labour was healing her bad mood and so she took more care when ladling the flour into the bowl and stirred it gently so as not to have flour dust coating both herself and the table. The spices were added, just a small spoonful of each, and gently folded into the mixture.

Finally, from a cupboard, Matilda took a tin box in which she would bake the cake. And then another, a smaller one, for Gundred's cake. Most of the mixture was spooned into the larger tin and this was put into the oven built into the fireplace.

"Now for the special cake… Gundred's spice cake," Matilda muttered.

Kneeling on the floor, and reaching into the cupboard, Matilda pushed aside jars of pickled vegetables, bags of oats, rye and flour. Then her fingers gently probed the wooden panel at the back and eased it along. It slipped behind another panel, revealing a small hollow in the stone wall of the house. Three small jars were removed, their stoppers hurriedly taken out and tossed on the table.

"Here we are: spices for Gundred," Matilda murmured as she looked into the pots. With a slight smile, she selected one and tipped a few tiny black seeds into the cake mixture. "Just what you asked for." She began to replace the stoppers but paused and tipped a few grains of white powder which settled upon the seeds. "And some of this. You want plenty of spice, don't you?"

The stoppers were carefully pushed back into place and the three jars gathered in one hand. They were placed in their hide and, with short jerky movements, the back panel of the cupboard slid back into place. Jars, bottles and packets were hastily moved back into the empty cupboard space and it appeared as if nothing had been disturbed.

Seeds and powder were soon hidden within the cake mixture, and Matilda pulled the cake tin forwards, ready to pour the mixture in. She hesitated, wanting to taste a little, just to check the flavour, but instead she spooned in another dollop of honey.

"A little sweeter would do no harm," Matilda whispered. Then she was done, and the smaller cake tin was placed beside the larger one in the oven.

Matilda took a peep at her sleeping son and a feeling of warmth spread throughout her body. How perfect he was curled up there, his cheeks soft and his hair tousled. Thankfully, he slept well, and she had plenty of time to tidy up.

The water, held in its three-legged pan above the fire, was hot. Matilda carefully lifted the pan and poured water into a large wooden bowl, already placed on the table. There was a smaller dish with soap, a scrubbing brush and a drying rag to hand. But rather than plunge the smaller mixing bowl directly into the warm water, Matilda took it to the back of the house, where she poured cold water from a bucket into the bowl and, with the spoon, she pushed any mixture free from the sides of the bowl. Then she hesitated – where to empty this dirty water? Not here on the ground? Walking to the end of the garden, she poured it deep into an area of brambles.

Back in the cottage, the smaller mixing bowl was washed again with soap and hot water, and placed on a thick rag to dry, where it was joined by the larger bowl and a selection of spoons.

Matilda hadn't realised how tense she had been until she sat with a goblet of wine, thankful the baking was complete. It was always such a rush to get these tasks done before Oliver was under her feet again. A pottage of leeks and grain was already cooking over the fire, and she only had to fry some fish when Henry came in. In these first months of pregnancy, Matilda felt weary and had suggested to Henry that they pay a young woman to help in the home when the baby came. Someone to prepare the meals and help with washing their clothes and the numerous linens a new baby would need. She would choose someone who was plain in looks and hard-working. It would not matter if they were a little simple, as long as orders could be followed.

By the time the goblet was empty, Oliver had woken and could be heard climbing out of his bed. The cakes were browned and, with her hands covered in thick leather mittens, Matilda eased the catch on the oven door and pulled out the tins, quickly placing them on the hearth.

"Hot, Oliver, hot."

The little boy, smelling warm honey and spices, began to creep closer.

"We'll have to wait for them to cool," Matilda told her son. "Now let's place them outside."

First the small tin, and then the larger. They were placed on a rough bench, just outside the back door. Matilda paused, looking at the smaller tin. *Is it safe to leave it there? Aye – I have Oliver with me and no one else will come meddling with my baking.*

Five minutes later, both Matilda and Oliver were outside again. Oliver carried a ball, which he began to kick around on the small patch of grass. The cakes were both tipped out onto wooden plates, to continue cooling, and with a quick glance back at them, Matilda followed her son onto the grass.

"*Mmm*, what's this? Honey and spices." Henry had walked through the cottage and swooped upon the cakes, holding the smaller one in his hand and sniffing it. "Still warm from the oven too."

"Hands off." Matilda forced a smile. "I'll cut you a slice soon enough, if you'll kick the ball to Oliver."

"I'll just take bite, shall I?"

Henry was teasing, and she knew it, but Matilda couldn't stop herself from snatching the cake from his hand. "This one's for Gundred. We have the larger one, for the three of us."

"I'll kick a ball if there's cake to come." Henry smiled down at Oliver who had raced over to be near his new father. "You'd like honey cake, wouldn't you? But first Ma wants to cut it, so we're not to snatch at it like poor folk would." He picked up the little boy and swung him high. "You'd be happy to break a piece off and eat it now, wouldn't you? Ma won't have it! We could gobble up that little cake, just you and I..."

Oliver laughed and screamed, as Henry swung him to and fro, sometimes tossing him in the air and catching him.

"You'll make the boy sick and then there'll be no cake," Matilda scolded. But with Henry at home and Oliver so happy, she felt a contentment not experienced in many years. When the new baby came, they would be a proper family. Henry would not question the child's early arrival into this world. He was a good man who harboured no suspicions or mistrust of people. She could learn from his even-tempered manner.

The cakes were placed on a wooden tray – not too close to each other – and taken into the house. Matilda wrapped the smaller one in paper and placed it high on a shelf. Then she cut generous slices of the spiced honey cake, put a couple of mugs of ale on the tray and a beaker of milk. She tossed a blanket over her arm; Oliver would enjoy sitting on the grass to eat.

The cake was devoured, and Matilda was able to rest, her legs outstretched on the blanket, while Henry and Oliver kicked and threw the ball. With the afternoon sun streaming into the garden, Matilda again felt a rare happiness. Soon she would deliver the cake to Gundred and then be done with having to be watched and taunted by the all-seeing old hag. Henry would care for her as Hugh never did; she would become more relaxed with Oliver and a good mother to the new baby. God would look over her if she prayed enough and did good deeds.

Henry strolled over. "Look, Ma. Oliver is turned all up-side-down!" He held the boy by his ankles and swung him lightly before gently lowering him to the ground."

"More... more!"

"Nay, if you were meant to have your head on the ground, then God would have made you that way! Now, I've got to get back to work and I'm sure Ma has things to do with you."

Matilda, sleepy from the warm sun, began to rouse herself. "Aye, we'll take that cake to Gundred and watch the fishing boats come in."

"Stay with Henry," the boy began to whine.

"Henry has to go back to work," his new father told him. "But what a treat to come by and have cake and ale in the garden, and ball games too."

"We'll walk Henry back to the shed." Matilda began to gather the empty mugs and plates.

"I'll carry you up high," Henry told the little boy.

"On your shoulders?"

"Aye, on my shoulders, although you know Ma worries to see you up there." He bent down and kissed Matilda lightly on the cheek. "You know I'll hold tight."

"Aye, he's safe with you," she smiled back at him.

The little family left the stone house on Fair Field Road and walked across to the wide shingle bank. Men were still hard at work in this area, smoking and salting fish or repairing boats. The keddle nets were stretched out between long poles in the sea, awaiting their catch of fish as the tide came in. Women sat on the stones, repairing nets or darning as they minded the young children who ran freely along the tideline. Older children gathered driftwood to burn on the open fires in their homes.

Oliver was extracted from his beloved Henry with the minimum of fuss and, with his hand firmly in his mother's, the two of them walked along the top of the beach towards the east end of St Nicholas Church.

"You *are* good to me, Matty. I said you would be. I said to myself that you'd be bringing along some spiced cake before the day was out."

"I've got Oliver with me," Matilda pushed the cake through the bars. "We'll just say a prayer for his pa and then be off back home."

"Aye, you've a nice cottage, you have." Gundred began to unwrap the cake. "Don't you worry about me, Matilda, when you're back there with your new husband and little Oliver."

Matilda had already turned away, "Oliver, don't jump on Pa's head… let's just kneel for a moment."

But Gundred was still talking: "It's been warm today. I sense there's a storm brewing. There'll be thunder and lightning before the day ends."

Matilda ignored her words but felt those black eyes on her back as she knelt beside Oliver, pressing his hands together.

"Dear Lord, may Pa rest in peace with you in heaven. Help me to know right from wrong and for my pa to be proud when he looks down on me. May I walk in your footsteps all the days of my life. Amen." They spoke the words together, Oliver's eyes closed tight as he concentrated on the rhythm of the prayer.

As Matilda turned away, she couldn't bring herself to send any words of goodwill in Gundred's direction. While they had been at the graveside, she had already heard the rustling of paper as the spiced cake was unwrapped. It was still slightly warm and rich with butter and honey. A tempting treat for the old woman...

Gundred had seen much over the years. She was a people watcher: a faint staining of a blush on the cheeks, a change in daily habits, a slight swelling of breasts and belly in a young woman, or the gradual fading away of an old man. She saw it all before any others had noticed those changes. Gundred listened too, not only to the words said, but the way they were said. The denial which flowed too quickly from the lips, or the insincere flattery. She heard the words which were left unsaid as eyes were lowered and the subject changed.

She lacked any attraction of face or figure. As a young woman she'd known that she would never be blessed with a husband and children. Her manner was too sharp to lure a man, her chin too pointed and her nose too crooked. Gundred didn't have any close women friends either – they didn't seem to take to her, or was she the one who didn't take to them?

She had made her mark on the town, nonetheless. People were drawn to her, gathering close to hear her words of wisdom. Wanting to know what messages she had received, or visions had been seen. They believed her every word and grasped at her advice. Others kept their distance, those were the ones who had something to hide, and Gundred had a special interest in them.

Young Agnes had been full of light and eagerness to talk of young love. Did Gundred believe in love, she had asked, and how would she know if a young man was interested in her? But it was when she stopped asking, claiming that she was to marry Will, and had no need to bother with such stuff, that Gundred knew she was up to no good. Then later, she had seen Agnes leave the village on the night of the storm, only to return scared and uncertain. But it was her swollen breasts and the damp milk-patches on her tunic, which led Gundred to piece together the story of the abandoned child.

To be placed in the anchorhold, within the walls of St Nicholas Church, had given Gundred a pride greater than she had ever experienced before. Her place in the community was clear and she marvelled at what faith the young widow had in her when Matilda asked her to spend her life praying in order to speed Hugh's journey through purgatory.

From her cell Gundred could see into the church and had watched the monks fawn over the mementoes of young Nicholas' life. She had also seen how often Matilda had made an excuse to pause and speak with Brother Gregory and wondered at the widow's attraction to him. From her position within the church walls, women seemed to fear her less than they did when she was free to roam the streets of Romney. They came and whispered their secrets and asked for advice – willingly given in exchange for a tasty meal. The more appetising the food on offer, the more care Gundred took to offer the best words of wisdom she could conjure up. More recently, she had offered to pray for the neediest. It wasn't strictly her place to do so, having been appointed to pray for Hugh, but as long as Matilda didn't hear of it...

Gundred felt as if she were a living saint of Romney – her words so sought after and her prayers of such value. She had become so filled with pride that she began to be less sensitive to the needs and feelings of those who passed within her domain.

What Gundred didn't see was the growing bitterness in the God-fearing Matilda. She didn't realise that when Matilda visited her husband's grave, she wanted to pray in peace and how the resentment towards the constant onlooker grew. Gundred, so proud of her status that led to many townsfolk now visiting her, became loose with her tongue as she taunted Matilda with hints of her all-seeing knowledge.

So, when she took her first bite of the moist spice cake, Gundred, who claimed to know so much, did not see that the cake was baked with hatred, not love…

At first it seemed that Matilda had overdone the honey and spices – the cake was both sweet and strong tasting, but it was still slightly warm and moist, which Gundred appreciated. There was a bitterness too, an after-taste which was not so pleasant. She would have to advise Matilda to check her spice pots. Another mouthful might soften that taste, after all there was plenty of honey, which was good and sweet.

It was after the third or fourth mouthful, while Gundred still puzzled over what ingredient caused such bitterness, that she began to tremble and experience cramping in her belly. Forced to bend double in order to ease the pain, she watched her fingers twitch uncontrollably as she clutched at her belly. Confusion struck as, with her body all hunched up, she was struggling to breathe. She must stand tall to open her airways, but her body was too weak, and the trembling had taken hold. She should stand to breathe, but no, she must allow herself to slide onto her straw-covered floor and stay all screwed up, for this was the only way to ease the stomach pain. But the cramps did not lessen, and the trembling worsened, and her head felt light as her throat tightened and her lungs were deprived of air...

Black clouds covered the afternoon sun, and the air took on a distinctive chill before those first heavy drops of rain were expelled over Romney. In the town, people ran to shelter. No one else would visit the old woman in the church that day.

Chapter Twenty-Four
Agnes

The strangers came along the beach track from the direction of Hythe, looking from side to side, their faces expectant. The men, knee deep in water, pulling in the keddle nets, observed the outsiders but made no comment. Those working at salting, tanning and barrel making just beyond the beach, glanced over, noting their arrival but too busy with their own tasks to wonder what brought them here.

The skies over the Marsh had taken on an ominous purple hue and already, to the west, the sun had been concealed. The air had become chilly, and the rumble of distant thunder could be heard. A summer storm would be upon Romney within minutes. It seemed that the newcomers were unaware of the change in weather – their faces were raised to the church tower of St Nicholas, which still basked in the July sun. One of them pointed to the church and, although they had been travelling for some time, their pace increased.

It wasn't until they reached the western end of the church and the group of four split – two to the tower and the others to the carving of the monk and newborn baby – that Agnes saw them. She had been looking out to sea, watching her father and brother bring the boat in, and had not noticed their approach.

"Joan," Agnes tapped her brother's wife on the arm. "Strangers by the church and there at the statue. Do you see the bags over their shoulders? Do you think…?"

"Pilgrims?" Joan's voice was full of wonder. "The very first… I didn't think, didn't really believe they would. He's still a baby!"

"There's been such a fuss, with Canterbury and the monks. They were sure to come." Agnes put her hands over her belly, protective of the unborn child.

She was weary, standing there on the beach, but not the debilitating tiredness she had known when the worries for Nicholas were all-consuming. This was the weariness of the last weeks of pregnancy when she struggled to find a comfortable position in which to sleep, and her lower back ached day and night. She shuffled on the shingle, wanting to sit, but knowing they must turn for home before the storm broke.

As those first heavy drops of rain fell on Romney, Agnes watched the pilgrims look to the sky with wonder. They had been unaware of the change in weather, not hearing the distant rumbles as they exclaimed over the church and statue. Like insects disturbed at their work, they turned and scuttled to the nearest shelter – the church tower.

"Come on Agnes, before the heavens open." Joan pulled at her, and they ran, Agnes finding it cumbersome to haul her body across the shingle bank to the limited shelter of the fish market.

They stood catching their breath, backs against an old stone wall, a roof of thatch above them and crammed amongst the rough tables on which fishermen displayed their catch. Although the tables were bare, the air was pungent with the stench of fish, which lingered in the crevices of the wood. Agnes screwed up her nose; pregnancy had made her more sensitive to those smells she had thought nothing of previously.

"I should be there, helping Pa and Robert," Agnes said, taking a step away from the shelter. "It's hardly raining."

"It will be," Joan said, "in no time at all."

Her words were barely finished before forked lightning slashed through the sky, which had prematurely darkened. Thunder followed with a low rumble and then the rain, lashing down upon the thatch and dripping through. It danced upon the darkened sea and drenched the men as they hauled their small boats above the high tide mark. No one would venture out to buy the fish while the rain fell with such force. Agnes and Joan watched as the catch was abandoned and the men ran, hoods low over their faces, towards the town.

"We'll have to take a soaking. This is no place to see out a storm, when we are just yards away from your fireside." Joan peered out towards the High Street crossroads.

"What about the pilgrims? What a welcome to Romney."

"You won't believe it, Agnes," Joan still looked towards the town centre. "Word of them has spread to Brother Gregory – here he is, braving the rain to reach them!"

"He must have had a message from the Lord!" Agnes sniggered. "For all that he is just plain Gregory now."

With his cape wrapped tight around him and body bent low, he scuttled along, not noticing the two women as he went to claim his prize. Three rooms awaited these pilgrims at the tavern belonging to his new bride's family.

Gregory was not married in the true sense, for he had taken monastic vows and no priest in Romney would marry him. But the tavern owner had no son, and his only daughter was so enamoured with the rogue

252

monk that she begged that they may live as if they were man and wife. All of Romney had watched the tale of their love unfold, as the men who supped ale at the Rome Tavern listened to the landlord's despair and his daughter's weeping. In turn they told their wives who gossiped with their friends.

Agnes followed Gregory's ambitions through the men in her life: her husband, father and brothers who occasionally met at the tavern. She heard of how Gregory impressed the landlord with suggestions of building a lodging house on the empty plot beside the tavern. He was sure the pilgrims would come and there was money to be made by whoever was quick enough to provide accommodation and nourishing meals. As she shopped at the market stalls, Agnes spotted the ring on young Magota's fourth finger. It gave her a degree of respectability as she shared her bed with the former monk.

No sooner had the landlord given the union his blessing, than shallow foundations were being dug and a wooden frame constructed. Gregory's confidence was such that he was certain there was no one who had more knowledge about the birth of Nicholas and his early months – other than his adopted family, he conceded. He spent hours replicating the books which told the story of the child's life, as first told by Brother Nicholas. Throughout the town it was whispered that if the pilgrims came, they would be well accommodated and entertained by Gregory. It seemed to Agnes that half the women were in love with him, and nearly everyone was in awe of his self-serving ambitions.

Sure enough, Agnes and Joan looked on as Gregory entered the church to seek out these pilgrims, and within minutes he was ushering the visitors through the driving rain, with the promise of shelter at the Rome Tavern.

"He was right." Joan watched until they turned at the crossroads and were out of sight. "They came."

"Aye, and Nicholas not yet a year old. I hope Cecily isn't bothered by them."

"She'll have her hands full with two babies. I saw her mother this morning and she said Cecily's pains had begun."

Agnes didn't reply as she dwelt on this news. Her thoughts were full of her own baby and the birth which would come in the next few days or weeks. The news that Cecily would be a mother before the day was out, made it seem all the more real.

Lightning ripped through the sky ahead of them, hit the deserted beach and, before they had commented on its savage forks, the thunder clapped above Romney. The storm was right upon them, relishing its moment, before it rolled on and over the sea.

"Now, before the next one comes," Joan pulled at Agnes, urging her on. It was no distance to her home behind the cobbler's, and unsafe to be out in the midst of a storm.

They ran as fast as Agnes could, Joan becoming her guide, past puddles and wet debris on the street. She flung open the door of the cobbler's and pushed Agnes in before her. Pausing for a moment in the darkness of the shop, Agnes felt her belly tighten and placed both hands on it. Leaning against the wood plank wall, she waited for the pain to subside, breathing slowly and deeply to calm herself after the race through the storm. Joan had gone ahead and appeared at the doorway to the living area.

"The fire's coming to life and I've lit a candle. Where's Will, do you know?"

"Nay, I'd expected him to be here, in the shop… but it's got so dark, and he can't work in this light." Agnes took a few slow steps towards the doorway.

"He'll have gone to the Jerusalem Tavern, to meet his brother." Joan stood back and allowed Agnes to walk through.

"Aye, he'll be at the Jerusalem. I can have a rest before he's back for supper."

"You do that," Joan agreed. "I've left the children with your ma for long enough and got no fish to show for it, but the men will bring some with them and I'd best get back." She paused, frowning at Agnes who was pale and looking down at her belly. "You don't mind being left on your own?"

"Of course not, I'll be glad of the peace and quiet." Agnes forced a smile. "Apart from the storm of course!"

"I'd best make a run for it and hope that my own fire is burning. I'll be soaked through for all that it's only minutes away." Joan had her hand on the latch and pressed it, holding the door steady in the wind. "I'll see you tomorrow then."

Agnes turned to sit by the fire, taking a blanket to wrap around her shoulders. But as she sat, the back door swung open, it hadn't quite caught on the latch. She sighed her frustration; why did everything feel like such a burden today? Surely her body was heavier than ever, and the baby must have settled in a different position. Heaving herself up again, she had just reached out to the door and was pushing it back in place when the second spasm came. Her belly tightened and, as she leaned on the door, with no strength to press the latch back into place, pains shot across her back and down her thighs. Gasping, she let the pain settle before opening the door – please God, let Joan still be there.

She was – at the end of the garden wrestling with the stiff gate. "Joan!" Agnes called. But the wind carried her voice back to her and out towards the coast. The gate came free, and without a backwards glance, Joan was scurrying across St Martin's churchyard.

Defeated, Agnes closed the door and turned back towards the room. Before she had reached the chair, a warm liquid came in a gush, licking at her thighs and forming a puddle on the stone floor. Agnes stood, looking down in dismay... something else to deal with.

She took a rag and mopped at first her legs and then the puddle. Then, thankful that she had done the washing the day before, Agnes pulled at her clean tunic and shift which hung on the wooden airer. She would have to change right here, in front of the fire. It was a relief to pull off her tunic and then the shift, wet from both the rain and her own waters. As she stood, naked with the clean shift in her hand, another spasm tore through her young body. Leaning on the table for support, she waited for the pain to fade. There was nothing else to be done. And, when the moment passed, Agnes pulled the clean shift over herself. She looked at the tunic but had lost the will to make the effort to dress any further, and merely wrapped a blanket around her shoulders before sinking into the chair.

Why did it seem so much more terrifying this time? Was it because she knew what was coming: this was no belly ache from rotten pottage causing the pains to course through her body. She didn't want to face it alone. Agnes needed her ma or Joan... or even Will. Of course, Will would be home soon, and he could fetch Ma and... another pain ripped through her. Instinctively she drew her knees up, so she was hunched within the cocoon of the chair.

In this way an hour passed, or maybe it was only fifteen or twenty minutes. With the sky darkened by the storm clouds and the pattern of the day interrupted, Agnes lost all track of time and merely existed in her own lonely place where the pain tore through her at regular intervals, lightning cracked in the sky above and the thunder rumbled and rolled out to sea. The rain was steady, giving a rhythmic beat on the thick glass of the kitchen window and seeping in under the door.

Then a rap came on the back door and Agnes looked up, a glimmer of hope cutting through her misery. The door opened and Mary launched herself into the kitchen, carried on a gust of wind. As she unwrapped her sodden cloak, her eyes were on Agnes and she saw that she was right to come... that her instincts had not been amiss.

"Agnes, sweeting, it's time. Your pains have come?" Mary knelt before her daughter, taking her hands in her own.

Agnes merely nodded her response.

"I knew it, I just knew you shouldn't be alone, and I sensed you were."

"Joan was here, but she didn't know..." Agnes whispered. "And Will, he'll be at the Jerusalem, but he'll be back soon, I'm sure of it."

"What use will a man be?" her mother smiled as she stood to check the water in a pan beside the dying fire. "We'll need hot water and I'll get the fire going."

"Joan put a log on before she left, but..."

"Aye, she's a good help but you couldn't keep it going." Mary placed the three-legged pot over the fire, which already had flames licking around the fresh logs.

Agnes tensed as the pain came again, holding her breath and wrapping her arms tight around herself.

"How often are the pains coming?" Mary asked.

"I don't know, Ma." Agnes let out her breath and inhaled deeply. "There's not much between them."

"You'll not think it now, but I've a feeling that you're going to be lucky. You'll have your baby in no time at all."

257

As the lightning became less harsh and the thunder a distant rumble, the sun broke through the clouds and cast its rays through the window and across the room. The table had a neat pile of clean rags upon it and the warm water stood in its pot beside the fire. Will had returned and been shooed from the room. Sent to work at his bench, he was pacing to and fro, making a poor show of tidying his workplace.

When she felt the need to push her baby out and into the world, Agnes had little time to reflect on the birth of her first child born in the pig shelter, just ten months before. She thought nothing of that old sow who had been her only support through the terrors of the storm. Now, with Mary beside her, ready to take the child, all Agnes' thoughts were on this moment.

The newborn was tiny, a couple of weeks before her time, but as she opened her mouth and roared, it was clear that all was well.

"You've a daughter!" Mary said to Will as he opened the door to peep through. "Just let me wipe her clean..." With a cloth, Mary cleaned away the birth fluids and swaddled the infant in a soft blanket.

"Well done, my love." Will bent down and kissed Agnes lightly on the forehead, while her mother placed her newborn daughter in Agnes' arms.

Agnes felt all the love, which had been shut away inside her, tumble out as she looked down upon the child she would keep and raise as her own.

Then she recalled Cecily, and asked, "Do you know, have you heard – has Cecily had her child?"

"Aye," Mary replied, "she had a daughter too, born just as the storm broke."

"Two daughters born to Romney," Agnes smiled and stroked her baby's soft cheek, then marvelled at her perfect rosebud mouth and delicate eyelashes.

Where was the monk who had been there when this story first unfolded and painstakingly written his account of the storm in curling brown ink on thick vellum? He was now in London. Having cowered before the archbishop and abbot and told of his vision that the child should remain in Romney, he had muttered about the need to spread the tale and departed.

On the day in which the first pilgrims walked into the town, the monk did not see the new lives begin with two daughters born to the town. Nor did he see Gundred lying dead in her anchorhold, her tongue black from the poison. He did not see into the home of Matilda, to watch her playing with her son and talking with her husband as if she had done nothing worse that day than forget to thank the Lord for her supper.

If he had been in Romney – praying in St Martin's, writing in the priory or admiring his own form carved in stone, would he have seen the murder? Would he have been aware of the births?

THE END

About the Author

Romney Marsh writer, Emma Batten, loves to combine her interest in local history with creative writing. It is important to her that historical details are accurate in order to give readers an authentic insight into life on Romney Marsh. She enjoys giving author talks about her journey as a writer, planning unique writing workshops and meeting her local readers.

What the Monk Didn't See is Emma's third novel.

Her first, *A Place Called Hope*, is set in the 16th century and tells the story of the lives of two young women living through the decline of the remote settlement of Hope on Romney Marsh.

Her second novel, *Secrets of the Shingle* is a mystery set on the wild, windswept wastes of the Dungeness peninsula in the 19th century and seen through the eyes of a naive young teacher.

But First Maintain the Wall is set in Georgian Dymchurch. Harry is passing through the village when the seawall breaches and events force him to stay. As an outsider, he struggles to be accepted and a tentative friendship is forged with a young woman who seeks answers to her past.

Stranger on the Point, a sequel to *Secrets of the Shingle,* is the story of a young woman's quest to fulfil her worth as the shadows of WW1 live on. Set in Dungeness and Ashford. This is followed by *The Artist's Gift set* during WW2.

Inspired by the pub sign for Botolphs Bridge Inn, *The Pendant Cross* introduces West Hythe and Lyminge in Anglo-Saxon times.

Still Shining Bright, a prequel to *Secrets of the Shingle*, again features Dungeness and Ashford. Cora and her daughter are brought ashore by lifeboat. With no home or possessions, they rely on the kindness of strangers and Cora must use her wit to survive.

The Sacred Stone returns to Anglo-Saxon times and features an ancient altar which is now in the British Museum.

For more details take a look at Emma's website:
www.emmabattenauthor.com